Once Upon A Blossom's Curse

Corset Strings and Cups of Tea

Audrey Lynn

To Richie,

For the countless ways you love me and support me on this author journey.

See if you can find the Dead references. They're just for you.

Author's Note

Once Upon a Blossom's Curse discusses emotionally difficult topics including sexual coercion, discussion of off page previous sexual assault, magical trauma, and off page loss of a family member.

It also contains on page consensual sex.

Any readers who are concerned that these topics may upset them or trigger traumatic memories are encouraged to consider their emotional well-being in choosing to read this story.

Contents

1

Genevieve

I shouldn't have had that fourth cup of tea. Of course, had I thought about how long-winded Lord Willoughby can be, I would have reconsidered drinking *any* at all.

I wiggle uncomfortably in my chaise, centered with Mother, Queen of Naseria and the members of her council flanking me on either side. Mother has always preferred to meet her councilors in this room, filled with understated elegance and creature comforts. It would be a relaxing place to enjoy an afternoon, if not for the current company. Light streams through the gossamer curtains, a perfect spring day just out of my reach.

Will Willoughby never stop his incessant prattling about the urgency of my reproductive capabilities? At twenty-eight, I'm considered behind on reproducing—over the hill. Yet, due to the nature of my blueblood gift, I've also become something of a difficult marital prospect, despite the fact that I will inherit the crown in two years' time. Goodness knows I've tried to find love, but love is a rather fickle thing, and when one is cursed to make every man fall in love with her, it begins to lose its value.

Nevertheless, the council and my mother can't seem to stop fearing for the security of the nation if I take the crown unwed.

By my age, Mother had already produced four heirs and would have her fifth before she took the crown at thirty. It's not as if I'm unaware of my duty to provide heirs, but with the brood my parents created, the kingdom needn't fret when there's a healthy line of heirs at the ready. Even still, I want an opportunity to have the life I've dreamed of—a family, children of my own, a companion to stand by my side when I take the throne.

This is why I've chosen my own husband. I can't waste any more years yearning for something I lost and will never regain. I can't hope for the love my parents share, or even the love my siblings will one day find. The solution is simple: choose a neighboring blueblood prince who can provide an advantageous alliance with Naseria. Prince Leland Frostclaw is everything I could want in an arranged marriage—kind, diplomatic, and loyal to his sister, Queen Kalise Frostclaw, in all manners of Icelantica's political needs.

I wish there were some way for me to escape—if only to find a few moments to myself. As I gently set my teacup down on the coffee table in front of me, the silk of my glove slips, and I nearly let the cup clink against its saucer. A small cough tells me the mistake didn't go unnoticed, and I breathe out slowly, trying to regain my composure.

Lord Willoughby is sweating so profusely I dare say he deserves a break of his own. He could do with a bit of mopping up before continuing to warn me about my womb's impending expiration.

Lord Fenweir, another stodgy old council member, barks out, "Princess Genevieve, have you considered whether the Frostclaw

Queen will claim your own offspring as her heir? What if she demands the child be raised in Icelantica?"

I can't keep the frown from my face at the utter shock of his suggestion. Why would Kalise Frostclaw ever want to claim my future children as her heirs?

"That wasn't on my list of concerns when I chose to marry Prince Leland. Why would you believe his sister would have any interest in our future children?"

My mother, Queen Penelope, subtly twitches her left eye in my direction. The indiscernible gesture goes unnoticed by the other council members and Father. But it's all too familiar to me. *Stand down. Let the men speak. Let them tell you what you've overlooked. Stay in your place.*

Lord Fenweir clears his throat just as I take a sip of tea, a phlegmy sound that makes me want to gag into my cup. I hold it back, because propriety allows a man to make bodily sounds in public, but of course the Crown Princess of Naseria would *never* do anything so crass as make an indiscreet noise or spit in her tea.

After Fenweir has managed to clear whatever blockage was in his throat, he says, "All our reports show that Queen Kalise will make no attempt to secure a husband for herself. Her gift is far too volatile for producing children, leaving the kingdom without an heir other than Prince Leland. If they believe they can secure an heir through you—"

This has gone on long enough. I interrupt him as politely as possible, sweetly replying to his illogical trepidations.

"Lord Fenweir, I hardly see this as a cause for concern. If anything, it only strengthens my desire to seek an alliance with Icelantica through marriage. My future child may unite the two kingdoms—or perhaps I shall have two future rulers. Now, do excuse me," I say, standing as I make my way to the door. The hem of my skirts slides across the polished marble floor, and I dart away before Mother has a moment to correct my terribly rude manners. I try to avoid her gaze but lose my resolve when I see her eye twitch, her mouth a firm, disapproving line.

The twelve other councilors rise as I pass, bowing low. They're all bluebloods, all from noble families that rose to power after the War of the Blood three generations ago—eight men and four women, bound to serve the Queen and the crown. Soon, they'll be bound to serve me. A part of me hopes some will choose to step down so I can appoint my own council, but that's probably too optimistic.

I reach the door just as Father shuffles forward, a bright smile on his face. I hold up a hand and give him a kind smile in return. "I propose we reconvene in fifteen minutes to finalize our discussions. We still have plenty to cover before Prince Leland and Queen Kalise arrive tomorrow."

The door is opened for me, and I make my way across the burgundy-carpeted hallway toward my private rooms. I just need a moment alone—a moment's peace without everyone trying to tell me what to do. Servants curtsy low as I pass, pausing their work to murmur, "Your Highness." I give a quick nod of acknowledgment before padding up a flight of stairs to the family's private wing and my own apartment.

Stepping inside feels like a weight has lifted from my shoulders. The sweet scent of freshly cut flowers fills the air, and I want to collapse on the pink velvet couch—or better yet, escape down my private stairs to my glasshouse, where I can finally slip off my silk gloves and tend to my plants. All rare tropical species from the southern continent, Kennon, so far beyond the reach of our own continent, Inver, that trade is arduous and nearly impossible. These plants are more precious than gold or jewels and have become my prized possessions: begonias with long, spotted leaves and soft pink flowers, delicate calatheas, and large, robust philodendrons fill my private sanctuary. All I want to do is tiptoe down the steps and disappear into my personal paradise.

But that will have to wait until evening. For now, take care of my needs, freshen my face and hair as best I can and prepare to return to the discussion on my upcoming wedding.

My wedding.

I dreamed for so long of this day as a girl. I always pictured it as the perfect love match, just like Mother and Father. But even then, I could only ever picture one boy. I thought we'd live happily ever after, ruling Naseria side by side.

Of course, there's no such thing as happily ever after. The boy I always dreamed of made sure it would never be mine. If the heartache I endured from Kieran Greenbluff wasn't enough, the manifestation of my gift—the moment all blueblood children dream of—turned my fantasy into a nightmare.

The gift of love sounded like a fairytale ending after Kieran abandoned me and was reported dead. When I realized my blueblood had blessed me with love, I thought I'd finally have someone who would see me for who I am—that I'd finally let go of the pain he left behind. Instead, my gift became a curse, for any man who touches me falls madly in love with me. But it's not true love. Lust is a better description, though such a term, when used toward the crown princess, is considered crass. Mother helped me settle on the term *love*, although what I've experienced at the hands of the men who claimed to love me was anything but.

Love implies mutual affection, but my gift deceives only the man who touches me, leaving me to feel the empty ache of another's desire. After years of learning how insidious my gift truly is, I've become resolute in giving up on love.

After all, the only boy I ever loved left me.

2

Genevieve

We're only children the first time I see Kieran Greenbluff. His father, the new head gardener of Fairbright, is being given a tour of the grounds while my siblings and I play outside. The boy follows close behind his father, but he keeps glancing back at us, curiosity sparkling in his grass-green eyes. The nanny tuts at him, telling him to show respect to the royal family, to mind his manners and run along.

He's filthy—all dirty nails, mussed dark waves of hair falling nearly to his chin, and a coat of mud caked onto his knobby knees. He looks like a child who has the freedom to splash in puddles and climb trees. A wild boy from a storybook.

All I see in him is my own longing, my own desire to be free, to feel the earth between my toes and muss up my pristine white frock. But as a princess, I'm not afforded such luxuries. Even at eight, I know such things only stir envy in my heart. And a princess should never feel such emotions.

A quick knock on my door signals that I'm being summoned back to the parlor to continue the discussion of my arranged marriage. A footman in emerald-green livery escorts me to the room, the doors swinging open as he announces in a clear voice, "The Crown Princess Genevieve Ashcroft."

The others rise and bow low, waiting for me to take my seat on the settee before resuming their own. I settle in, adjust my skirts, and sit up straight to keep my corset from pressing against my soft middle. Small talk hums through the room, and I glance to my right at my brother. It's a small relief to see he's joined us. Gabriel, only two years younger than I, has taken naturally to his role in the military, representing the crown's interests in all military affairs.

Gabriel gives me a wink before asking, "How are you holding up, Genny?"

I shrug and murmur low enough for his ears alone, "As fine as can be expected. I'm just tired of these people interfering in my decisions."

Gabe runs a hand through his fiery red hair—hair like our mother's. Mine resembles no one in particular, except perhaps my youngest brother, Darian. With its raucous blend of yellows and nearly pink, Mother settled on calling it strawberry blonde, while Father nicknamed me Peach for its likeness to the delicate hues on a ripe fruit's skin.

"I think you need to accept that this will be your lot in life," Gabe says. "Old men meddling in your affairs."

I roll my eyes in a most undignified manner. "As opposed to you, the second born *and* giftless, who spends your life as you please. Which, from all accounts, means bedding every willing woman in the kingdom."

His lips quirk into a faint smirk, jest coloring his tone. "Don't believe all the rumors you hear. There are many women who only dream that I've bedded them and enjoy spreading salacious gossip. What kind of gentleman would I be if I contradicted a lady's word?"

I suppress a grin. If even half the rumors of my brother's escapades are true, that's far more than I care to be acquainted with. Ever since Gabriel didn't receive a gift at twenty, he's worked twice as hard to make a name for himself in other capacities—much to the Ashcroft family's chagrin.

He and my youngest sister, Marielle, are both giftless, despite their fine blueblood lineage. The first generation of gifted bluebloods—those exposed to the mineral helachite—are probably rolling in their graves, knowing their sacrifice to unite the blessed has faded into nothing more than blood stained the color of ink rather than crimson.

Gabe grows serious, lowering his voice to a near whisper. "You know the rot is spreading, right? She's trying to keep it from you."

I know immediately who he means—Mother. The rot has been seeping into our borders, even appearing near the Naserian capital, Crawford. It's eating away at the land, and there seems to be no cure, though the concentration remains contained. If Mother's keeping its spread from me, she's breaking her promise—and failing to prepare me for the crown I'll inherit in two years.

"Why would she do that?" I ask, turning slightly to be sure no one else can overhear. I know the rot is caused by the misuse of helachite—the whole country knows this—but what I don't understand is how it's happening. Helachite is now highly guarded, prized for its ability to grant nearly magical gifts to bluebloods and create technology that has transformed life across the continent of Inver.

"She claims she doesn't want you to worry, with your wedding approaching," Gabe replies. "She knows how much pressure you're putting on yourself. But I've seen the damage. You need to be included in these conversations. Don't let her shut you out."

I can't help a soft, undignified snort. Nobody tells Queen Penelope what she should or shouldn't do—not even her council. To expect her to listen to her children is foolish.

"You try telling her what to do," I mutter.

He raises an eyebrow as the doors open, and we stand before I curtsy low as my mother and father's names are called. "Queen Penelope and King Consort Hugo."

My mother gracefully dips into her seat, a comfortable yet imposing chair resembling the throne two stories below us. My father takes his place at her side, sliding his hand into hers with a striking mix of tenderness and deference. The harsh lines on my mother's face seem to ease at his touch.

All I can hope is that Prince Leland will be like my father: kind, gentle, and willing to stand by my side when I take the throne. From all accounts, he is that sort of man, with his gift as a peacemaker and his natural diplomatic skills. I hand-selected him as my future consort. Since I know that my own gift—my curse—will inevitably affect our relationship, and that he will love me in whatever false form my curse casts upon him, I find it prudent to choose a man with attributes that will serve the crown as well as my rule in Naseria.

"Shall we continue our previous conversation?" my mother asks, a saccharine smile on her face that fails to disguise the weariness in her eyes. "We will no longer discuss the necessity of Princess Genevieve securing an heir. She knows her duty to the crown. Instead, I want to ensure she has no plans to change her mind."

I keep my expression neutral as I meet her brown eyes. They're the same shade as my brother's, but without his warmth or softness—hard, like chips of flint. All the gentleness has long escaped her, except when it comes to my father. He alone seems worthy of her warmth. It wasn't always that way. I remember, as a child, how she would welcome me into her arms, how she once seemed to crave our company. But years of being queen have eroded all that away. She's warned me that the crown will devour who I am and mold me into something else entirely—and her own harsh gaze has long made me believe her.

I meet her eyes and say evenly, "I have no intention of going back on my word, Your Majesty. As you know, a love match like yours and King Hugo's isn't possible, and I wish to do my duty to the crown to the best of my ability. Prince Leland possesses the qualities I find agreeable in a husband, and an alliance with Queen Kalise will secure our kingdoms against the growing unrest along both our borders with Wylan. Nothing on my part has changed in the *many* discussions we've had."

I shouldn't add that last quip, but if she wants to insult my decision before the entire council, I'm more than capable of offering a retort.

Her left eye twitches again before she composes herself. "Yes, dear, but all the council is aware of your gift. They've also been informed of the—" She pauses, unsure how to broach the subject of my volatile power in public. It's something we've long avoided speaking of. For years, we've pretended it wasn't a problem, hoping it would simply go away. It hasn't—and I've grown tired of waiting to secure a future for myself. "Of your reaction when someone encounters your gift."

A low murmur ripples through the council chamber. Gabriel reaches for me, squeezing my gloved wrist, but I don't dare meet his eyes.

"Genny..." he cautions softly.

I don't need his warning. I know my role. I know what propriety—and the crown—demand of me.

Shortly after I received my gift, my mother tried to hide its power. At first, I thought the love men felt for me was true, and I brought them to my bed, seeking a balm for the heartache I'd suffered only a year before. But I learned quickly that what I sought and what I received were two very different things. Worse still, the men I trusted were all too eager to boast of our encounters.

The few attachments I did form ended abruptly when I realized their affection was only a hunger to be filled by my gift. My mother quietly named it the gift of love amongst the court, but as I grew older, I understood that love wasn't what I'd experienced. To call it love was an insult to what I once felt long ago. Yet calling it anything else was deemed improper. So the rumors spread, and in time I closed myself off to all advances, all physical contact with others.

I began wearing gloves every day, a common precaution in a court rife with erratic magic that can spread through touch. I refused most men's advances, but the rumors of my impropriety had already taken root. My mother did her best to contain the worst of the gossip, but it was too late. She feared for my marriage prospects—and rightly so. With a tarnished reputation and a gift that drives men to obsession, I was already a lost cause.

My father speaks up, a rare thing for him to do at a council meeting. "Penelope, dear," he begins. He's the only one who ever addresses my mother so informally in public. "Princess Genevieve has grown over the years. She's learned to control her gift and has kept any scandal at bay for years. If this is what she wants, she knows how her gift will affect her marriage, and you should accept her decision."

My mother gives a minuscule nod before replying, "Very well. Keep Prince Leland at arm's reach until the wedding ceremony. I do not want him exposed to your gift until the arrangement is settled. There is also the matter of Mr. Morris Blackwell to discuss."

Lord Fenweir clears his throat again, the sound grating my nerves. "Yes, Your Majesty. Unfortunately, Mr. Blackwell will be arriving tomorrow. We attempted to delay his visit until next month, but he indicated that if we do not host him in the coming month, he will bring the discussion of his intercontinental railway line to Wylan."

My mother's lips quirk as she delicately passes her teacup to a lady in waiting. "The railway is already in place through much of Icelantica. If Mr. Blackwell has already formed an agreeable contract with Queen Kalise, I see no reason to delay his visit. If anything, Prince Leland and Queen Kalise may help us secure the line through Naseria."

I've heard discussions of the mysterious railway magnate, but I assumed he would visit while Prince Leland and I took our honeymoon. It's a relief to hear that his arrival will occur while I'm still at Fairbright Palace. I'm eager to be involved in the decisions regarding where the railway will be placed, and fascinated by his ingenious use of helachite. I know it must follow the naturally formed lines, bonding raw helachite with his processing techniques to power the machines. Like Naseria, Icelantica is rich in helachite, and Mr. Blackwell has had smashing success developing a new transportation system throughout the bitterly cold country.

But I also want to better understand this man—a man of unknown redblood origins who now possesses more wealth than anyone else on the continent. The famed self-made magnate is responsible for creating Blackwell Industries, the most expansive mining and industrial firm in Inver. He's strategically based in southern Icelantica, where he has access to the three largest countries on the continent. He holds mining rights in all three and commands the most extensive stockpile of helachite in existence. That rare mineral—once the cause of wars, the source of blueblood lineage and gifts—is now controlled by a redblood. How very ironic.

The discussion around his schedule dies down, and finally my mother stands to dismiss the meeting. Her dark eyes meet mine, and I know I'm expected to wait and speak with her privately. Gabe catches my gaze and immediately knows I'm being summoned. We're both far too familiar with our mother's expressions. He smirks before rising and moving toward the door, clearly making his escape before he's drawn into an unwanted conversation.

Once the room is cleared of all but a few servants, I approach Queen Penelope. "Mother," I say, curtsying before she gestures for me to sit in my father's vacant seat.

"Darling," she begins, and I do all I can to appear the adoring daughter I once was. "I don't want you concerned about negotiations with Mr. Blackwell. Your duty is to secure this marriage. Prince Leland still has the right to change his mind until the contract is signed. Let me handle the railroad agreement, and you focus on forming an attachment to the prince."

I shake my head. "I have a right to be involved in these discussions. By the time the railroad project is completed, I'll be the one on the throne, not you, Mother. Further, Prince Leland and I have decided to sign our marriage contract as soon as possible."

Her lips tighten before her face softens. "Genny, dear, my most earnest wish is to see you succeed as queen. But your wedding is far too important for you to be distracted by business matters."

I unclench my hands, willing them to relax. Is this how she'll always treat me? Like a child? At twenty-eight, I'm only two years away from my coronation and her abdication. And yet, she still acts as if there's all the time in the world before the transfer of power.

"Mother, I insist on being in those meetings."

She exhales sharply, trying to mask her exasperation. "If you insist, my dear. But you must understand—Mr. Blackwell is not a gently bred blueblood. He's known for his crass behavior and harsh temperament."

"All the better to learn how to negotiate with redbloods now, before the crown is on my head."

Mother scowls, creases forming between her brows. "The man has been a thorn in my side since he purchased the mines to the north. Always sending complaints about the conditions. Well, if he wasn't happy with the conditions, he shouldn't have purchased them!"

I think of Gabe's warning. *She's hiding things from me.* I don't know why, but she clearly doesn't want me involved with the helachite rot. "Is there corruption from tainted helachite in the mines? I want to know what's happening with the spreading rot."

Her lips draw into a thin line. "There's been little progress, as I already told you. It seems contained for now. As for the mines—of course the helachite is corrupted. It's a volatile mineral."

"Please, Mother, be truthful. I need to be prepared before I take the crown. Don't hide crucial information from me." My voice rises in frustration as I blurt out, "I won't have it!"

I've crossed a line, but I don't care. Not when the future of this kingdom depends on my readiness to rule. Her stare is so sharp it takes everything in me not to look away.

"*You* won't have it?" she repeats, her voice low and dangerous. "Don't forget, Genevieve—*you* are not queen yet. Remember who wears the crown. I will decide how much you need to know to govern in two years. For now, secure your husband."

With that, she stands and sweeps from the room, her elegant skirts whispering across the marble floor.

Genevieve

The air is sweetly scented with cherry blossoms and hyacinth blooms. The soft blue sky, shrouded by downy white clouds, settles my nerves as I stand awaiting Prince Leland's quickly approaching carriage. My future husband is in that carriage, and the very thought sends a current of apprehension down my spine.

Does he understand what it will mean to be my king consort? Will he be able to bear my gift long enough to make an heir?

Leland Frostclaw is my last hope—to find a husband, to fulfill my duty to my country.

Love isn't even an option.

A team of six snow-white horses rounds the corner, followed by three other impressive carriages, and I can feel my heartbeat matching the thud of the approaching hoofbeats. Regardless of my own feelings, this marriage *must* happen.

The lead carriage slows to a halt before the gathered assembly outside Fairbright Palace, and I can't help but wonder what Prince Leland is thinking as he sees his new home for the first time. Does he admire the steep gabled roof and stately granite exterior? Does he notice how it seems to glitter in the spring sunshine?

A hand brushes lightly against my gloved fingers, and I glance down to see my sister, Astoria, at my side. With light brown hair, hazel eyes, and spectacles, she has a more subtle, dignified beauty than the rest of us. As my dearest companion and closest sibling, she's attuned to my every inclination. No doubt she's noticed the anxiety rising in my chest.

"It's going to go well," she says bluntly, the seriousness in her tone evident as a soft breeze loosens stray strands of hair from her chignon. Astoria is dear to me—so dear that I try not to burden her with the complicated parts of my life. Her gift, foresight, is what she considers entirely useless. Coming in short spurts and only foretelling the immediate future, Astoria tries to avoid using it. I let out a slow, steady breath. At least this time, her sporadic visions have proven useful.

"I just want the meeting over with. The anticipation is too much," I mutter, linking elbows with my sister. A pointed throat-clearing draws my gaze to Mother's stern expression, and I release Astoria's arm, though I long to cling to her like a lifeline.

"Here he comes!" Astoria whispers as a footman dressed in Icelantica's navy livery opens the coach door.

Not a man, but a woman steps out. Her skin is alabaster white and her short-cropped hair the color of watery sunlight on a winter's day. But it's her eyes that catch my attention—two chips of ice-blue meeting my gaze. I curtsy to the Queen of Icelantica as she approaches with regal stride. Her soft green traveling dress makes her pale skin nearly glow, and two fluffy white foxes trail close behind her.

I offer my most courteous smile and curtsy low. "Queen Kalise, what a pleasure."

"Princess Genevieve," she replies stiffly, her own curtsy stilted, before turning to Mother.

Beyond her, a tall man steps from the carriage, unfolding himself to his full height. He's slim—not exactly thin, but lacking the heavily muscled build of some men. My heart stutters as Kieran Greenbluff's lanky teenage form flashes through my mind. If he'd survived, would he have filled out like other men, or would he have remained slight, like my future husband? I push the thought aside and turn my focus back to Leland Frostclaw. Thinking of a long-lost lover will not do while I meet my fiancé.

Prince Leland walks with easy grace. He's obviously a man of leisure and courtly courtesies, with perhaps the occasional fencing lesson to keep fit. His hair is the color of autumn wheat, and his pale skin holds a warmth his sister's lacks. But his eyes are the same frosty blue. As he approaches, he offers a generous smile that eases some of the tension coiled within me.

"Princess Genevieve, at last we meet!" He takes my hand and presses a chaste kiss to my silk glove. The gesture is warm, and he seems genuinely happy to meet me. "You look even more beautiful than your portrait."

"Prince Leland, it's a pleasure to finally make your acquaintance," I reply with a smile.

He bends, nearly a bow, in a casual motion of deference. "I feel as though I already know you, after all our correspondence. Fairbright Palace is just as you described—it even sparkles in the sunlight."

His words ease my apprehension, allowing a faint sense of calm to settle in. This decision was the right choice for everyone. He's read my letters and even remembers my words, just as I remember his. I know this is the start of a happy matrimony—arranged or not.

"Please come in. You must be exhausted from your travels," I offer.

"I'd be delighted," he answers, offering me his elbow. The height difference makes this a bit of a challenge as I slide my hand into the crook of his arm, and I'm glad I chose to wear heels today. When we link arms, I catch my mother's slight nod of approval as she guides Queen Kalise toward the palace doors.

The courtiers of Icelantica stream out of their coaches, following as we make our way into the palace. Although my attention is on Prince Leland, I can't help but wonder if the mysterious Mr. Blackwell is amongst their retinue.

As we walk, I ask about their journey, and Prince Leland shares an entertaining story about traveling across a newly finished stretch of railroad through Icelantica by locomotive.

"The train's carriages are so smooth our soup course held steady, even as we moved at an astonishing speed. Princess Genevieve, I think it's fortunate that Mr. Blackwell traveled with us. If you would allow me, I'd be delighted to continue working closely with him to secure the railway line through Naseria. He's becoming something of a close friend, and I believe that with his expertise, our two countries can be linked by more than marriage in no time."

I smile, thankful that Prince Leland already has a working relationship with the magnate and can assist in securing this new technology for my kingdom. "That would be most helpful, Prince Leland."

He looks down at me, our eyes meeting and holding. "Please, it's my hope that you'll consider calling me Leland when we're in private."

A bold request, especially since we've been formally acquainted for only a matter of minutes. But in less than a month, we'll be husband and wife. In this case, decorum be damned.

"Of course, Leland. Please call me Genny. It's what my family calls me in private."

We enter our family parlor, a less formal setting than I expected Mother to arrange for the Icelantican delegation. But as we settle in, I see the merit of a more intimate arrangement. Present are only our family members, Queen Kalise, Prince Leland, and the young general of their army, General Pryor Darrow. From Leland's correspondence, I know he's close friends with the general, and it's no surprise they'd invite him to join us. Like Queen Kalise, General Pryor exudes a stern, cold presence that will take some getting used to.

My siblings look at me expectantly, and I try to maintain an easy countenance as I take a seat in a wingback chair. A servant arrives with a tray of refreshments, but I accept only a cup of tea, my nerves still too high to stomach food.

There's a stilted silence as everyone settles into place, and I find myself at a loss for words to fill the void.

Prince Leland—*Leland*—smiles at my siblings as he takes a seat near me. Queen Kalise sits beside Mother, stroking one of her foxes in her lap with a gloved hand. The other fox leans against her skirts, staring adoringly up at her. Mother glances at them but makes no comment. But the expression on her face tells enough. She's always been against animals in the palace.

"Please, tell me your names," Leland begins, breaking the silence. Gabe opens his mouth to speak before Leland lifts a hand. "Better yet, let me have a guess. Princess Genevieve has shared so much about you all, I feel as though I already know you."

Gabriel's expression mirrors Queen Kalise's bored disinterest as Prince Leland correctly guesses my siblings' names.

"You, of course, are King Hugo. And you must be Gabriel, the second oldest, with your mother's features," he continues, gesturing toward my brother. "And you must be Astoria. I've heard the most about you!"

Astoria offers a courteous smile as Leland turns his attention to my youngest siblings. "So that makes you Princess Marielle, and you must be Prince Darian."

Marielle—ever the one to test Mother's patience—gives an exaggerated yawn in reply, while Darian smiles politely.

"Well done, Prince Leland," my mother remarks with an indifferent smile that doesn't match her cordial words. "We wish to welcome you and Queen Kalise to Naseria—and to our family."

"We're honored," Queen Kalise replies coolly. "We look forward to many years of unity between our two kingdoms."

She carries that same measured tone that makes me wonder if becoming queen inevitably turns one cold and affectless. Queen Kalise is known across the continent for her frosty demeanor. What I didn't expect was how much of her I'd see reflected in my own mother.

Unlike Queen Kalise, Mother is known for her warmth and generosity—qualities tied to her gift of fertility and life. It has brought rejuvenation to the kingdom that many praise her for. Fertile fields and rich harvests are useful to people, unlike a cursed gift of love.

"It certainly is an enthusiastic match," Gabe drawls, his tone bordering on insolent.

I glance at him in surprise at his boldness.

"In what way?" Queen Kalise inquires, her cold eyes fixing on my brother.

"It is not our custom to arrange marriages in Naseria, and thus far, I've found the practice lacking."

His words carry a bite I didn't expect from Gabriel, and my cheeks flush with embarrassment.

"And what, Your Highness, do you find lacking in this arrangement?" Queen Kalise quips back.

"Please, let's be cordial. Prince Gabriel doesn't agree with my reasons for choosing an arranged marriage." My voice is quiet, threaded with the humiliation his words stir in me. Yes, we've argued about this arrangement before, but this marriage is *my* decision, and I won't be bullied by my younger brother out of my right to choose a husband.

Prince Leland studies me with mild curiosity, his chin tilted slightly, and I find myself wondering whether he too faced resistance to our match. Most of all, I wish for a few moments of privacy with him—an opportunity to let go of this stifling awkwardness.

As tentative silence settles once more over the parlor, I search for something to say. "Should we discuss our plans for the next month?"

Queen Kalise nods, and Leland glances her way before she speaks. "I would prefer to return to Icelantica in twenty-one days. My kingdom needs me there. Prince Leland has expressed no objection to an expedited timeline. I trust that's no trouble for you, given your willingness to sign the marriage contract ahead of time."

"Oh—you wish to attend the wedding?" I ask, surprised to realize I may be married sooner than expected.

"I would never dream of missing my only brother's wedding."

Leland adds, "Kalise and I are all we have for family. My move here hasn't been without inconvenience to her court, and I'm willing to accommodate her schedule."

I summon my most understanding smile. "Of course. That shouldn't be an issue."

Mother gives the slightest tip of her head—her subtle sign of approval—and silence descends again. After a moment, Mari says brightly, "I look forward to the engagement announcement tomorrow night at the ball."

Gabriel clears his throat but says nothing. Finally, Leland's companion, General Pryor, breaks the quiet. "A masquerade, is that correct?"

"Yes," I reply as the others sip their tea. "We'll remove our masks midway through the evening to announce the engagement."

The two queens exchange cool glances, the silence settling around us like a cloak.

"A masquerade ball. What an original idea," Queen Kalise remarks, passing her teacup to a servant. "Do excuse me. I feel fatigued after the journey." She rises, her foxes scattering around the hem of her dress, and everyone stands to bow as she departs. "Prince Leland, General Pryor, please meet me in my suite in about half an hour. There are some matters I wish to discuss before I rest."

Both men agree, and Mother rises as well. "I should also take my leave."

My father crosses the room, taking my gloved hand in his. "This will all work out, Peach," he whispers encouragingly before following her out.

"Excuse me, I must be off too," Gabriel mutters, making for the door without another glance.

When it closes behind him, I turn to my new fiancé. "I apologize for my brother's behavior. He wasn't speaking for me."

Leland smiles, and I catch the faintest hint of dimples. While his sister's eyes pierce like shards of ice, his hold a gentleness that soothes, like a gently flowing stream.

"My sister can be a bit of a beast as well," he says lightly. "This hasn't been easy for her. She doesn't want to lose me at her side, but as we've already discussed in our letters, the benefits of our union outweigh our families' misgivings."

"It's for the greater good," I agree, taking in the face of my future husband. He's everything I imagined—kind, gentle, handsome.

And yet, all I feel toward him is a steady certainty that this will have to be enough for me.

It must be.

4

Genevieve

My body stiffens as I see Mother and Father's somber expression greeting me at my rooms. They never have reason to come to my private quarters—not unless something is wrong.

"What has happened?" My voice betrays me; the nervous rush of what could be coming hits like a wave. There are only a few weeks left before I receive my blueblood gift. Nearly twenty years old, and already I've felt a heaviness beyond my years since Kieran's departure. The day he betrayed me—leaving without explanation—was the day my heart threatened to shatter.

"May we come in?" Father asks gently, and how could I deny him when he's treating me like spun sugar, all delicate fragility.

"Yes, just... what is the matter?" I ask, leading them to the soft settee in my sitting room.

Mother's face reveals nothing, but Father looks on the verge of breaking himself as he takes the chair across from me.

"We received news—tragic news," Mother says. Her tone carries a softness so foreign to the Queen of Naseria.

"What? Please, just tell me."

She nods before continuing. "Kieran and his father have both perished in an accident."

My heart thuds against my chest, breath trapped inside me as I fight to inhale against the restraints of my corset. I try to speak, but all that escapes is a keening cry—a sound I didn't know I was capable of making.

"H-how? Where?" The words slip from me before the crashing weight of their meaning hits.

Kieran is dead. He's never coming back to me.

The ballroom is resplendent tonight. Crystal chandeliers cast a luminous glow over the room, and every available space bursts with spring blooms—peonies and ranunculus, early season roses and cherry blossoms fill the corners with vivid color. As I walk down the marble stairs into the radiant ballroom, polite applause echoes through the room as everyone bows. *So much for anonymity.* The attention keeps me steady on the steps, and my younger sisters follow behind.

We each chose dresses inspired by birds for the masquerade. Marielle wears brilliant shades of yellow to represent the warbler. Her mask, encrusted with yellow topaz, is adorned with soft yellow plumes. The bright, cheerful colors match her ebullient spirit. Of the three of us, she's the one who sparkles with bold grace. Despite her vibrant attire, I catch a glimpse of tiredness beneath her eyes before we don our masks, as if she's once again struggling to sleep well.

Astoria chose a more muted palette: the pale greys and blues of the heron. Her soft silk gown cascades around her, a subtle beauty that suits my sister, who would prefer nothing more than to blend into the backdrop. Her mask has been fitted to accommodate her spectacles, concealing them perfectly. She'd never want the compliment, but I whispered how beautiful she looked before we took to the stairs.

I chose to match Prince Leland as a pair of swans. My white bodice is cut just low enough to reveal the top of my full bust, the lace overlay exposing the delicate ties of my corset in the back. The skirt is fashioned from thin strips of lace, gathered in thick bundles to imitate a swan's feathers as it glides across the water. My hands are gloved in white silk that reaches past my elbows, leaving only a hint of bare skin at my upper arms. A pearl-and-feather mask conceals my face, and for once, I feel beautiful and mysterious.

Mother and Father are already seated at their thrones, each guest presented to them despite the supposed anonymity of the evening. There is a giddy eagerness in the air, as there always is during a ball, and I can't help but feel emboldened by the atmosphere.

Mari and Astoria come to my side, each linking an arm through mine, their silk gloves brushing the bare skin of my upper arms.

"Do you see Prince Leland?" Mari asks.

I shake my head, scanning the crowd. Masks of every color and shape conceal the faces that bow to me. Of course, everyone knows who I am. My hair gives me away, even with the white mask. I recognize some of my dearest friends, including Lady Clementine.

"Most likely he and Queen Kalise are being inundated by courtiers seeking their favor and attention. It isn't often we host another monarch," I say as a servant offers us glasses of sparkling wine from a glittering tray. We each take one eagerly, and as I take my first sip, I spot the tall, stately figure of Leland's friend, General Pryor. His dark skin and long white hair makes him stand out even amongst the dazzling crowd, despite his navy evening wear and blue-black mask. He looks decidedly Icelantican in a sea of Naserians.

I tug my sisters along, knowing that Leland will be nearby. But he isn't speaking with Leland. He's deep in conversation with a large, muscular man with olive skin and black hair—but it's his eyes that make me gasp. Brilliant green, they stir a prickling awareness in me I haven't felt in nine years.

"What is it?" Astoria whispers, and I shake off the haunting sensation of recognition.

"Nothing. I just nearly slipped," I reply, finishing my glass of sparkling wine in a quick gulp.

The stranger's green eyes—flecked with gold—stare back at me from behind a mask of raven feathers and black diamonds. His evening suit shimmers iridescent black, tailored to emphasize his broad, well-built frame. He and General Pryor make sweeping bows, giving us room to join their conversation.

General Pryor speaks in the same measured tone he always carries. "Your Highnesses, may I present Mr. Morris Blackwell?"

The man doesn't break his penetrating gaze as he takes my gloved hand, drawing it to his lips for a kiss. My heart races, and I struggle to keep from trembling in his grasp.

His eyes.

They're so familiar to Kieran's that it's like seeing a ghost. But in every other way, he's wrong—too dark, too tall, far too strong to be the boy who once stole my heart and left this world for good. What I can see of his face reveals a sharply defined jaw and angular features.

"It's a pleasure to make your acquaintance," I say, keeping my voice light and steady.

"The pleasure is mine, I'm sure, Princess Genevieve."

Not Kieran's voice. Not with that faint Icelantican lilt and the deeper timbre I don't recognize. He also didn't call me Gen—the nickname only Kieran ever used for me, despite our vastly different stations in life. He was never one to care about social status, or the fact that I'm a blueblood princess and he was a redblood gardener's son.

What am I thinking? Of course it isn't his voice.

Kieran has been *dead* for nine years. My mind can't help but drift back to the last time I saw him—to the hurt in his eyes. I did that to him. I was the reason he left. I chose the crown over him, betrayed him for my kingdom, and then he left me, breaking my heart in the process.

I pull my gaze from Mr. Blackwell as I see a flash of white approaching. "Ah! There you all are! Princess Genevieve, I see you've met Mr. Blackwell." Prince Leland's smile gleams behind his white, pearl-encrusted mask—the twin to my own—and I force a smile as I make room for my intended. I continue to feel a current of emotion rush through me, especially as I notice the man still watching me with an intensity that sends a shiver down my spine.

Leland leans close, his gloved hand brushing my bare shoulder. "The music is about to begin. Queen Penelope requested that I bring you to her. We're to begin the first dance with your mother and father, as well as Queen Kalise and Prince Gabriel."

"Of course. Excuse us," I say to the others, and Leland takes my hand, offering his arm to escort me. His touch isn't unwelcome—it's simply there. Glove to glove, in the most proper manner.

"I hope your day was good?" Leland asks, reminding me that we haven't seen each other since yesterday afternoon.

"It was, thank you for asking." A good day only if one enjoys the endless process of gown fittings, hair styling, and having little time to oneself. "How was your first full day in Naseria?"

"Splendid! General Pryor, Mr. Blackwell, and I had the pleasure of making use of your well-stocked lake. King Hugo and your brothers were excellent hosts, and we all left with a full creel of fish."

"You must be quite the fisherman, then. I'm happy you had the opportunity to enjoy our lake. My father loves nothing more than to host a day of fishing. Do you often fish in Icelantica?"

We make our way past guests dressed in their finest, the chandeliers scattering light across the crowd. We're nearly to the dais where the three monarchs wait.

"Unfortunately, not as often as I'd like. Our lakes stay frozen for seven months of the year, and I'm often too busy to find the time for ice fishing."

This surprises me. "I know you've mentioned your duties to Icelantica, but are you busy most days?"

I think of my own father—the way he always made time for us as children, even when our mother couldn't. How he still spends his days entertaining guests or visiting shop owners in Crawford. He's always socializing, always sharing his warm smiles at redbloods and bluebloods alike, even when Mother is buried in endless meetings.

"My sister utilizes my skills—and my gift—often in her court. She is very private and prefers that I take a more active role in the kingdom."

I glance at the woman seated beside my mother. Her back is rigid, her visible features drawn in a harsh line. She looks utterly unapproachable, and I can see why she depends on Leland to rule.

"What will she do without you in Icelantica?"

Leland's gaze shifts to his sister. "It will be difficult for her, but I think it will also give her the opportunity to become the ruler I know she can be."

I nod, feeling a pang of guilt that I'm taking Queen Kalise's only family—the one person she seems to rely on so completely. I knew this from our correspondence, from his letters describing how much she depends on him, but I assumed he wouldn't have agreed to this match without her blessing. Perhaps I was wrong.

We reach the platform where the monarchs sit, and I curtsy as Leland bows low. My mother and father rise and make their way to the ballroom floor, Queen Kalise following behind. My brother meets her with another bow as he takes her gloved hand. There's a tightness between them, as though both would rather walk barefoot across crushed glass than take the other's hand.

The gaslight chandeliers dim. The music begins. I feel Leland's hand rest lightly at the small of my back. My hand finds his shoulder, and we begin a fluid dance. It's an upbeat, energetic song, just as Mother prefers.

"You're an excellent dancer," Leland murmurs near my ear. His head bends, his lips only a breath away, his closeness tickling my exposed skin. "You tolerate my lanky body so well." His tone is self-deprecating, but I smile behind the mask.

"You're too harsh on yourself. Word of your dancing skill reached me long ago." He sends me into a heart-thudding twirl before drawing me back in. "Did you think I'd choose a husband who couldn't share one of my favorite pastimes?"

He chuckles before spinning me again. "No, we cannot have Princess Genevieve standing by the wall because her flat-footed husband cannot dance properly."

"We must certainly avoid that disaster." As he pulls me close, I wish I felt something more—a spark, a flutter—anything beyond this quiet sense of contentment. Leland makes me laugh, he dances beautifully, and yet I feel no romantic stirring for my future husband.

It's all simply... fine. I know there is a chance romance might come later. It will, in time—I'm sure of it. Until then, we'll make do with friendship.

As the music fades, the court and guests descend onto the floor, partners lining up for the first dance with the court.

"Shall we?" Leland asks, and I agree. It's true, I love dancing. I love the feeling of being swept away by my partner, and knowing that Leland is a good dancer makes it easy to partner with him again.

This song is just as lively as the last, and Leland pulls me close enough to border on indecency—which isn't difficult to do in Queen Penelope's court. But we aren't the only ones. Other couples are already quite close, emboldened by the semblance of anonymity. As we dance, we talk and laugh together. The more time I spend with Leland, the more certain I become that I can make this work, even if our marriage is destined to be founded on friendship and little else.

After our second dance, Leland helps me find another glass of sparkling wine, and Lord Ambrose—one of my mother's councilors—asks me to dance. I accept, even though I know he's not the most talented of partners.

Leland assures me that he'd like to dance with me again before our engagement is announced, then leaves to ask Astoria to dance. Unlike me, Astoria prefers to observe the balls from the edges of the room, and I'm surprised to see her gloved hand in his.

The dance with Lord Ambrose is a slower tune, which spares my feet from being trampled too many times, but once is quite enough.

After that, I dance with several dignitaries and lords until Astoria pulls me aside, insisting I have a drink and something to eat.

"You'll exhaust yourself if you continue like that, and they still haven't even announced your engagement!"

I take small sips of lemonade and bites of a savory dish.

"What do you think of Prince Leland?" I ask. She's danced with him twice, and I hope she's formed an opinion.

Astoria looks thoughtful as she gazes at the dancers. "He seems to fit your requirements for a husband. His experience helping his sister rule Icelantica will be invaluable, and he appears to be a man with a charming disposition."

I purse my lips. "But?"

Astoria shrugs, and if I could see her whole face, I know she'd be giving me that exasperated look she always does when she thinks I'm overthinking. "But what? You've been clear about what you want in a husband. I think he'll do well enough."

My shoulders slump slightly before I catch myself and stand straight. "I like him. He's kind. It's just... I don't feel any romantic inclinations toward him yet. And I worry."

"Give it time," my sensible little sister replies. "You've only just met, and you shouldn't put unnecessary pressure on yourself. I understand your reasons—your gift, the time constraints. You want to feel *something* for him before he's overtaken by your gift, but forcing the matter won't help."

I take a deep breath. "You're right. It's just that I need this to work with him. Everything depends on this union being a success."

Astoria shakes her head, probably already weary of my worries. As the music slows, I notice a man approaching us. In the dim light of the ballroom, it takes me a moment to realize who it is.

It's Mr. Morris Blackwell—and my traitorous heart leaps when he takes my hand and asks me to dance.

5

Genevieve

I hold my breath for the first count of the dance, trying to calm my nerves as I feel Mr. Blackwell's hand slide down my waist. Lower, lower still—so low that it makes me give the tiniest squeak. But despite the quiet chuckle that tells me he heard, he doesn't move his hand higher. Instead, I see his full lips tilt into a smirk.

To make matters worse, Mr. Blackwell isn't wearing gloves, and the scrape of his calloused hand against my lace bodice sends a tingle down my spine. It's odd that a man of such wealth has the build of someone accustomed to manual labor. Not for the first time, I wonder how he came into his fortune. Of course, it would be rude to ask, so I stifle my curiosity. His other hand remains on the gloved part of my upper arm, a small relief that I don't have to worry about my curse overtaking him. But the gentle press of his fingers and the roughness of his callouses through the silk of my gloves heat my blood. There's an intimacy between us that is startling, and yet I cannot bring myself to ask for more space. It's as though my own curse is finally working its way through my body—and it's happening with the wrong man.

He leads me across the floor with graceful movements that seem incongruous with his large, muscular frame and those roughened hands. The candelabras cast him in a soft glow, and for a moment it feels as though the rest of the dancers fade away, leaving only us and the music.

"Mr. Blackwell, you're an excellent dancer," I remark, trying to break the silence hanging between us. His eyes are fixed on my face before drifting lower.

He pulls me closer, and I can feel the heat of his body against mine. My heart quickens as he leans nearer. Although the resemblance to Kieran is there, it's his distinct features that undo me—the precise tailoring of his suit emphasizing his strong build, the proud jawline visible beneath the raven-feather mask. He's a gorgeous man, and I've quite forgotten myself when he lifts me, spinning me before catching me effortlessly. Honestly, his form should be a thing of study. Observe: the perfect male specimen.

"You flatter me, Princess Genevieve, but I'm nothing compared to your betrothed." His voice is deep and smooth, the slight Icelantican accent more pronounced as he lowers his face near mine. The gold flecks in his green eyes are astonishingly similar to Kieran's, but where Kieran's gaze once brimmed with warmth, his carries a shadow of harshness. Kieran was all easy smiles and brash confidence.

"Prince Leland is very skilled, but you have a natural grace. You must dance often at Whitehurst."

Mr. Blackwell lets out a low scoff. "Does this surprise you, Princess?"

He says *princess* as though it's an insult. Perhaps it is to him—a self-made man, without even a blueblood's gift to aid his success.

"Certainly not. Although a busy man like yourself must find it difficult to make time for such frivolous activities as dancing."

His eyes pierce me as he dips me low enough that my breath catches. Would he dare drop me? His lips curve into that easy smirk, and I'm not sure whether he means to hold me steady or prove me wrong by letting me fall. He looks as though he might do it just to spite me.

"Do I look like a man who wastes his time on frivolous activities, Princess?" he whispers in my ear. They way he says it is almost indecent. This near, I can smell the spice of his cologne—expensive, no doubt, but beneath it lingers something familiar. Something that makes my eyes sting.

It can't be.

He can't be.

I feel lost in the sensation of this powerful man holding me close. The familiarity in his embrace is like the touch of a ghost, and I suddenly need to get very far away from Morris Blackwell. I can't stay here—not when being in his arms feels so good, something I never expected to feel again.

"I don't think there's anything frivolous about you, Mr. Blackwell." My voice comes out choked, and I flush with embarrassment at my candid words.

The song ends, and Mr. Blackwell releases me before bowing and taking his leave without another word. He seems as affected by our nearness as I am. I jump when I feel Mari's hand on my shoulder. Her eyes are wide, and a mischievous smile peeks from beneath her mask.

"Genny, what was happening between you and Mr. Blackwell?" she asks, linking her arm through mine as she tugs me across the ballroom toward Astoria.

"Whatever do you mean?" I ask, recovering my demure posture.

"It means the entire court saw how you two were dancing. It was positively exhilarating!"

I blanch at Mari's words. If the whole court saw me move in a way that could be described as *exhilarating*, then our dance will be the subject of gossip by morning. "Did Mother say anything?"

Mari plucks two more flutes of sparkling wine from a passing servant before handing one to me. I shouldn't drink it—not with the riotous feelings still stuttering through my veins, not when it feels as though I've just been in the arms of a man I was never meant to see again. Still, I take a generous sip, hoping the wine will bring me back to my senses. "She was busy dancing with Lord Willoughby, but Queen Kalise looked ready to intercede."

"And Prince Leland?" I can't believe I behaved so scandalously in front of my betrothed—just before our engagement is to be officially announced to the court.

"I didn't notice him. Perhaps he stepped out?"

I scan the room but don't see Prince Leland anywhere. I need to speak with him, to check on him and present a unified front before our announcement. We need to dance again, to laugh and flirt together in front of the court. It's crucial that the kingdom knows I'm committed to this marriage.

I finish my sparkling wine in a less-than-ladylike gulp before turning toward the terrace. "I'm going to look for him. If Mother asks for me, make up some excuse."

Mari's lips quirk into a wide smile. "I'll be sure nobody remembers your dance with Mr. Blackwell."

"Mari..." I warn, knowing my vibrant sister loves nothing more than to make our mother miserable with scandalous behavior that leads to salacious gossip.

She flicks her gloved hand at me. "Genny, this is what I live for."

I turn away, trying not to dwell on what trouble she'll cause next. At the last ball, she was caught in a compromising position with a redblood on the very terrace I'm now walking toward.

My skin tingles as I step into the cool night air. A man stands in the shadows on the far side of the terrace. He's tall, but in the darkness I can't be sure if it's Leland.

"Prince Leland?" I call before the man turns.

It isn't Leland. In fact, it's the last person I should be approaching alone in the dark. I should turn and leave, but Mr. Blackwell is already facing me—and I can't look away. I freeze as he approaches with purposeful strides that make my skin prickle. When he reaches me, he's so close I can feel the heat of his body near mine. I gulp in a breath, knowing I should step back, create distance between us. But even as my mind urges me to move, my body leans toward him, drawn by the familiarity of his scent and the pull of his warmth—an attraction I seem powerless to resist.

Mr. Blackwell lifts a hand to my face, brushing a stray lock of hair aside. His fingers caress my exposed cheek, and I pull back, afraid that in my heightened state I'll pour my gift into him.

He doesn't press me further. Instead, he raises his mask to reveal a face so familiar, yet so changed, I don't know what to think.

"Kieran?" The name catches in my throat, a stilted word carried on dusk's breeze.

"Hi, Gen. I've returned to you."

My Kieran looks at me like a phantom from my past. It's him—and yet, it isn't. His jawline is sharper, his nose crooked where it was once straight, and the dark brows shadowing his eyes hold a hardness they never had before. A faded scar slices across the right side of his forehead. I bring my hands to my face, knocking my mask to the ground as I stifle a cry.

Then everything around me begins to spin, the world blurring from my vision.

6

Genevieve

When I wake, I'm lying on something soft and supportive. My eyes focus on Gabriel's and Astoria's faces, close enough to startle me. Their masks are off, and both wear expressions marred with concern. I'm no longer outside; instead, I'm on a couch in an alcove beside the ballroom. These small sitting rooms have curtains that can be drawn, but from the light I can make out past Astoria's head, they haven't been.

"Slowly, Genny. Don't sit up just yet," Gabriel mutters when I try to lift my head from the pillow.

"What—what happened?" Memories of Kieran's caress, of the way he called me Gen, rush back, and I force myself upright despite Gabriel's admonishment. "Where did Kieran go?"

Astoria and Gabriel exchange a puzzled look. "Kieran?" Astoria asks, her brows knitting as she glances toward Gabe. His expression is unreadable as he gives her a slight shake of his head.

"Mr. Blackwell *is* Kieran Greenbluff." My words come out in a hiss, and disbelief only deepens on my siblings' faces.

"Genny, Kieran has been dead nine years. I spent all day with Mr. Blackwell. Do you think I wouldn't recognize my closest friend?" Gabriel's voice is so quiet I have to strain to hear him. I glance around again, noticing the crowd just beyond us. We have an audience, and Gabriel doesn't want our words carried to the court.

"But—but he was there. He was..." I let the words die on my tongue as I see two masked figures approaching.

It's Mother, and behind her, Prince Leland. She lifts her mask, studying me closely. "Darling, you must be overtired. Prince Leland has offered to escort you to your rooms."

I hesitate. We're supposed to declare our engagement to the court tonight. I need to convince the entire kingdom—and Prince Leland's retinue—that I'm serious about this marriage. "The engagement announcement?"

"Your health is the priority," Leland answers with a gentle smile. "There will be another day for that."

I nod as he places his gloved hands on my upper arms, helping me stand and offering steady support that, to others, looks like a gentleman escorting a lady—not a woman clinging to a man she hardly knows like a last refuge. I straighten my spine, despite the fact that all I want to do is collapse. I don't make a fuss as Leland leads me toward the door, though I'd much prefer it were my father—or even Gabriel—walking me back to my apartment. I don't know how I can face Prince Leland, not with the confusion running rampant through my mind.

The only man I ever loved, the one who broke my heart, a man I thought *dead* all these years, has returned. And returned for me. But that path is closed. My duty is to my people and to Leland now. I can't let Kieran—Mr. Blackwell—distract me from that duty.

"Your sister said you had another glass of wine. Do you think it caused you to become overset?" Leland asks as we walk the halls toward my rooms.

I shake my head. I cannot tell him that the man he believes to be a trusted friend is someone I once knew intimately.

"Do you know how I got inside?" I inquire. "The last thing I remember was walking onto the terrace to find you."

His grip on my arm is light, offering just enough support to steady me. It's polite and gentlemanly. "Unfortunately, I stepped away with my sister and General Pryor. I suppose Prince Gabriel found you."

"Of course. You weren't there." I nod as I pull the key to my apartment from a discreet pocket hidden in the folds of my skirt. "Thank you for escorting me to my rooms."

His eyes meet mine, two cool chips of ice, but his face is warm, his expression sincere as he asks, "May I join you in your sitting room? Just to get to know you better."

All I want is a moment alone to sneak down to my glasshouse and calm my raging nerves. But how can I refuse him? We were supposed to grow better acquainted tonight, and with the court distracted at the ball, this may be one of the few moments we have alone together for days.

"Of course. Come in." I open the door just enough for him to slip through, ensuring no one sees us before locking it securely behind us. A fire crackles in the grate, and a small plate of refreshments waits on the sideboard.

"Would you like anything to eat?" I offer, gesturing toward the food. I've had little since early afternoon, but I can't eat now—not with my mind flashing back to Kieran's face.

"Yes, actually—I'm famished," Leland says, helping himself to cheeses, cured meats, and vegetables.

While Leland makes a plate, my mind drifts to Morris Blackwell. He *must* have been Kieran. No one else has ever called me Gen. But why would he stay away from me all these years? Why did he leave me in the first place? His brief letter of farewell was so curt, so harsh, and I never understood why.

I think back to the night I brought him to this very room, not as a friend but as a lover. How he touched me with such reverence, such adoration. No one has ever treated me like that. Our whispered words of love are etched into my heart even now.

The argument we had afterwards all because I was afraid of what the court would say after Kieran asked me to marry him—shouldn't have ended us so easily. He shouldn't have left after one difficult moment. The way he avoided me for days afterward stung deeply, and as a young woman, I hadn't known what to say.

I bring my attention back to Leland, who gives me a warm smile as he pulls out a chair for me. I sit beside him, letting him tuck it closer to the table.

"Would you like anything?"

"Perhaps a cup of tea." There's a fresh pot, steam curling from the spout.

"Of course. How do you take it?" he asks with a casualness people rarely use with me.

"With a bit of milk, please."

Leland walks to the sideboard, his white evening wear still perfectly pressed. He moves easily through the room, as though he's already comfortable in the space—and it puts me on edge. Few people other than my closest family or servants have ever entered my private quarters, not since I learned the effect my magic can have on others.

When he returns, he joins me at the table and offers another one of those friendly smiles. I only wish I weren't so distracted—so tangled inside—that I could at least try to enjoy this moment. It's what I've been hoping for: a chance to get to know Leland, to make this engagement into something more than a contract.

But now I don't know if I can, at least not this evening.

Not with my emotions twisted in knots over Kieran's return.

I wordlessly sip my tea as Leland talks about the various members of the court he's already become acquainted with. Try as I might, I can't seem to focus on the mundane conversation; my thoughts keep spiraling with the knowledge that Kieran is at Fairbright Palace. I still don't understand why he's returned after all these years—and now he's disappeared before I can even ask him why.

Abruptly, Leland frowns at me, pulling me from my distraction. Did he say something I should have answered differently? I can't even recall the last thing he said.

He stands and runs a hand through his sandy-blonde hair. "I should go."

"Please, stay. I'm happy to have your company." The lie falls flat, and I know I haven't been convincing. I'm not even convincing myself that I want Leland to stay.

He shakes his head, a hint of disappointment in his expression. "No, I've intruded on your evening. After fainting, you should be in bed resting, not listening to me prattle on. It was rude of me to impose like this."

I rise with him, relief washing over me. I'm so tired. I need time alone, time to think about what I'm going to do and let my emotions settle.

"I apologize that I haven't been a better host. Can I see you tomorrow?"

He steps closer, his brilliant eyes sparkling. "I'd like that. Genny, I want nothing more than for our engagement to lead to a happy union."

I offer my gloved hand, and he presses it to his lips. "I want that as well. Tomorrow, then?"

"I look forward to it," he replies as I unlock the door. As I watch him walk away, I see him remove his mask from his jacket pocket and slide it back over his face.

The sigh of relief that escapes my lips as I close the door behind me makes me ashamed. I should want to spend time with my fiancé. I shouldn't be distracted—or thinking of another man. Even if the thought of marrying Leland fills me with doubt, I have a duty to both our countries to fulfill our alliance. It's the only way to prevent the growing unrest between our borders and those of Wylan. It's the practical choice for producing heirs and being the queen Naseria expects me to be.

Besides, Kieran has had nine years to return to me. Nine years, and not a single letter. No indication that he wanted me back, or that he was even alive, for that matter. Why would he return now, only to build the railway? He didn't want me. He left me and forged his own path without me.

It's been so long since he left that I know I can let the past die and work with him in a professional capacity—after I recover from the shock of seeing him alive. As queen, I won't have a choice but to work with people I may not like. This will be no different.

I slide off my gloves, stretching my fingers before moving to the armoire to take out a dressing gown. Reaching behind my back, I work at the laces of my corset. It's not the easiest task, but at least this gown doesn't have intricate buttons over the corset, and I'm so desperate for a bit of solace that I don't want to bother my lady's maid,

Trudy, for help. Knowing her, she's probably downstairs flirting with the handsome footman I've seen her talking with.

Once I've changed out of my ball gown and into my dressing gown, I slip on a pair of older slippers with sturdy soles and grab the oil lamp from my dresser. I make my way to the bookshelf, knowing it isn't a book I need tonight—it's an escape to my private glasshouse.

Pressing on the book that isn't truly a book feels like second nature, the worn latch clicking out of place as I swing the secret door open and step into the drafty stairwell. The scent of wet stone and damp air clings to my skin, but it's a comfort to me. It's the scent of freedom.

I push open the heavy wooden door that leads to the private family gardens of Fairbright Palace, taking steady steps as I cross the lawn to my safe haven. Tucked away in a far corner of the gardens, my glasshouse is all my own—a hothouse built for my collection of rare tropical plants. Plants so unsuited to life in Naseria that, at sixteen, I begged my mother for a place to store my growing collection. It's been mine ever since. My refuge and sanctuary from life at court.

As I open the glass door, the humid air settles over my skin, the scent of earth and greenery hanging heavy in the air. But that's not all. There's another scent here—a spicy, masculine scent.

I'm not alone in my glasshouse after all.

7

Kieran

Gen's lips part as she lets out a gasp. So I *did* catch her by surprise, waiting for her here in the glasshouse. She's still as predictable as she was nine years ago. There's no place my princess would rather be than retreating to her glasshouse after the shock of seeing me again. She still comes to this small room—the place I helped build with my father for her, all those years ago.

She looks even better than I remembered: the rich strands of peach and honey in her hair, the way her dark-blue eyes shine with surprise. She makes a sensual little gasp through her parted lips as her gaze meets mine.

I want to devour that sound and draw even more from her. I want to explore her fuller figure and trace the changes in her body over all these years. But most of all, I want to make her ache and hurt. I want to ruin her for the way she ruined me.

"It *is* you." Her voice comes out as a hoarse whisper, and she takes a tentative step closer—bare arms outstretched before tugging them back to her sides. There's a hardness in her expression that I've never seen on her sweet face. "How? Why are you here?" She gestures to the small space we share.

"I told you I was back, Gen." *Back to make you pay.*

She bites her lower lip, just as she always has. A hand slides to her chest, and I take in the sheer nightdress she's wearing.

"But—but you're dead. You…"

Her voice sounds raw with pain—pain I never expected from her, not after all these years. I thought she'd forgotten me long ago, especially after hearing the rumors of her gift and the power she's wielded over other men.

"Why did you think I was dead?"

She turns away, her attention fixed on a begonia with long, speckled leaves. The names of these rare plants come back to me like old friends. This one, in particular, is the hybrid my father and I bred—white speckles framed by green and pink. Begonia Gen. The plant I gave her when she turned seventeen, shortly after I realized I loved her.

"We received a report not long after you left," she mutters, her gaze still averted.

"Ah. That should have been limited to my father. But in a way, you're right—Kieran Greenbluff died long ago. I'm Morris Blackwell now."

She looks up at me, hurt flickering in her eyes. Why does she care? Why does she look like she never recovered from my disappearance?

"You never came home. All these years—why return now?"

I want to reach out and smooth the pain from her face, but that goes against everything I've planned. I didn't expect to feel anything for her. Not after so many years, and not after everything I've endured to get here. Not after I let every feeling for Genevieve Ashcroft die.

"I'm here strictly for business, nothing more." I cross my arms as she stares at me with wide, wounded eyes. "By the way, I hear congratulations are in order."

I can't stop watching her every movement—the tiny prickles on her skin at the mention of her engagement, the way she turns her face to avoid my gaze.

"Thank you."

"Prince Leland is a good man. You're lucky to have made such a match." The words taste bitter. I pity Leland for being attached to such a woman, and yet I'm still as drawn to her as I was when I was young. I don't tell her that I encouraged Leland to pursue the match. Not because she deserves him, but because I know Leland can fix the broken pieces of this country. He can make improvements that will benefit redbloods across Naseria, including the miners I once worked beside.

"I am, indeed. It's an arrangement that will benefit both our kingdoms."

Ah, she admits what Leland already told me. This isn't a great love match. It seems both of them are approaching their union with the same pragmatism Gen always had.

"Still so practical, Gen?"

She wrinkles her nose at me. "Don't call me that. I'm Princess Genevieve, and you're Mr. Blackwell now. Of course I'm still putting my kingdom first. That will never change."

I snort. Of course, that will never change with Genevieve Ashcroft. Nothing has ever been as important to her as her duty to Naseria—not even the love I once had for her. She broke any hope that she'd choose me long ago, but the way she tossed me aside after a childhood of friendship and years of mutual love still stings. Especially how her rejection led to the hell I endured deep underground in the helachite mines.

No, Genevieve Ashcroft doesn't know what love is. Not toward me and certainly not with the rumored conquests she's taken, thanks to her cursed gift. Soon she'll be as brittle and broken as her own mother, that damned crown of helachite atop her head. And I'm willingly letting Leland pursue a marriage with her.

"That's not what the rumors of your behavior a few years ago indicated. Tell me, *Gen*—did you enjoy breaking all those men's hearts?"

She looks at me as if I've struck her before hissing, "Don't speak to me with such impertinence. You have no idea how I've struggled."

How dare she speak of struggling when I've been through the depths of hell and back to become who I am today. How could *she*, a spoiled princess, ever understand what it is to struggle? To suffer?

I let my eyes linger on the pale nightgown, her ample breasts above a soft stomach unbound by a corset. The changes in her body make her all the more beautiful—soft and lush and as poisonous as a sweet pea.

"It looks to me like you don't know what struggling is."

"Why are you looking at me like that?"

I give her the smallest hint of a smile as I keep my eyes on her. "You've grown into quite the attractive woman, Gen. I can see how you've broken so many hearts."

She wraps her arms across her chest, only accentuating the tantalizing curve of her breasts. "Just stop. Just—leave."

I smirk at her distress. It's delightful to watch her squirm. "No, I don't think I will."

Her face tightens as she looks at me—really takes me in—as if she's finally noticing all the differences in my appearance before changing the subject.

"How did Gabe not recognize you?" She takes a tiny step closer, her curiosity getting the better of her.

I'd rather be flayed alive than share how the helachite in the mines shifted me, changed me in unnatural ways from the inside out. I'm no longer that bright-eyed young man with a soft face and lanky frame. I'm not a lot of things I once was, but what I am now is strong enough to take on the Ashcroft family's degradation.

"Princess, there are many things about Morris Blackwell that I would never disclose to you. You're likely the only one capable of recognizing me." I don't want to dwell on how easy it was for her to see through me. Within moments of making eye contact in the ballroom, I knew she'd seen past my false identity. I'd planned to ruin her without revealing myself—but this should be more satisfying.

She scoffs. "They already think I'm mad. You mean to say nobody will believe it's actually you?"

I laugh at her frustration, and she looks at me with such malice. I want to bottle it up and keep it, to replace every memory of her devotion. I want to remember her anger, her hate, and erase any last trace of the love she once showed me. Just as I'm no longer Kieran Greenbluff, she's no longer the beautiful, loyal girl I once believed loved me.

"No one will believe you, Princess." I should leave, let her simmer in the disgust that mars her pretty face. Except I can't, not without knowing the truth. "Tell me, how long did you wait after the news of my death to warm your bed with another man? One week? Two?"

Gen looks at me with a scathing hatred that shouldn't sting as badly as it does. She raises her hand, and I brace for the burn of her slap. I crave it, actually.

But instead, I'm struck with a hard, blunt object. She's thrown her damn shoe at me. I can't stop my laughter—long and hard—only causing her ire to flare further.

"I should have known Genevieve Ashcroft wouldn't lose her composure enough to touch me with her bare skin. Well played, Princess."

With that, I slip past her into the darkness of the night. Music and laughter drift through the still air, the ball continuing in some far-off corner of the palace. I have no intention of returning.

I make my way toward my rooms, knowing the long night will be best spent studying geological surveys of Naseria. Work is the only thing that will keep my mind off the revolting desire I still feel for the woman who ruined my life.

8

Genevieve

"Psst... Gen!" *A whisper from across the empty hallway catches my attention as I walk toward the schoolroom. I'm already late for my lessons, but I know that voice immediately.*

It's Kieran. He's the only one who ever calls me Gen. His disheveled hair and toothy grin are all I can make out as he pops his head out of the door to the servants' stairwell. I glance around, making sure I'm not being observed, before darting across the hall in a very unladylike fashion that would have Mother scowling. Kieran closes the door behind us.

"I got you an apple," he says, playfully holding it out for me to grab.

I reach for the fruit, deep red and golden in the muted light, but he pulls it back toward him.

"Can I have the first bite?" he asks, and there's a hunger in his eyes. Kieran is always hungry. At twelve, he's shot up in height, and no amount of food seems to fill him.

I smile at him, knowing he'll never deny me anything. Not when we've been the best of friends for four years now. "I thought it was a gift. You cannot take back a gift once it's freely offered."

He gives me a mock bow and holds out the apple again. "You're right, Princess. Where are my manners?"

Just as I reach for it, he pulls it back and takes a bite from the sweet flesh before tossing it to me. My reflexes are nothing like his, and I miss—the apple hits the floor with a thud.

"Kieran! Why would you do that? You're supposed to be my best friend!"

"Who better to tease you than your best friend?" He walks past me, picks up the apple, and takes another bite before opening the door.

"We'll be late for lessons now, and I didn't even get an apple for it!" I moan.

"You're welcome to some. It's delicious!" he says as he starts down the hallway, turning back to wink at me. "You just have to catch it first."

"You seem distracted," Astoria whispers as we walk into the family breakfast room. It's blissfully empty, no doubt most of the family is having breakfast in bed after last night's festivities. "Did you get any rest after you left the ball?"

"A little. I went to the glasshouse after Prince Leland left last night."

Her eyes light up, immediately homing in on Prince Leland's late-night visit. "Did you get to know him better? Are you feeling more confident about the engagement?"

I shake my head quickly. "I was tired. He stayed for a few minutes, but I just wanted to be alone." I should tell her about Kieran, but something inside me keeps me from speaking, knowing that not even my best friend and sister will believe me—that the man posing as Morris Blackwell *is* actually Kieran. I already know Astoria and Gabe didn't believe me last night. I don't need to embarrass myself any further.

After Kieran left, I took my time to calm down and think about what I should do next. The best I came up with was to ignore him. Keep our interactions professional and brief, and move forward with my engagement to Leland.

I'm not the only woman who's had to unexpectedly face someone from her past, and it doesn't change my situation. I don't want anything to do with this man who lied to me, who left me, and let me think he was dead all these years.

"Well, if it makes you feel any better, no one saw Mr. Blackwell after you left. Gabe is furious that he'd cause you such a fright. He was even muttering something about the need for a duel."

My hands shake, and my ears ring at the thought of Gabriel and Kieran dueling. Maybe Gabe doesn't recognize Kieran, but Kieran knows Gabe, and I can't imagine him fighting his former best friend.

"Don't say that, Astoria. The last thing I want is for Gabe to get in a fight with that man," I mutter as I walk toward the sideboard laden with breakfast sausages, eggs, toast, and a delicious fruit salad filled with imported fruits from the kingdom of Malin to the south. My stomach grumbles at the scent, and I remember just how long it's been since I had a good meal. I fill my plate before taking a seat in one of the cushioned dining chairs.

"Can I ask why you thought he was Kieran Greenbluff?" Astoria fiddles with her spectacles, nervous to broach the subject. I should tell her the truth, but Kieran's words echo in my mind—*no one will believe you*—and that probably includes Astoria.

"He looks like Kieran. It's his eyes. And he called me Gen."

Astoria doesn't bother to disguise the shock on her face. "Gen? That's rather forward for a man who's supposed to be working for us."

I nod, and we fall into a comfortable silence until Mother walks in.

We both stand and curtsy deeply as she gives a swift wave to release us. She marches toward the sideboard, a frown on her face. After taking her usual place at the head of the table, she finally addresses us.

"Good morning, girls." *Girls.* At twenty-eight and twenty-five, we are both still just girls to her. We always will be until we're wed—and even then, I don't know how my mother will relinquish control over us, or over the kingdom for that matter. She's bound by Naserian law to abdicate the throne on my thirtieth birthday, but there are times I doubt she will. I cannot imagine my mother in any role other than queen. My grandfather, the former king, seemed delighted to slip into retirement, moving to the coast where he spent his final years in quiet solitude. But Mother has always had more drive, more ambition to cling to power.

This is another reason I need this marriage. In her eyes, a married daughter has more legitimacy to the throne.

"Good morning, Mother. I hope you slept well."

She gives a brisk nod before focusing on her breakfast. A servant pours her a steaming cup of tea before making herself scarce. Mother has dark circles under her eyes, though her hair and dress are immaculate. She's tired, certainly, from the late night, and the strain on her face gives her a slightly imperfect air to her otherwise flawless presentation.

The door opens, and Prince Leland enters with General Pryor. Leland looks fresh-faced and smiles broadly. I didn't expect him to be invited to our private dining area, but it's not unusual for us to have important guests join us at meals.

Dread dips in my stomach. Would Kieran be given such privileges? I don't want to see him in my family's intimate quarters. I don't want his presence overshadowing the only part of my home that feels like my own. But that's what he's already done, isn't it? Coming into my glasshouse uninvited, something no one ever dares to do.

The nerve of him, thinking he still has a right to enter my private sanctuary, fills me with bitter rage. I think back to his insults, the way he perused my body and dared to say I didn't understand what it was to struggle. What right does he have to make such assumptions? Especially after his remarkable rise to power, going from a gardener's son to one of the wealthiest men in Inver.

"Good morning, ladies! Your Majesty! What a fine day it is!" Leland says with such earnest gusto it makes me cringe a bit. Mother's left eye twitches slightly, the only sign of her irritation at being addressed in such a way after a late night.

"Good morning, Prince Leland. General Pryor. It's so nice of you both to join us," Astoria replies, all demure manners and bright smiles.

"Good morning," I add, returning my focus to my half-eaten meal. I don't even know how to meet Leland's cheerful presence, knowing that I must marry him, even when my mind is so distracted by Kieran.

"Prince Leland, please feel free to sit next to Genny," my mother says when she sees him heading toward the opposite side of the table. "We can loosen the rules of propriety here, of course. General Pryor, there are a few matters I'd like to discuss with you," she adds, and he moves to the far end of the table, taking the seat beside her.

Prince Leland smells of freshly laundered clothing and clean male skin. It's a warm, inviting scent—but nothing as captivating as Kieran's, which haunted me throughout the night. Leland's morning coat is pressed, his hair perfectly styled. He looks every bit the part of a prince and moves with a fluid agility that is objectively attractive.

I just need to get to know this man better. In my mind, I begin listing things I already like about him. He's handsome, a skilled dancer, has an easy grace about him, and is a kind and cheerful man. All good qualities in a husband.

"I thought more about how I intruded in your rooms last night. I want to apologize. You were tired, and I shouldn't have imposed on you," he murmurs. Thick, light-brown lashes dip over his ice-blue eyes, and I can see how easily a woman could fall for his good graces and easy smiles.

"It wasn't an intrusion. I invited you in—no apology necessary," I insist, letting my gloved hand brush his arm. A small gesture, but I hope he sees I'm trying. "In fact, I'd be delighted to spend more time with you today."

Before Leland can respond, the door opens again—and Kieran walks in. He's wearing a black morning coat and black shirt with a black cravat: a dark expanse of a man who knows exactly how to make a statement. Like yesterday, his hands are ungloved, so unorthodox in courtly blueblood society. Ungloved hands are considered crass, something only working-class redbloods would do. Of course, that's because most bluebloods' gifts are more curse than blessing, and accidental touches can result in accidental releases of unwanted power.

Astoria glances in my direction, and I take a steady breath, suddenly very fixated on my remaining sausage.

"Blackwell! Good to see you this morning!" Leland greets in that same cheerful tone that makes my mother's eye twitch. "Please, join us."

I look up as Kieran takes a seat directly across from me, his eyes piercing mine as I offer a courteous nod. Leland turns to me and asks, "You had the privilege of dancing with Mr. Blackwell last night, did you not?"

His smile remains, but I wonder if he's heard rumors of our dance and is testing me. My mind drifts back to the way Kieran held me close—the brazen desire in his eyes, the way I got lost in his embrace, forgetting the dangerous gazes of the court analyzing my every move, every reaction.

"We did. Mr. Blackwell is a skilled dancer," I answer, meeting his eyes while lifting my teacup to give my hands something to hold.

"It was a *pleasure* to dance with you, Princess," he drawls, not breaking eye contact. I feel my cheeks heat, thinking about the closeness of his body to mine. The way I had to fight myself from leaning further into his touch. Even before I knew it was Kieran, my body had responded to his familiarity in a damning manner.

"It's a shame we couldn't see the two of you dance for the engagement announcement."

The nerve of this man—to feign ignorance of what prevented us from announcing our engagement. I open my mouth, close it again, and Astoria steps in.

"Correct me if I'm wrong, Mr. Blackwell, but you were unable to stay at the ball very long, were you not?"

I could hug her. My brilliant, wonderful sister who stands up for me when I need her most, even if speaking out is something she's been trained not to do. The attention turns to her, and I see her cheeks flush.

Mother clears her throat. I hadn't realized she'd been paying such close attention to our conversation. "I was expecting a dance of my own with you, Mr. Blackwell. I believe it was the first time I've had a partner choose *not* to dance with me."

My eyes widen. He didn't fulfill his dance with the queen? That kind of insult is unheard of, though conversely, he did it to wait for me in the glasshouse.

"I apologize, Your Majesty. I had a personal obligation that needed to be seen to."

"Personal obligation?" Mother's words are laced with venom as she holds Kieran's glare. *Does she recognize him?*

Mother was always too busy to notice the budding friendship between me, Kieran, and Gabe. Father always allowed the gardener's son to join in family games and even instructed the tutors to teach him alongside us. It wasn't until I was a teenager that Mother took an interest in the young redblood—a negative interest, of course—forbidding me from continuing a friendship that had begun to blossom into something more. That's when I stopped listening to her and made our rendezvous secret.

I didn't listen to her, and it turns out she was right all along. I should have avoided Kieran Greenbluff.

"Yes, Your Majesty. I look forward to the next opportunity we have to dance," he says. His tone is cool, and it's clear he won't be discussing it further—even with the Queen of Naseria.

Mother seems to accept this response as she continues, "About the engagement. It's unfortunate that we couldn't announce it last night, especially with the expedited timeline. I discussed the changes with Queen Kalise and Prince Leland. We have a new plan in place, and the announcement will be made in five days."

Five days? I wanted it announced immediately, just so we could move forward quickly. "Why wait?" I ask, looking from Leland to Mother.

"I hope you don't mind," Leland replies. "Since we couldn't do it last night, I wanted everything to be perfect next time—and there were some items I'd like to arrive first."

Mother's eye twitches. This wasn't what she wanted; that's evident enough from her frown.

Kieran chimes in, "How wonderful. It will give the two of you more time to get to know each other. You must have so much to learn about one another."

"We've been corresponding for over six months," I retort, not deigning to look at him.

"You'd be surprised how much you can learn about a person through correspondence," Leland adds, and I feel his gloved hand press against my arm. A subtle touch, reassuring and possessive all at once.

"I wouldn't know. I hate correspondence," Kieran mutters with a disgruntled look on his cocky face.

"That's not a surprise, coming from a busy man like yourself," I counter, meeting his eyes with an intensity to match his own. "There are all sorts of things one can learn through correspondence—little joys and interests, and of course news, like whether there's been a death. Or perhaps changes in occupation."

He scowls at me, and the scar on his forehead seems to darken. "Not all of us have such luxuries, Princess."

Mother clears her throat, and I catch her harsh stare out of the corner of my eye. *Back down. Don't over-speak.*

"Yes," Leland adds hesitantly, trying to smooth the tension. "Had it not been for our letters, I would never have learned so much about

Princess Genevieve's love for tropical plants. Or how she enjoys picnics with her sisters and walks through town."

Kieran snorts, an indignant expression on his face. "Prince Leland, you could learn all that in an afternoon. Even I can tell she's devoted to her sisters. Or that she finds dancing invigorating and enjoys her own company more than being with others."

I turn from his glare to Leland, who's looking at me as though realizing how little he truly knows about me. How could he know all my preferences when we are only just beginning to learn one another?

Prince Leland looks away. "Yes, well, all in good time, friend," he says to Kieran, but his embarrassment is plain. He knows we're strangers trying to make the best of our situation.

Astoria glances at me, a grimace on her lips.

Queen Penelope doesn't bother to hide her irritation. "Mr. Blackwell, I believe you have meetings to prepare for. Genevieve, darling, perhaps you and Astoria should take Prince Leland into Crawford. He must know how much you love visiting town—from all those letters."

I nod in agreement. "Excuse me. I'll go prepare for a trip to Crawford."

As I rise to leave, Kieran meets my eyes. There's something unreadable in his expression, beyond his open disdain. *Is it longing?* Surely not. My cheeks heat. He must stop looking at me like that. If he doesn't, everyone will suspect there's more to us than I'll allow.

Leland looks from his friend back to me, and I turn away, afraid to reveal too much of my own treacherous heart.

9

Genevieve

The fresh air blowing past the barouche carriage is just what I need. Astoria and I sit side by side, waving to the friendly townspeople as we pass. The scent of apple blossoms drifts through the air, and the clean cobblestone streets remind me how much I love visiting Crawford.

The capital of Naseria, Crawford has found a neighborly balance between bluebloods and redbloods, leading to a harmonious life amongst former enemies. I've traveled so little outside the city that I often wonder if the rest of Naseria shares this balance. Mother would have me think so, but as I grow older, I've begun to doubt her word. Yet she still controls all aspects of my life. A tour of the country for my honeymoon will be just the thing to allow me to make my own assessment of the state of Naseria.

Leland was gracious enough to take the seat facing the opposite direction, saying he preferred the view of two beautiful women to that of the road into town. The remark turned Astoria a shade of crimson

I've only seen in a tomato. She didn't complain about joining us, but I know it must be uncomfortable for her to accompany Leland and me as we try to get to know each other better. She would never disobey Mother's orders, but I think she'll be more than happy to slip off into the city for some time to herself.

As we bump along the cobblestone road, a silence settles over us. Usually, a trip to town relaxes me. I look forward to time away from Fairbright, but today it's all I can do to calm the nerves coursing through me.

"It's such a treat to be in warmer weather. We're still deep in winter's grip in Icelantica," Leland says, breaking the silence as he leans his head back to take in the blue sky, scattered with soft white clouds.

"I don't know how you endure such long winters," I reply, placing my hat at my side and reveling in the sunshine on my face. I know I should cover up to prevent further freckling, but the sun feels too good, and its warmth soothes my fractured spirit. Astoria doesn't dare remove her hat, but she tips it back just enough for the sunlight to illuminate her pale face.

"A long winter is part of life in Icelantica, and it's welcome there. Cozy evenings by the fire, ice skating on the lake, skiing the trails outside the castle—all fond memories of my childhood. But I think I'll enjoy these changes," he muses, smiling at me.

The carriage stops outside my favorite bakery and tea shop, The Wild Rose. I want to share my favorite parts of Crawford with Leland, so a stop here had to be first on our list. Lady Clementine, the owner, is a dear friend, and I need her to meet him.

The first time I brought a man here, it was a gangly boy. The memory of sharing a sweet with Kieran—of the surprise on his face at the frosted delicacies—fills me with warmth. We were only eight then, and Father allowed Kieran to join our outing. It was shortly after

Kieran arrived at Fairbright, still a skinny wild child. Father had to warn him to slow down or he'd make himself sick from all the sugar. Kieran's father had just been appointed head gardener, and Kieran had recently lost his mother. I think that's why Father encouraged us to play with him. But before long, he became the boisterous companion who joined the Ashcroft children in all our adventures.

After that, we'd sneak into The Wild Rose every chance we had to share a sweet and cup of tea. But those visits became fewer as we grew older—the gap between a blueblood princess and a redblood gardener's son too vast to ignore. Eyes were always on me, always reporting my behavior to the queen, and soon I was separated from anyone Mother deemed a bad influence. Especially redbloods like Kieran or Clementine.

Now I'm bringing my blueblood betrothed with me. The irony is not lost on me that I've done exactly what I once promised Kieran I'd never do—marry for the crown. But he did exactly what he promised never to do—leave me without fighting for our love. We both broke those promises so long ago, it hardly matters that our words of love have turned sour.

Leland steps out of the carriage first and offers me his hand, waving the footman off. I appreciate that he takes the time to help others, a rarity amongst the blueblood gentry. After he releases my hand, he offers the same courtesy to Astoria. She curtsies to him and turns toward me.

"Genny, would it be alright with you if I went down to Crawford Paints?" Astoria asks. While I know she tries to visit the shop as frequently as possible, I also suspect she wants to escape watching the fragile relationship between Leland and me unfold.

"Of course, go have fun! Maybe Mr. Guthrie will be there to instruct you," I quip with a coy smile. I know shy Astoria is attracted to the owner of Crawford Paints, but she's far too reserved to let her true feelings be known.

"Are you an artist, Astoria? I would love to see your work!" Leland says enthusiastically as he steps closer to me, his tall frame blocking the sunlight that had been falling on my bare face.

"Wouldn't we all? Astoria keeps her artwork under lock and key. I fear there may be booby traps involved," I tease, and see Astoria's cheeks flush. I shouldn't have embarrassed her in front of Prince Leland. Her naturally reserved disposition makes it difficult for her to open up to others, and I know she would rather keep her artwork private.

"They're nothing—really. Just a way for me to fill my time. I enjoy mixing the colors and the seclusion my art affords me."

"The pressures of royal life can be exhausting," Leland agrees. "I understand the need to find an outlet. I keep a few hobbies for myself as well."

I look at him, wondering what this charismatic man could possibly keep to himself.

"Very true, Prince Leland. I look forward to hearing all your opinions on our capital city. Enjoy your time together!" Astoria replies before parting from us, a footman walking close behind her as they make their way through the bright streets.

The bell announcing our entrance into The Wild Rose rings as we step into the shop. Scents of freshly baked pastries and pots of tea fill my senses, but it's the bright, cheerful voice that greets us that makes me smile.

Lady Clementine Hanford stands behind the counter, flour smeared across her cheek and a dusty apron tied around her waist. "Genny!" she exclaims. "What a wonderful surprise! You escaped the palace at last."

I feel Leland tense beside me, likely surprised by her casual greeting toward the crown princess. But Clementine is one of my oldest and dearest friends. We've never followed societal norms—nor would we now that she is a duchess.

"Clemmy, you know I'd be here every day if I could," I say as she comes around the counter and embraces me, careful to avoid the bare skin on my arms. She's a redblood and has no gift herself, but she understands the customs bluebloods follow and the caution many of us practice.

"Lady Clementine, I want you to meet my fiancé, Prince Leland Frostclaw of Icelantica."

Clemmy curtsies. "It's a pleasure to make your acquaintance, Prince Leland."

Leland bows, taking her hand. "The pleasure is mine, Lady Clementine." He doesn't seem surprised that my dear friend is a shopkeeper covered in flour, and he treats her no differently than my sisters.

"Please, everyone calls me Clemmy. I wasn't born an aristocrat—that would be my husband, Lord Griffin Hanford. How I ended up married to a duke is still a surprise to me!"

My friend's marriage to my cousin is still new. It was a scandalous rise in power on her part, something much of the court still hasn't adjusted to. Especially since Griffin was considered quite the catch amongst the blueblood ladies.

Leland smiles, not missing a beat. "You make a marvelous duchess."

"I still don't know how you convinced Griffin to let you work in The Wild Rose each day," I add. I wasn't sure Clemmy would take on the role of duchess so easily, but she and Griffin seem to have found a balance and mutual respect.

"Well, he had no choice if he wanted to marry me, like he so desperately hoped. The Wild Rose is a part of me, just as it was a part of my mother and grandmother." Her tone is so matter-of-fact that it catches me off guard. I think about my own curse, about the burden of becoming queen. Those things are a part of me too, but will Leland learn to accept them?

"Lord Griffin is a good man," I say, happy for the love my dear friend found.

"Enough about me, take a seat and let me get you some refreshments." Clemmy bustles off like a wild wind, pulling out chairs for us at an intimate table toward the back of the shop. Its white lace tablecloth and porcelain place settings are pretty with understated grace. I always love the attention to detail Clemmy gives every part of her business, and I'm proud to see my friend find success, love, and happiness.

We sit, and Clemmy leaves us as she whisks away to the kitchen. I can hear her talking and wonder if her mother is back there, or perhaps the new shop girl helping today.

"She's lovely," Leland murmurs, looking around as he takes in the space. "And I can see why you enjoy visiting The Wild Rose. Is there anything in particular I should order?"

"Oh, I don't think you'll be given much of a choice. Clemmy usually decides for us when I visit. She's always trying to stuff me full of her latest creations."

"Ah, well, have I told you that I have a weakness for sweets?"

"Is that so, Prince Leland? Tell me—is that your hobby? Are you secretly a baker? Or merely a connoisseur of baked goods?"

"Unfortunately, I've never baked a thing in my life, so no, that isn't my secret hobby. But I will admit to having impeccable taste when it comes to pastries. One of the best palates on the continent, in fact."

"Then you're in for a treat," Clemmy calls from behind the counter, clearly eavesdropping, before she sets four plates on the table. Each is laden with delicate pastries—one filled with cream, another a cinnamon roll dripping with thick white frosting.

"You've outdone yourself this time," I say, choosing the cream-filled pastry.

"Not at all. These are simply what remained after the morning rush. Prince Leland, do you have a preference in tea?"

"Anything strong will do. We had quite the night last night."

"Didn't we all?" Clemmy replies with a grin. "I was there—and very disappointed I didn't get more time with you, Genny. What kind of friend are you?"

"You know I'd have run to your side if it weren't for my duties." The truth is, I was completely distracted after meeting Mr. Blackwell before the first dance and trying to focus on the engagement announcement.

She laughs, patting the flour from her apron. "Don't worry, I was far too occupied with my gorgeous husband to notice you snubbing me."

Of course she was. Even after a year, the two only have eyes for each other. I hope their devotion never fades. Clemmy deserves it.

"Regardless, I should have made an effort," I murmur, and she shrugs, her black curls bouncing with the movement.

"I'll brew your tea and let the two of you become better acquainted."

Leland bites into a raspberry-topped confection. Cream smears across his bottom lip, and his tongue darts out. He lets out a small moan before bringing his attention back to me. "Based on my superior palette, I can say with unquestionable assurance that this is one of the most exquisite things I've had the honor of tasting," he remarks with a chuckle.

"Tell that to Clemmy. She'll be over the moon to have a foreign prince praise her baking." I wish his little sounds—the way he licks the cream—stirred something inside me, but instead I force a smile. Nothing. Why can't I feel more for this man than a friendly indifference?

"I think I will. She has an openheartedness that so many of us lost a long time ago," he continues before taking another bite and letting out a soft groan of pleasure. The way he eats his pastry is utterly improper, and I wonder if he's doing it on purpose.

I take a bite of my own pastry, trying to ignore my wayward thoughts. It really is delicious. "I don't think I've seen you not want to make someone smile yet. Tell me, is there anyone you don't like?"

A shadow crosses his handsome face. "You know what it's like to have a gift that controls others' emotions. My gift—bringing peace and reducing conflict—has made me naturally more inclined to bring happiness to others."

"So it's not always what you'd prefer to do?"

He meets my gaze and shrugs, as if he too struggles with the weight of his gift. "It limits my own natural responses at times. I find that, over time, I've accepted my role as the one in the room who can bring a sense of calm, or a slight smile to someone sad."

"Does your gift work through touch?" I ask, curious if that's why I've felt instantly comfortable around Leland while also feeling nothing romantic.

"It's more potent that way, but no. Just my presence can bring about feelings of well-being and peace in others. I think my sister—and possibly your mother—may be the only ones immune to its powers.

And Mr. Blackwell, for that matter. The man is unflappable, especially for a redblood."

I let out a small, strangled cough at the mention of Kieran. There's a fearlessness in him that wasn't there when he was younger, as though very little can stir him now.

Clemmy sets down the teapot and pours us both cups of stoutly brewed black tea into delicate porcelain cups before she smiles and walks away. She's no blueblood, but she doesn't need a gift to recognize when her customers are deep in conversation.

"I wonder if it has something to do with their own willpower," I muse, curious about what happened to Kieran to give him such a resolute disposition.

Leland takes a sip of his tea and studies me thoughtfully. "Most likely it does. My sister has closed herself off emotionally to everyone—including me. But what about your gift? You never wrote about it, although I have to admit, I've heard rumors."

A twisting sensation settles in my stomach. Mother's words come back to me, urging me not to allow Leland to experience my gift before our wedding.

"It's—it's something I prefer to avoid. After I realized how powerful my gift is, it became more like a curse."

Leland reaches for my gloved hand, taking it in his. "I understand. Of course, I've had similar effects with my own gift. I wonder—would you allow me to experience it before our wedding night?"

My body stiffens, and I have to work not to pull away. What does he expect me to say? Then I take a deep breath. This is fine. We need to work through our differences, and the guilt of keeping so much from him weighs on me.

"Perhaps," I reply, taking a drink of my tea to clear my mind. "I think it would be best if we continued to get to know one another better first. There's a park nearby with some beautiful gardens. Shall we make our way there?"

10

Kieran

I'd rather be back in the mines than sitting in this parlor with Queen Penelope, King Hugo, and Gabriel—oh, and the council breathing down my neck. I knew sitting in this room with the people I blame for my father's death wouldn't be easy, but I need to do this if I'm going to get my revenge on Gen. Only, she's not even here. Instead, she's off entertaining Leland.

Damn, I wish I didn't have to involve Leland in all this mess. He's been nothing but courteous to me. Hell, he even believed in me when no one else thought my idea for a railway system would work. He listened as I explained my theory about using the veins of helachite, along with processed helachite rails and wheels, to power the locomotive. And here I am, allowing him to marry into this pit of vipers. At least Queen Kalise is here to witness the lack of integrity she's agreeing to. Her two white foxes lie at her feet, quietly sleeping. The creatures hardly leave her side, but from Queen Penelope's expression, I can tell she doesn't share Kalise's affection for them.

The Ashcrofts don't even understand that they're the source of all that's wrong with this country. That valuing blood over people, a damned mineral over lives, is the true rot in Naseria.

"Can I see the most up-to-date maps of the helachite deposits in Naseria? The ones I reviewed last night were rather dated, and my surveyors will be arriving in the next few days."

"Of course," Gabe says, giving me a piercing stare. Does he recognize me? I thought that was impossible. These bluebloods don't really understand the impact helachite can have on a person. They think the initial exposure three generations ago was all it took to make them a superior class of people to redbloods, but what's their long-term plan as the tides turn? Gabe himself is a walking example of a blueblood—someone whose ancestors were exposed to helachite at dangerous levels—who lacks the gift. Despite the indigo color of his blood, he doesn't have any special power the queen seems to value so much.

I wonder if it's strained their relationship. She's always had an odd level of disinterest in her children's lives. I study the way they look at each other—Gabe's face pinched, her icy glare. There's never been affection between the queen and her children, but does she still have favorites?

A footman provides the map in question, spreading it on the table, and my eyes immediately drift to the far corner along the coast where Naseria stands between Icelantica and the Beral Sea—a place where my worst nightmares and all my current success were forged. A place so rich in helachite that its levels are easily destabilized when disturbed. Add in over a century of mining, and the entire area is crumbling. Now I get the honor of owning that whole fucking mess. Better me than someone who doesn't understand what's at stake—what's happening to the people trapped in inhumane conditions that have gone on for far too long. At least I can be the change the region needs, even if it should be the government doing it.

"Tell me, who from the council or government has checked on the mines in the north?"

Queen Penelope gives me a puzzled look. "We have a liaison who visits twice a year, but you should know that, Mr. Blackwell, since they've been incorporated into Blackwell Industries."

"That's why I'm curious *who's* representing your interests in my mines. Since taking possession, I haven't heard from a single council member or royal. It's a sharp contrast to how Queen Kalise and her council have handled the transition to Blackwell Industries ownership in Icelantica."

Kalise studies me with cool, knowing eyes. She's a cold bitch and terrible bore, but she's a shrewd leader and serves her people in a way I can't help but admire.

Queen Penelope scowls. "And what is the contrast, Mr. Blackwell?"

"Prince Leland and a team of inspectors were there within two months of the mines' transition from its former owner. We've had a close partnership for several years now, resulting in the railway line and growth of their kingdom. Meanwhile, I've never heard a word from your government, Your Majesty."

Her scowl deepens as she turns to one of her council members. "Explain why there haven't been inspectors to see the Blackwell mines."

The man—a middle-aged fellow with thinning hair and a rounded figure—looks as if he wants to crawl behind the furniture. "I—I'll look into the situation immediately."

Queen Penelope raises an eyebrow as the man sinks further into his chair. "Well? What are you waiting for, Lord Tabbish? Go!"

The man nearly leaps from his seat, knocking into the side table and sending a plate of food crashing to the floor.

Gabe steps forward, clearing his throat. "If I may speak, Your Majesty?"

She gives a subtle nod.

"This region isn't highly populated and has tended to be fiercely independent," he explains. "It's one of the richest helachite veins on the continent, and we see the benefits of its wealth throughout the country. But since the mine owners have, up until this point, done satisfactory work, we've chosen to let their judgment in how they operate stand."

I hold back the curse I long to let loose. The blood of his people, of redblood laborers, was spilled every day in those mines for far too long. Too many miners still suffer from the former owner's so-called satisfactory work. My own sleepless nights, haunted by the poisoning my body endured, still plague me. The sweat and convulsions that seize me are things these bluebloods must have forgotten over the generations, though I don't doubt their ancestors—those who grappled for power and tore this continent apart for their greed—suffered just as I do.

But I don't say anything. I keep my rage contained. My former friend's privileged life of comfort and ignorance should be held against him, but not here, not now.

"Tell me, Prince Gabriel," Queen Kalise says, a cutting edge to her voice. "Is it Naseria's habit to accept the word of a business owner over ensuring nothing untoward is happening to your citizens?"

"Well, Queen Kalise, we typically trust business owners to manage the best interests of their workers. We've had very few complaints using this system of trust with the mine owners. Should we be concerned about how Mr. Blackwell is operating his mines?"

She snorts and rises, her tall, willowy frame towering over Gabe as he remains seated. "I take it you've never been inside a helachite mine. We keep ours highly regulated, as Mr. Blackwell knows. But that's a story only he can tell."

Gabe looks at her in disbelief, then turns to his mother. "Do you know what she's talking about?"

King Hugo speaks up, and from Gabe's expression, it's clear that's a rare occurrence. "We've had an excellent relationship with the former mine owner, Mr. Wells. It's unfortunate he had to sell, but we look forward to deepening our commitment to our citizens working in the helachite mines, as well as to the future railway workers. The discovery of helachite is still recent, and the advances that you, Mr. Blackwell, and others have made in its uses are revolutionary. I think we, as a country—and as people who share Inver—should keep our focus on the progress this remarkable mineral has brought us, and on its benefits."

Rage floods my veins, and it's all I can do not to lash out. "King Hugo, if I may be so bold, the mines were in deplorable condition when I purchased them. A rotten blight had spread so deep we needed to decommission several shafts due to their deterioration. I've personally seen to the medical expenses of the former miners suffering from helachite poisoning and conducted an investigation into what went wrong in northern Naseria. I brought the report, if you're interested in reviewing it. Progress or not, I will not put my business's profits over the well-being of its workers—and I refuse to work in a country that doesn't value the lives of its own citizens. Even the mines I acquired in Wylan, while not up to Icelantican standards, were better maintained and more regulated than those in Naseria."

"A rotten blight? Helachite poisoning?" Gabe frowns, lifting a hand. "Your Majesty, does Princess Genevieve know any of this? I think we should wait for her before continuing these discussions."

"Princess Genevieve has more pressing matters," Queen Penelope says, her gaze locking on me. "I do not want her or Prince Leland interrupted."

Queen Kalise looks horrified. "I can't be a part of this. And Mr. Blackwell, I suggest you wait for Prince Leland before proceeding. My brother would never want to be excluded from these discussions. May I have that copy of your report?"

"Of course, Your Majesty." I pull a copy, a thick bundle of typeset pages, from my briefcase, knowing she'll at least be interested in reading it. I could have given her a copy when the marriage discussions began, but Naseria needs Leland more than she does. "I agree. Knowing Prince Leland, and knowing he'll be consort before the railway line is complete, he'll want to understand how the Naserian government has treated its helachite miners."

She stands, taking the report, and I follow, collecting my briefcase. I give Queen Penelope and the others a curt nod before trailing Queen Kalise to the door. A footman opens it for us, and we step into the hallway. Before it even closes behind us, she turns on me, icy rage in her eyes, the chill of her gift radiating across my skin.

"How dare you not share this information with us before Leland committed himself to this marriage! The contracts are already written. We need this alliance if we're to create a united front against Wylan. You, of all people, know what they harbor within their borders."

Gooseflesh rises on my arms, and I don't know whether it's from Queen Kalise's frosty gift or from memories of the beasts—twisted and tortured by helachite—that still haunt me. An army of creatures so abominable I know exactly what she fears.

"Mr. Blackwell!" Gabriel calls after us, and I turn to face the man I once knew so well.

Queen Kalise looks positively murderous as she spins on her heel, refusing to acknowledge the prince.

"Mr. Blackwell, you mentioned a rotten blight in the mines. Can we speak privately?" he asks, sweeping his flame-red hair from his eyes, concern etched across his face.

I give a quick nod. I don't even know why I do it, but I follow him without hesitation.

11

Genevieve

Leland places a hand on the crook of my arm as we walk toward the gardens in Covington Park. Low grey clouds are replacing the clear blue sky from earlier, and I wonder if we're about to be caught in one of Naseria's spring rains.

"I want to apologize," Leland says, leaning close to my ear as we walk deeper into the gardens. Fresh blooms of peonies hang heavy on their stems, while pretty lilacs perfume the air with their sweet scent.

"For what?" I ask.

"I shouldn't have been so forward in asking about your gift. Both of us are strong-willed, and we have powerful gifts. We'll learn to navigate how to manage that together in our marriage."

I haven't had someone speak so frankly about my curse. Typically, when a man is curious to feel its effects, it's all pawing and quick gropes. Perhaps it will be the same with him, despite what he says, once he feels my gift fill his senses.

"Thank you. It's good of you to say you're committed to working with me. My gift has always felt more like a burden—especially when I was younger and didn't understand its potency." The words come out tight. I dislike speaking about my gift with anyone, but this conversation matters. If we're to turn this arrangement into a real marriage, we have to work past our challenges—and my gift will likely be the first.

Leland lets out a small huff, nodding. "My sister has lived for over a decade in fear of her own gift, and I've only seen it cause her more harm than we already suffered."

We take a seat on a park bench. This conversation feels far too heavy for a walk in the park, but time is limited. Best to face these things head-on.

"We've all heard rumors of what happened to your parents when Queen Kalise's gift manifested. Is it true?"

Leland lowers his head for a moment before looking into my eyes. "If you're wondering whether my sister killed our parents—yes, she did. It was never her intention. She was angry with my father for a secret he'd kept from all of us, and her gift manifested in that anger. She's always been distant and serious, but after she froze them, she all but shut herself off from others. The only companions she allows are her foxes. She hasn't had a lady's maid since the incident. She even cuts her own hair, unwilling to let anyone touch her."

"What of heirs?" I ask, recalling Lord Fenweir's claim that Queen Kalise would take my child for her own.

He shrugs, looking at me with a shyness I haven't seen in him before. "I'm her only heir. I don't think Kalise will ever take a husband, but if she did, it would be in name only. So the future of my kingdom—and yours—rests in our offspring."

"No pressure, of course," I say, trying to lighten the conversation. I've always carried the burden of producing Naseria's next ruler, but knowing I'm also responsible for another kingdom's future is something I don't want to dwell on.

"Heirs know nothing of pressure, do we?"

"Especially not heirs of terrifying queens," I quip—and immediately wonder if I've overstepped propriety. Leland bursts into laughter, startling a gentleman walking by.

"Let's vow not to let our future heirs carry the same burdens we have," he proposes, extending his gloved hand.

I take it, certain this is a vow I want my children to know I've made. "To no longer burdening the heirs." We shake, and a sort of kinship blossoms between us.

We both chuckle before falling into companionable silence. I take Leland's hand and lead him toward a pond dotted with water lilies, wisteria climbing over an arch near the bank. He squeezes my hand before letting go, turning toward me as he dips his face closer to mine.

Feel something. Anything.

Butterflies.

Fluttering.

Excitement.

But all I feel is the same comfortable companionship I've known since our first meeting—and I'm beginning to wonder if that's simply an effect of his gift.

"Genny, I don't want to be too forward, but I'd like to give you something."

I look up at his cool blue eyes, at the gentle smile and the way his hair falls across his forehead. He takes my left hand in his, and I'm at a loss for words as he removes my glove and slides a ring onto my finger. It's white gold, set with a clear diamond framed by light-blue stones.

"I wanted to make this official. Will you marry me?" he asks, and I can hear the hesitation in his tone. Does he hesitate because he doesn't want this—or because he doesn't know if I'll say yes?

"Yes, Leland. I'm honored to marry you," I say, smiling up at him, but as the words leave my mouth, I see Kieran in my mind. His haunting emerald eyes, the loss and longing I've harbored in my heart for so long.

He nods, leaning closer, as though he feels obligated to seal this moment with a kiss. A sickening twist curls through my stomach. I don't want to reject his affection, but I cannot kiss him—not when the feeling of my gift makes me ill, not when my mind is on another man entirely.

I step back, ever so slightly, and Leland leans his head back, looking at the darkening sky. "Looks like rain. Should we make our way back to the carriage?"

"It's probably for the best." I take my glove from his outstretched hand, slipping it on over the large ring.

"Please let me know if you'd prefer a different ring. That one was my mother's, and she was very fond of it. Even if she wasn't always fond of my father."

"It's perfect, really," I reply.

"I hope so. Kalise suggested it was bad luck to give you a ring from an unhappy marriage, but my mother was a good woman. She was kind to everyone, and I'd like to see a part of her with my wife each day."

I take his hand in mine, giving it a gentle squeeze. "I'm honored to have a piece of her with me."

I lead him along a shortcut, a wooded path seldom visited but more direct to the carriage from where we stand. Ferns skirt the edges of the trail beneath towering trees. As we walk, an unfamiliar scent drifts through the air—a rancid, rotten smell that stings my eyes. I lift my handkerchief to cover my mouth and nose.

"What is that?" Leland asks, voice muffled behind his own handkerchief. Then he grows still. "I've smelled that once before—along the border near the Beral Sea. It came from rot spreading in an old mine. Mr. Blackwell showed it to me. Corrupted helachite can become a spreading rot."

I nod, scanning the forest, and see the source immediately—a dark, brownish-grey gash in the earth, pulsing and steaming. The stench makes me want to flee, yet I can't look away.

"There it is," I breathe. "But how can the rot be spreading through the center of Crawford?"

Leland keeps his face covered as he takes my hand and pulls me back from the foul pit. "It doesn't make sense. According to Mr. Blackwell, the rot is linked to over-mining and prolonged exposure to helachite."

"The nearest helachite mine is a day from here. We need to return to Fairbright Palace at once. I'll have to send another footman ahead to let Astoria know a new carriage is on its way for her."

12

Kieran

"Tell me all that you know about the rot," Gabriel presses, a smallsword in his hand. We're standing in the training hall, a place I once knew well, back when I was permitted to train with him. As a gardener's son, I shouldn't have been given such freedom, but King Hugo felt sympathy for me after my arrival. Once Gabe, Gen, and I became close companions, I was allowed to do anything the Ashcroft siblings did.

I see it clearly now: I was a sort of pet to the Ashcrofts. A red-blood companion meant to entertain the young crown princess and her siblings—but always to know my place. To never hope for more than what was freely given. Striving for more, hoping for the love of a princess, was strictly off-limits.

He gestures for me to choose my own weapon, so I reach for a smallsword meant for training. How did we end up here? From agreeing to speak privately about the rot to preparing to duel in a practice ring?

I stare down at the blade in my hand. It's not as though I haven't kept up my training. Yes, there were years where I didn't see the light of day, let alone a weapon, but since then, I've made good use of my elevated position and found time to hone my swordsmanship again.

"You do practice, do you not?" Gabe asks, a hint of his old cocky grin tugging at his lips. He was always an arrogant prick, even when he was my best friend.

"Of course. I just wasn't expecting us to discuss the state of your mines while fencing."

Gabe shrugs, the motion so familiar it catches me off guard. Something inside me twists—familiarity, and yet distance so vast it feels foreign. "I always practice at this hour. It's a routine I refuse to miss. Now—about the rot."

He walks to the court and takes his position, waiting. I oblige him, curious to see if my renewed training is enough to overtake a prince.

"Many of the mines along the coast were so far gone when I purchased them that I permanently closed them and took it as a loss. I wouldn't wish my greatest enemy to work in those conditions."

He raises his sword, swagger returning to his step. "Do you have many enemies, Blackwell?" The way he says my name cuts, and he attacks with such speed that it nearly takes me by surprise as I quickly step to block his offense.

"You'd be surprised how many people hate a man for rising above his station." I counter in a quick, rhythmic tempo that's been drilled into me since childhood. His lunge is predictable—the same move he's relied on all his life—and I deflect it easily. The gleam in his eye turns feral as he advances again.

"And how many people fell during your rise, Blackwell?" he snaps, his strikes growing sharper, more exacting.

"I thought we were talking about the rot, not my business success." I counterattack, forcing him onto the defensive as I swipe and parry.

He growls in frustration as I catch him off guard. "Rot, yes. Cases have been reported around the country."

"Impossible," I snarl as we move in a steady rhythm of back and forth. Despite the years I spent trading a pickaxe for a sword, we're still evenly matched.

"It only spreads when the land can no longer bear misuse. But that's not what's happening here. That leaves only one way it can spread."

We're close enough now that I can see the sweat dripping down Gabe's face—but it's the anger in his eyes I don't expect.

"Someone is misusing helachite, causing the rot to spread."

The thought shocks even me: helachite rot, intentionally unleashed across the kingdom. I use a quick parry that was once my signature move, a reflex so ingrained I forget I should be trying to keep Gabe from recognizing my swordsmanship.

He drives his elbow into me, shoving hard. It takes everything I have not to stumble. "Kieran—it *is* you."

I falter at the sound of my real name. He drops his sword, lunges forward, and punches me square in the face.

The blow lands hard and fast. I hit the ground with a thud.

"Gabe! No!" A feminine voice fills the training hall, and my vision blurs as I try to make out the figure rushing toward us.

"He left you!" Gabe's voice is venomous as he spits the words at Gen. Of course, it's Gen. "He has to know what that did to you. He deserves worse than to be knocked out flat."

I want to protest—that the only reason I left was because of her, that leaving cost me everything I'd ever valued—but I can't find the words as the two of them stand over me.

"It doesn't matter," she counters. "It's in the past. I don't want you hurting him on my behalf. He's absolutely not worth it."

Slowly I push myself up on my elbows, my vision sharpening on the siblings. "How did you recognize me?" I ask.

"Your fencing style," Gabe replies. "It's evolved, but hardly at all. You need a better instructor, by the way. Felt like I was fencing with a novice—you were always terribly predictable."

I nod. I should have known he'd see through me. "Did you bring me here to test that—to see if I was who you thought I was?"

Gabe scoffs. "Of course, you idiot. I don't know how you didn't see it coming. Genny told me who you were, but I didn't believe her until I watched your mannerisms in the meeting this afternoon."

I stand, unsteady, feeling the swelling in my cheekbone grow. "Now it's off to tell Mommy, is it?"

Gen snorts. Gabe rolls his eyes. "Why would we tell her? She's kept far too much from Genny for us to trust her."

I'm not surprised. Every interaction I've seen between Gen and her mother shows that the queen still treats her like a little girl, not like a woman about to be crowned. And for her part, Gen doesn't seem to mind being stuck in the same role for the past nine years. It only proves she's as complicit as her mother in Naseria's problems.

Gabe picks up his sword, stepping closer to me with the casual ease of a cat toying with its prey. "Tell me what you're really doing here, Kieran. Why return now after nearly a decade of lies?"

"I've been nothing but truthful. I've worked closely with Queen Kalise and Prince Leland for years. Your mother heard of my plans to build an intercontinental railway and contacted me herself, hoping to secure the line through Naseria."

"Enough," Gen cuts in. "Gabe, Prince Leland and I came across the rot in Covington Park. We need to speak with Mother immediately."

Gabe shakes his head, then looks at Gen. They lock eyes, speaking in that wordless way only siblings can. That irritating connection between them is something I've never understood. Some things never change.

I step closer to Gen, watching the heat rise in her cheeks. Her reaction makes me want to reach out and brush my fingers against her soft skin. "I can tell what you're doing, Gen. We're going to be working closely for years if I agree to build the railroad through Naseria."

She retreats, moving nearer to her brother, who's still holding that damn smallsword. "I'm ready to find a different contractor. We don't need Blackwell Industries for our railway."

I can't hold back my laugh. There's no one else on the continent capable of safely developing helachite infrastructure. My patent—secured in Icelantica, Naseria, and Wylan—on the process for safely manufacturing raw helachite guarantees that. I wouldn't trust anyone else to handle the mineral safely.

"That's impossible. Furthermore, if you don't believe me, ask Gabe what you missed while off with the prince. Queen Penelope is intentionally keeping things from both of you."

Gabe's eyes meet mine before he says, "It's true. It seems Mother is trying to isolate information from you."

I close the space between us. "If you want the truth, meet me tonight. You know where."

"Absolutely not," Gabe barks out, disdain evident on his face. "Who do you think you are, Kieran? If you want to meet with her, you'll meet with me or Prince Leland as well. Or just tell us what you know now, you ass—we're already here."

Gen brings her gloved hand to her brother's arm, and I catch the glint of the rock on her ring finger, even through the fabric. A jealous pang cuts through me, and I have to consciously relax my jaw as I stare at Leland's ring on her gloved hand. Did he touch her? Did he feel her gift?

"I'll be fine. If Kieran knows Mother is keeping information from me, I'll meet his demands. After all, he wouldn't dare touch me."

"Call me Blackwell. You'll slip up soon, and everyone will be wondering why you're calling me by the name of your dead lover."

"Right. Blackwell, then," she replies, her sapphire-blue eyes studying me.

Gabe regards me darkly and lifts his sword toward my stomach. "If she reports anything untoward, I will personally disembowel you."

I look at Gen, ignoring her brother and his blade. "You have my word that you'll be safe with me, Princess."

13

Genevieve

"Come on, Gen!" Kieran cries, gripping my mitted hand and pulling me into the soft snowfall blanketing the Ashcroft family gardens. The chill in the air makes me shiver despite my heavy fur coat. Snow is rare here at Fairbright, something that happens once or twice a year, and this snowfall shows no sign of relenting.

"I shouldn't," I insist, glancing toward the windows where someone might be watching. At fifteen, I've been reprimanded about decorum enough times to know that the crown princess should not, under any circumstances, be seen gallivanting through the gardens with a redblood boy.

Even if that redblood boy is my best friend.

Kieran looks back at me, giving a gentle tug that draws me closer to the warmth of his body. "Please. For me? I know you shouldn't be seen with me, but I've missed you."

My heart threatens to crack at his words. I haven't been as good a friend to him lately—the expectations on my behavior growing, the pressure of my every move being reported to Mother.

"Okay, just for a few minutes. You know I wish I could stay longer, but I shouldn't if we're alone. People will talk."

Kieran steps closer, and I can make out the snowflakes clinging to his lashes. My blood feels heated, and I know my cheeks are turning pink. The more I pull away from Kieran, the more he seems to fight the growing divide between us.

"Princess, please don't tell me you care what others think of us. It's always been us, and I'm not going to let that change."

There's a strange seriousness in his eyes, so foreign to him that my protests die on my tongue. "No, of course not, Kieran. You're my best friend. Nobody can change that."

He leans closer, close enough that I wonder if he might kiss me. My heart thunders in my chest. Do I want him to? Does he actually feel something more for me than friendship?

"Genevieve Ashcroft! Come inside before you catch your death!" my lady's maid shouts from the open door. I pull back from Kieran and run toward the warmth of the hall. Before I step inside, I glance back at him—at the strange devastation on his face.

"Can I get you anything, Your Highness?" a servant asks. I shake my head before taking a seat on the settee. Supper was an extravagant affair that went on far too long as I tried to hold a conversation with the two council members flanking me on either side.

Meanwhile, my mind raced through the many courses as I thought about meeting Kieran— not just because I want to hear what he has to say about how the rot might be spreading, but admittedly because I want to spend more time with him.

I hate the way I'm naturally drawn to him—how, all throughout supper, our gazes kept locking. The way I could hear his voice carry over the other conversations, catching snippets of him all night. How I kept having to stop myself from joining his conversation, if only to study the way his accent has changed.

It was torture, and now all I crave is an end to my discomfort. But there is no end to this agony. I just have to learn to live with Kieran's presence. Because, if all goes well, he will be in Naseria for many years to come, building the railway lines along the helachite veins that cut across our country.

I'll be queen. The one overseeing the project.

And married to Leland. *Married.* I cannot possibly allow myself these stolen glances, these desires to draw closer to the man I once called my own.

Astoria slips into the seat beside me. I know she returned safely to the palace without issue, but we haven't spoken since then. There's so little privacy in the parlor, but I'm desperate to tell her about the events of the day.

"I'm so sorry we had to leave without you," I begin as she takes a glass of wine.

"Don't apologize, Genny. What I wanted most was for you to have time with Prince Leland."

"No, we shouldn't have left like that. Did the other carriage find you alright?"

Astoria nods and takes my hand, her fingers brushing the ring beneath my silk gloves. "I hope everything was alright? The coachman said there was an incident."

I shake my head, keeping my voice low. "Prince Leland and I found rot in Covington Park. We left for the palace immediately."

The color drains from Astoria's cheeks. "So close? But how?"

"I wish I knew. Mr. Blackwell says it's from misuse of helachite."

Astoria glances across the room to where Kieran and Leland are deep in discussion. "You spoke to Blackwell? Did he apologize for his forwardness?"

I can't keep his true identity from Astoria, not with Gabe already knowing who he is. I lean in close, lowering my voice so no one can overhear. "He *is* Kieran Greenbluff. He admitted his identity to Gabe today."

To her credit, Astoria keeps her face neutral as she scans the room. "And has it changed how you feel about your marriage to Prince Leland?"

"It has complicated matters. I feel confused, especially since I see Prince Leland as more of a friend than a lover."

It's an honor to be given Leland's mother's ring, but I think back to how I pulled away from his touch. The cold, distant feeling I already have toward my fiancé makes my chest ache. This isn't what I wanted. I never thought I would have a loveless marriage, but that's what I'm forcing on both of us. That's what my curse will punish me with.

"Prince Leland and I got to know one another better, and I introduced him to Clemmy. Of course, he loved her immediately. But I feel as though I'm pursuing this arrangement for our kingdoms only."

I look past Astoria, and Kieran winks at me from across the room. The brazen lack of propriety from that man makes me want to march over and hit him with my shoe again. He's purposefully drawing attention to us, and I fear it will ruin everything I've worked for to secure this alliance.

Doesn't he understand we're being watched? I'm being watched. Even as the thought crosses my mind, I see the subtle twitch of Mother's eye and turn to see Queen Kalise looking at Kieran.

"Genny, are you alright?" Astoria asks, her voice barely a whisper.

I force my attention back to her, trying to ignore everyone else in the room as I count down the minutes until I can politely excuse myself from the parlor. "I'm fine. It's just that Kieran keeps looking at me. It's unnerving."

"How do you think he managed to injure himself in Fairbright? Please tell me it was your doing." The swelling in his cheek has reached his eye, and a deep shade of purple is already setting in.

"He deserved it—but it was Gabriel. He knocked him flat on his back."

"Did he give you an explanation for why he left?"

I shake my head. "No, and I don't think he plans to. He's insinuated that it's my fault. But it doesn't matter. I need to do my duty to the crown. Prince Leland is here, and I need to concentrate on feeling *something* for him."

I purse my lips and look at the clock on the mantle. It reads eight forty-five. That seems like a perfectly acceptable time to make my exit. "I need to lie down. It's been a long day." I stand and approach Mother, feeling Astoria close behind me. Maybe she's just as desperate as I am to leave tonight.

"Your Majesty," I say, dipping low. "May I be excused? I find myself quite fatigued."

Mother studies me, and I see some sympathy in her brown eyes. She looks worn down and almost envious as she gives me a brief nod. "Get some good rest, dear. Astoria, you're excused too. Good night," she replies, before turning back to the councilor she invited to our parlor.

I turn and wonder what else my mother is keeping from me. Is she even now sharing information with a councilor that I have a right to know?

Astoria walks beside me as we make our way into the hall. "Do you ever wonder what life would be like if we weren't part of the royal family?" she whispers.

"Of course. For one thing, I wouldn't be asking my mother's permission to leave a room at twenty-eight. Being royalty means shrinking yourself to fit the expectations of an entire kingdom."

She nods. "Anyone in Mother's presence must ask permission to leave. Royalty or not."

I think about how that permission will be for me soon. I will be the one who carries the burden of releasing everyone from a room—all because some former monarch decided they wanted absolute control over everyone's comings and goings. I don't want that burden. Perhaps I'll do away with such a silly custom.

"Honestly," Astoria says in a voice so low I almost don't hear her. We stop at my door, and I can hear the rustling of my lady's maid in my apartment. "If I weren't royalty, I think I'd be much happier."

"It's easy to say that, but you are the wonderful woman you are in part because you're Princess Astoria Ashcroft."

She looks at me contemplatively, her brow slightly furrowed. "I'm twenty-five. I've been able to do *nothing* on my own merit, and I feel exhausted by it. The crown constricts me from being who I want to be. I understand how you can't imagine separating yourself from the crown—you'll bear that weight one day—but for me? The third child in five, I just wish to shed its burden from my life. Yet I know I'll never be permitted that right."

I do the only thing I can for my sister: I pull her close and hug her. Astoria is deeply private and only reveals small details to me. There's something else she isn't telling me, but from the tired circles under her eyes and strained look on her face, I know this isn't the time to press her further.

"Would you like to come in?" I ask, knowing full well that I need to meet Kieran.

She shakes her head. "No, a hot bath should cure my melancholy."

"I love you, Astoria." The words come so naturally when I say them to her.

"I love you too, Genny. Good night." She pads down the hall before stopping at her door.

I open mine and come face-to-face with Kieran. He's made himself at home on my settee, looking obnoxiously proud of himself.

14

Genevieve

"**J**ust take the key, Kieran," I say resolutely. At sixteen years old, this feels like the most reckless decision I've ever made. Allowing a boy—not just any boy, but Kieran—to have the only other key that reaches my private apartment through a secret passage feels audacious. I know if Mother ever found out, I'd be in more trouble than I've ever faced.

She doesn't like all the time I spend with Kieran—how I choose him and Clementine over other companions. But they understand me better than anyone else, the exception being Astoria. It's different with Kieran and Clemmy. They're not my siblings. They choose to love me for who I am, not because I'm a princess or a sister.

"Gen, I don't know. You could get in a lot of trouble," he replies, and I know I've truly thrown caution to the wind if even Kieran thinks this is a bad idea.

"I'm already being told who can be my companion. I'm worried that if you don't have a way to see me, we won't be able to play together any longer. Just hide it so no one will find it."

His face is serious—far more serious than it usually is when we're together. "Let's hide it together. Then, if you need to take it away, you can."

I nod in agreement as he leads me to a large, well-manicured rosebush in the family gardens. He lifts a rock from the border and places the key beneath it.

"There. When should I come to your rooms?" he asks, and there's a shyness in his voice, as if he's not sure my offer is real.

I think about it, knowing how often people come through my private chambers. "We shouldn't use it too often. People will grow suspicious. How about on the full moon? That will give us once a month to catch up."

His brow furrows. "Okay. Yes. But only because I miss you, Gen."

"You must stop doing this!" I exclaim, the words coming out with a bitter punch. "It's one thing for you to show up in my private glasshouse, but here? In my apartment? My lady's maid could appear at any moment."

He leans forward, elbows resting on his large, muscular thighs. He's so much bigger than I remember, grown into his lanky body in a way I never imagined possible. Mostly because, in my mind, he's never aged beyond nineteen. He cocks his head in my direction with pure arrogance.

"And that would be a problem. Why? It's not as if we're in a compromising position. Oh, but that's already happened to us before, hasn't it?"

His eyes pierce mine as he licks his lower lip, a diabolical grin spreading across his face. My frustration builds as I catch myself staring at his soft mouth, his harsh laugh filling the space. "If you think for one moment that I would *ever* allow us to be caught alone together, then you're delusional."

I close the gap between us, tugging at the cuffs of his sleeve and he stands, towering over me. I can feel the heat of his body against mine, the spicy scent of him filling my senses. I step back, and he follows. He's so close I have to tilt my head to meet his gaze—a mistake, I realize too late.

"No, you're right, Gen. This is much better." His hands stroke my covered upper arms, and I steel myself against his touch, grabbing his wrist again and pulling him toward my bedroom.

"Actually, this just keeps getting better and better." Kieran laughs as I close the door behind us. "What exactly are your intentions with me, Princess?"

"Stop this, you infuriating man!" I snap, letting go of him and striding toward the bookshelf and the secret passageway beyond. The passage is already ajar, and I look back at him, my expression hard with anger. He has the gall to laugh again, loud and deep.

"When I found my key, I wondered if it was an invitation meant for me specifically, or if you've shared the location with your other lovers. Third rock from the rosebush in the gardens along the wall. The roses are immaculate, but I couldn't help wondering who's doing your pruning these days."

My breath catches in my throat. I haven't thought about that key in years. At first, I left it hidden, hoping he'd return to me—but that never happened. Not until now. And now, I wish I'd taken it back years ago. "Give that back to me!"

"I don't think I will. It was given freely to me, remember? Tell me—have you shared your secret entryway with Prince Leland?"

I shake my head, still speechless that he remembered after all these years.

"No, of course you didn't. There's nothing romantic between the two of you. Sure, he's a decent man and will serve his purpose, but there will be no private trysts between you before the wedding, will there?"

"That's none of your business," I retort, grabbing a candlestick and stepping into the darkened stairway. He follows me inside, and I hear the soft click of the bookcase closing behind us.

I can feel the heat of his breath on my neck as he murmurs, "You're right—it's none of my business. But you make every encounter with your fiancé so painfully stifled I can't help but think back to the way you once moaned in my arms."

I turn around, gripping the stair rail. "I'm not that girl anymore. *You* ruined that girl."

He huffs out a bitter laugh, stepping down to the same stair as me. "*I* ruined you? Oh, Gen—you're going to find out just what it looks like to be ruined by me."

His hand brushes a loose strand of my hair, and he rubs it between his fingertips. Can my gift fill him like this? "What do you mean?"

The shadows cast by the candlelight dance across his face as he says, "Only that you've asked about my true purpose in returning to Naseria. It's you, of course. To see you ache and suffer the way I have.

To see you long for me and beg, all while you try to convince yourself that you want another man."

I pull back from his touch. "Why? Why, Kieran? You've made a good life for yourself. Why ruin mine over something that happened in the past?"

He's closer now than ever. His lips caress the shell of my ear, and my heart thrums in my chest. "Because I can."

Then he slips past me, down the final steps and out into the gardens. I follow after him. Not because I want to be near him another moment, but because he still hasn't shared what he knows about the rot—the entire purpose of this damned meeting.

When I step into the dark gardens, he's gone. I walk to the far wall where I once hid a key long ago for a boy I once loved. It's not there, which means Kieran still has the ancient, secret key to my private rooms. A key that is impossible to replicate or replace.

15

Kieran

That interaction didn't go as I planned. I had every intention of telling Gen everything I know about the rot. I even thought of convincing her to join me at Huntley House, to see the state of the helachite mines in Naseria for herself. She might just do it. She and Gabe both seem to want to know what's really happening in this country, to hear the truth of how their mother has governed.

Yet once I was in her apartment, I had an inexplicable urge to make her hurt as much as she hurt me. I don't like the way she makes me feel—so brash, so reactive. I shouldn't be letting her affect me like this, not after living without her for so long.

The gardens are quiet as I tuck the key into my pocket. I plan to make use of it before I'm through with Genevieve Ashcroft. I sneak along the inner wall of the Ashcroft family gardens before ducking behind a large maple tree. Using the low branches, I boost myself over the walls protecting the family's private grounds from public view. It's the same old place I used to slip out as a boy, and the familiarity of it sends a pang through my chest.

I dust off my evening coat and make my way toward the main entrance from the gardens when I hear someone call out, "Blackwell! Is that you?"

It's Leland and Pryor. Of course it is.

"What are you doing skulking about the gardens?" Pryor asks, suspicion sharpening his tone. General Pryor has always been wary of me—and for good reason, I suppose. He's Leland's closest friend and confidant. I'm a nobody who's risen to power and befriended a prince. I never planned it that way, never had ulterior motives to get back at Genevieve through the Prince of Icelantica. No, our friendship is genuine. Still, it won't last much longer if he ever discovers my connection to Gen.

"Just taking an evening stroll. That's allowed, is it not, General Pryor?"

He shrugs, taking a drink from a flask before passing it to Leland. "Rather odd, isn't it? Walking so near the royal family's private gardens. Almost like you were trying to find a way in."

I scoff at his accusation as Leland hands me the flask. The amber liquid burns smoothly down my throat, warming my chest. Icelantican grogg, of course. They can't get enough of the stuff—not with those long, lonely winters.

Leland gives me a mischievous smile. "Pryor and I have a running bet. He believes Princess Genevieve won't go through with the wedding. I think she will. What are your thoughts, Morris? You seem rather observant of her. Care to share your own prediction?"

"I don't see why she wouldn't marry you. You both need the alliance if Wylan continues its abominations."

Pryor looks at me like he knows what I've said is only a half-truth. "Yes, but she's not attracted to him. It's obvious. In fact, I think she fancies you more than Leland. She can't keep her eyes off you."

Leland lets out a bitter laugh, taking another long drag from the grogg. It isn't like him to drink heavily, and I wonder if he suspects there's more between Gen and me.

"That's because I'm far more attractive than this scarecrow," I jest, but the words fall flat.

Leland frowns, studying me. "I've seen how she looks at you. I don't demand a love match—I knew that wasn't going to happen—but I'd like my future wife to show *some* enthusiasm for me. Did you know she wouldn't even touch me? She doesn't want me to know what her gift feels like until we're wed."

An angry gnaw of jealousy blooms in my belly. The idea of Gen's gift filling Leland, making him lust after her, makes me feel ill. I'm going to need to make myself scarce after the wedding, just to keep myself from losing my composure with Leland.

"Do you think the rumors about her gift are true?" Pryor asks. We've made our way through the manicured public gardens and are approaching the veranda that leads into our wing of the palace.

Leland lowers his voice. "She's told me so herself. I don't want to make her uncomfortable, but what if marrying her is a mistake? I would never want to make that commitment if her gift is something neither of us can tolerate. I'm not capable of committing to a lifetime of celibacy like Kalise—but I'm not going to marry someone who's repulsed by my touch."

"What did you expect? You knew her gift made men 'fall in love.' That's a polite way of saying wanting to fuck her," Pryor says.

"Enough!" I snap, and both men look at me in surprise. "There are servants everywhere. We don't need to be overheard."

I think about what Gen said in the glasshouse—how she's suffered—and a gnawing dread fills me. What has she gone through because of that curse of hers?

The thought vanishes as a woman's scream echoes down the corridor. We run toward the sound and find a maid standing over a prone male form dressed in the forest-green livery of a Naserian footman.

"He's dead!" the maid cries, and I see the spreading rot consuming the body. No, this shouldn't be possible.

There's a nefarious misuse of helachite within Crawford, and it's infiltrated the palace.

"Is it the rot?" Leland asks, pressing a handkerchief to his face. The smell is vile, but it's nothing I haven't endured for years. I roll the body over. There's very little helachite rot can do to a man already poisoned by it as I have been.

"Blackwell, are you mad? Don't touch it!" Leland shouts, but I ignore him. The rot seems to be coming from the servant's mouth, as though it's pouring from within.

"Get Princess Genevieve," I order a nearby servant. Leland looks perplexed. "The queen will do nothing. Get Prince Gabriel as well. Tell no one else what you've seen."

Pryor glances down at the spreading mess on the carpet. "I'll get Queen Kalise. She should know as well."

Leland steps closer to the body, but I wave him back. I can't have the Prince of Icelantica exposed to helachite rot.

"Oh, it's fine for you to endanger your life, Blackwell, but not mine? I see," he protests, though he stays back.

"The damage was done to me long ago. You know that."

Leland shakes his head. "Right. Your former life in the hardscrabble mines of northern Naseria."

Gen arrives quickly, dressed in a robe, her hair tied back in a loose braid—and I think back to the sheer nightdress she wore in the glasshouse. The swell of her soft, unbound breasts must be hidden just beneath the thick fabric she wears now.

Leland doesn't seem to notice the precious jewel before him, and that makes my frustration throb inside me. He doesn't deserve her if he cannot even see what's before him.

"What's happened? I was told there's been an emergency," Gen says as she approaches the body. She covers her ungloved hand and gasps as she studies the dead man.

My words come out harsh as I tell her, "You have a problem, Princess. A very big problem on your hands."

She looks from me to Leland. "I see that. Did anyone witness who killed this man?"

"We found him in the passage. The servant girl was screaming," Leland explains, just as Gabriel arrives. Behind him, Queen Kalise carries one of her foxes. She's dressed in a robe, her short bob slightly mussed as though she'd already been in bed. Her other fox circles her feet, then pads toward the body.

She gives a sharp whistle, and the fox tucks itself around her ankle. "This is unacceptable," she hisses, fixing Gen with an icy stare.

"Well, it's not Genny's fault!" Gabe retorts. "How can we have a dead servant in the halls of Fairbright?"

"Dead from rot—because your country has allowed it to go completely unregulated," Kalise counters.

"What would you suggest we do, Queen Kalise?" Gabe's tone is cutting as he gestures toward the scene.

"First of all, grow a backbone and stop allowing one woman to make bad decisions. Leland, I don't know if you should continue with this."

I rise from my kneeling position, wiping my hands on my trousers. "You'll regret not forming an alliance if the Wylan situation isn't dealt with swiftly. You think this is a problem? Just wait."

Gen frowns at me. "What do you mean, exactly?"

"He's referring to the Wylan forces massing at the border," Gabe interrupts.

I shake my head. "That's not what I mean. They're weaponizing helachite in ways that should never be allowed."

Gen gives me an exasperated scowl. "Why didn't you say so sooner, K—Mr. Blackwell?"

Leland looks between us but says nothing as Queen Penelope strides into the corridor. "No!" She glances around the group. "What are you all doing standing over this man's body? Can't you see he's contaminated? Are my other children here?"

"Only Gabe and I," Gen answers.

The queen gives an authoritative dip of her chin. "Get this mess cleaned up. Not a word of it, do you hear me?"

So the truth of a death—possibly a murder—in Fairbright is to be buried? I should have assumed as much.

"There needs to be an investigation," Gen insists.

The queen's eye twitches as she studies her daughter. She looks as though she's about to rebuke her, but her expression softens. "Yes, you're right. Of course. Gabriel, can you make a formal report?"

"I'll take the body," I offer. It should be me. I'm the only one who can safely do so. No one protests as I move to lift the man. It's not the first time I've shouldered the weight of someone lost to the rot. A servant I recognize from my years in the palace steps forward to help, but I wave him off and tell him instead to lead me to where we should place the body.

I deposit the deceased man in the palace's medical clinic and wash up, scrubbing any trace of rot from my hands. The servant brings me fresh clothing from my rooms, and I change. It's imperative that I keep all traces of the rot from spreading further. After removing the key to Gen's secret staircase, I toss my soiled clothing into the incinerator.

Once finished, I return to my own rooms, but I'm so filled with restlessness that I know I won't be able to sleep. It's not as though I sleep on a good night, anyway. The key to Gen's room sits on my bedside table, and I keep looking at it, wondering if she's still awake.

Wondering if she's thinking of me, even now. I shouldn't be having thoughts of her—not when I've vowed to break her heart and ruin her. Perhaps I've misjudged her influence in this country. Even so, her willful ignorance of her kingdom's problems is inexcusable.

But I can't stop thinking of her.

I pick up the key, study the old brass design, then set it back down. Only moments later, I retrieve it and slide it into my pocket before heading for the door.

I just want to see her, to know if she's still awake. I could share what I know about the rot and how it spreads.

The night is late, and the palace is silent as I make my way through the gardens, plucking a few stray rose blooms as I go.

The secret door creaks as I turn the key in the lock, the stairwell humid and damp. At the top of the stairs, I ease the door open and step into the darkness of Gen's bedroom.

I can make out her sleeping form in the middle of the bed, the steady rise and fall of her breathing. Her hair is loose, cascading around her face and pillow. She's so beautiful—just like one of her rare flowers. I place the roses on her bedside table and turn to leave when she lets out a little sigh.

A sigh that makes my treacherous heart thud. She rolls to her side and murmurs, "Kieran, don't leave me."

Does she know I'm here? Her eyes are shut tight, but how can I refuse her, even in her sleep?

"Never," I whisper, taking a seat in the chair.

Sleep overtakes me with a gentleness I haven't felt in years. When I awake, the watery light of dawn filters through the window. Gen still sleeps deeply in the bed, and I leave the room—a shadow cast in the night, gone by daybreak.

16

Genevieve

Only two weeks remain until the wedding, and I should have known that Prince Leland would choose a garden party to announce our upcoming nuptials.

"Where will the garden party take place?" I ask, and Leland gives me a knowing look.

"Somewhere I know you'll love."

It feels good to have a surprise, for someone to take the time to plan something based on what I actually want. For days now, I've awoken to flowers at my bedside, from simple garden blooms to rare delicacies. I hope they're from Leland, a secret gift he's sneaking into my room through my lady's maid, Trudy. But I suspect it's Kieran. He hasn't spoken to me since the death of the servant. The spreading rot probably only adds to the growing list of things he hates about me and my family.

Leland and I are settled in the carriage when someone else steps forward. I'd hoped we could have had more time alone. It's been so difficult to find even a few moments together, between the busyness of the wedding preparations and the obligations of the crown. Kieran's broad frame fills the doorway, and he meets my eyes, his lips curling into a grin.

"Mind if I join?" he asks. I'm tempted to say yes, I do mind—but I don't want Leland to know just how familiar Kieran and I are. What if it changes what he thinks of me? What if he no longer values our alliance, knowing I was once in love with his close friend?

But Leland answers first. "That would be wonderful, Blackwell. In fact, I've wanted the three of us to have a private moment together. I think we'll all get along splendidly once the two of you are better acquainted."

Kieran takes the seat across from us, his long, muscular leg close enough to brush the hem of my full skirt. "I think you're right, Leland. Tell me, Princess, do you think we'll get along alright? Have you had any redblooded scoundrels as companions?"

His foot taps against mine—and stays there—the contact between us sending an unwanted current through my body.

Leland looks at both of us, a sly smile on his soft face. "No teasing my bride, Morris!" He glances at me and adds, "Mr. Blackwell has an abominable reputation, but he has a heart of gold. He's dedicated to improving the lives of the helachite miners, railway workers, and their families. Did you know he's created a workers' organization for his employees? They can request higher wages, seek free medical assistance, and are provided comfortable accommodations through their employment. He's brilliant, really, the way he's built entire communities to better their lives. I don't think there's a man like him on the entire continent."

"You flatter me," Kieran mumbles, and it's the first time I've seen him look uncomfortable. He turns to the window, and I feel the warmth from his shoe leave me.

"It's not flattery. You're an innovator in both mining and engineering—as well as social progress. The world is a better place thanks to you, Morris. I only wish others knew how much you've done for those with less than us."

The man Leland describes sounds far more like the Kieran I once knew and less like the cold, distant Morris. Finally finding my voice, I say, "Mr. Blackwell, what made you decide to become so innovative in how you treat your employees?"

His eyes meet mine, his expression hard and unyielding. "I've experienced the worst the mines can offer, and I rose above it. The least I can do is ensure no one ever experiences the hell I lived through in your kingdom's mines, Princess Genevieve."

A chill creeps down my spine, and I press my leg closer to Kieran's. Maybe he never came back to me because he couldn't. He's alluded to it before, and perhaps I've been too blind to realize there were reasons beyond our argument that kept him away.

Leland lets out a quiet tut of his tongue, shaking his head. "Dreadful, what you went through, Morris. Just awful. But you're out now, aren't you? You're ensuring what happened to you never happens again." His words are honey-smooth, and I feel myself calming. Kieran, though, looks at Leland with the same hard intensity he gave me.

"Don't pull that shit on me, Leland. You know it won't work." He turns back to the window.

"Of course." Leland sighs and slides his gloved hand into mine.

The carriage comes to a smooth stop. Kieran jumps up as though he can't wait to leave, opening the door before the footman even has the chance. He's gone before I can say another word.

"Don't worry about Mr. Blackwell. He has these moods. His past is painful, but he's a good man. In fact, it was he who suggested I accept your alliance. He pointed out all the good it could bring to both of our kingdoms."

Kieran is the one who suggested Leland proceed with our arrangement? "Was he? Did he have a reason to suggest our match?"

Leland offers me his hand as I exit the carriage, steadying me, then rests it in the crook of my arm. My sisters and brothers are walking toward me, as are Queen Kalise and General Pryor.

"I believe he suggested that I would be a welcome influence in the kingdom."

"What do you mean by that?" I ask, desperate to know more before our families close in around us.

"I said he's a kind man, but he's also a shrewd businessman when it comes to dealing with bluebloods. Perhaps he thought we could continue our work in Naseria together. But does it matter? We're uniting our countries—and our lives—in only two weeks. Now, let's make our engagement official, shall we?"

I nod, my head spinning as Leland leads me toward Covington Park. What game is Kieran playing here? He seems to genuinely value his friendship with Leland, and yet he's promised to ruin me.

I've been waiting for him to destroy everything I've worked for, but he's kept his distance. In fact, the carriage ride over was the first time he's said anything more than a few polite words to me in days. Perhaps he's had a change of heart.

Gabe told me they met privately, and Kieran disclosed the former state of the helachite mines in Naseria to him. Gabe's descriptions were abhorrent, and if Kieran suffered in those mines, as he and Leland suggested, then I can better understand why he wants to see change in my kingdom.

Kieran refused to share more details with Gabe about what happened to him after he left Fairbright Palace. After the conversation in the carriage, I can see why. He's never seemed this upset before, and until now, he's been nothing but arrogant and composed. I scan the park, searching for him.

I can't find him within the crowd of festively dressed aristocrats and redblood townspeople in their finest. Children have smoothed hair and girls wear crisp pinafores, while boys run through the sunshine in short pants.

The park is decorated in Icelantican blue and Naserian green, with lush scarlet begonias cascading over poles that hold up the ribbons. It's a beautiful sight, and I can't stop the smile that spreads across my face as people cheer for the royal family.

"You organized all this for me?" I whisper as Leland leads me toward a dais.

"I did. I wanted to make it up to you. We'll announce our engagement right away, then there will be dancing. After that, refreshments from The Wild Rose and other local businesses, highlighting the best of Crawford. This evening, there will be more dancing and fireworks under the stars."

"Really?" It's incredibly thoughtful of him—the kindest thing anyone's done for me.

This marriage is going to work. We respect one another. He's kind and considerate, just what I hoped for in a husband.

Clemmy whistles loudly through the crowd, her husband's hands wrapped lovingly around her hips.

I can't stop smiling as I walk through the cheering crowd. "Thank you, Leland. It's beautiful. You're such a good man."

We walk up the dais and take our seats on the two middle chairs. Our families follow close behind. Once we're all seated, the orchestra begins to play a cheerful tune. Bluebloods and redbloods alike mingle and dance.

That's when I see Kieran. He's off to the side of the event, leaning against a tree. His eyes are trained on me, and he dips his head when we make eye contact. I turn my attention back to the crowd, taking in the jubilation and trying to ignore the gnawing guilt rising in my chest.

Finally, the music stops. The crowd grows still as Queen Kalise and Queen Penelope step forward.

My mother addresses the crowd, her vibrant voice carrying across the park. "We are honored to have you all here today. From redblood shopkeepers to blueblood lords and ladies, today we gather to celebrate the engagement of Princess Genevieve to Prince Leland of Icelantica. Together, our kingdoms will forge a future united against our enemies, join our two countries through a revolutionary railway system, making travel easier and accessible for all."

The crowd bursts into cheers as Queen Kalise slowly raises her hand to call for silence. I look toward Kieran, but he's no longer where I last saw him. I scan the crowd as Queen Kalise begins talking about a new partnership, but I can't find him anywhere. My heart sinks, and I try to focus on her words.

Leland places his gloved hand over mine, gently pulling me toward the queens. "Kalise called for us. They'll give their blessing on our betrothal now."

I suck in a breath, strained by the tightness of my corset. "Right."

My mother places a hand on my shoulder, and Queen Kalise does the same. Even through the glove, I can feel the chill of her touch.

They both say the traditional blueblood blessing for an engaged couple—one I'll hear countless times today.

"May your marriage be filled with the gift, fruitful and joyful in abundance."

My stomach tightens. The gift has never been a gift for me. I hate it and secretly pray that my children will lack its curse, just like Gabriel and Marielle.

After they release their grip on us, Leland and I stand across from each other, not quite close enough to touch, but near enough that I have to tilt my head up to look at his face. He winks, and I give him a quick, reassuring smile.

This is good.

This is the right choice for me.

"Give her a kiss!" a man from the crowd shouts.

"Kiss her!" another adds, and suddenly the people are all yelling and cheering for us to kiss.

Leland hesitates, then steps forward, wrapping his arms around me. My heart thunders as I glance at Mother. Her face holds a bright, practiced smile—the false smile of a queen maintaining appearances. But her eye twitches as she looks at me.

The crowd cheers louder, the shouts for a kiss growing bolder as one of Leland's hands slides to the small of my back and the other to the back of my neck. "Is this alright with you?" he asks.

I nod. What else am I to do in front of such a vocal crowd? "Just make it quick."

He gives a steady nod as his face comes closer to mine, so close I can smell his scent. I close my eyes, hoping to feel anything other than the waves of anxiety flooding me as Leland's soft lips press against mine.

For a moment, all I feel is a rush of calm. This is a good thing.

His lips move against mine, and I don't stop him as he pulls me closer, the crowd roaring with approval. Then my gift begins to surface—a rush of warmth filling our embrace—and I feel the instant Leland senses it.

A hungry desperation overtakes him as he tries to deepen the kiss. Instantly, I pull back, and he looks down at me, panting, his eyes wide with uninhibited lust. His grip tightens as he leans in again.

It's nothing I haven't experienced before, and disappointment washes over me like ice water. "That's all for now, Leland," I whisper. His hands fall as he steps back, but there's still that wild gleam in his ice-blue eyes, so foreign to his gentle spirit.

I turn from him, afraid to see what my gift has done to a man I wanted to build a life with. I don't know why I hoped it would be different with Leland. My curse flooded him just as it did every other man.

I risk a glance back, and the lust in his eyes has turned to disgust. That, too, happens to men—especially the good ones. The ones who can't stand to face what my gift turns them into.

I turn away again and find Kieran's hard stare near the front of the crowd. I don't know if he's jealous or plotting his next move, but I fight the urge to run to him. He's not my safe haven anymore, and my gift would fill him just as it would any man. It doesn't matter if he's the only man I've loved. He's still not right for me.

"I'm sorry. That was—unexpected," Leland mumbles, turning to Queen Kalise before leading her to their seats.

Cracks show in my mother's false smile as she addresses the crowd once more, announcing the evening's events.

Then I hear Marielle's ear-splitting scream from behind me, and chaos erupts on the dais. I turn to see a dark rot spreading across the platform, my sisters running for the edge. I freeze, the corruption eating away at the wood beneath my feet as everyone else flees.

Leland is gone. The queens are nowhere to be seen. And still, I can't move.

Before I can force myself to react, Kieran is there—tugging me against his hard chest, his hand locking with mine as he runs, pulling me with him.

17

Kieran

"Let me go!" Gen shouts, but I only tighten my hold on her delicate wrist, tugging her along the trail deeper into the woods surrounding Covington Park.

"I can't do that, Gen," I say, pulling her faster, harder, as people scream and shout behind us. I block out the chaos. My one goal is to get Gen away from the rapidly spreading rot as quickly as possible. I can't stop to think about the reasoning behind my actions.

I hate this woman.

I hate her for every way she's hurt me—for how she forgot me so easily. For the loss of my father and the years I suffered from the same rot festering deep in the helachite mines. I hate her for kissing Leland just to please a crowd of people who don't give a damn about her life.

But even knowing all that, I couldn't bear to see her frozen on that dais, the rot spreading like floodwater as the rest of her family fled. As her fiancé fled.

No one even seemed to notice that she was the only one left standing there, immobilized as the entire structure began to split apart.

"Kieran, I have to go back! I need to know my family is safe."

I shake my head, tugging her toward an old willow at the edge of the lake. The rot never spreads into water—it can't survive in damp conditions. That's what makes the helachite mines such a living hell: the heat, the dry beat of mineral dust pounding against hot air underground.

I've seen too many people lost to the moldering helachite. Seeing it close in on Gen made something inside me snap. Even if I can't have her, I can't watch her die from the same malady that took my father.

I part the willow's branches and pull her inside, guiding her to lean against the trunk. She's gasping for breath, one hand pressed to her chest. Her damned corset is so tight, cinching her soft waist to an obscenely slender size. No wonder she can't breath—the fucking thing is strangling her.

"Turn around," I bark, setting my hands on her shoulders and turning her to face the trunk.

"What do you think you're doing?" she demands, struggling against me as I pull at her dress, revealing the corset beneath. I ignore her jerking movements, working the laces loose. She gasps, dragging in a deep breath.

She turns around, arms crossed over her chest to keep the gown from slipping. The fabric hangs loose, leaving only her thin shift beneath.

"You didn't have to do that. If we're seen—"

I cut her off. "Yes, if we're seen like this it would be a tremendous scandal—but that's the least of our worries. First the murder, now this? Gen, how bad has the rot become in Crawford?"

She shakes her head, her wavy peach locks tumbling over her shoulder. "The other day at the park was the first incident I'm aware of. The constables haven't found the killer. They must be here now."

Of course they haven't. Queen Penelope all but admitted there would be no punishment for the guilty party. "Has your mother shared anything about the spread of the rot in Naseria since we last spoke?"

She looks at me with such disdain I want to smooth it from her face until she's panting in my hands. "Since we talked? Kieran, last time we spoke privately you threatened to ruin me. You didn't even share what you knew about the rot! Now look at me!" She tries to turn, but I cage her in with my arms. "Lace me up. I can breathe again."

I move closer, feeling the rise of her breasts against my shirt. She's so lovely. Watching her sleep these past few nights has been my own punishment—seeing her full, beautiful body resting before me yet being unable to show her my true feelings.

Now she's here before me. She's as close to mine as I can have her, even after that terrible kiss. No, Leland and Gen would do nothing but condemn each other. I see it now: their two gifts are their own torturous rot. She's mine. She always has been.

"No," I murmur. "I don't think I will. I like seeing you mussed."

"Stop this!" she cries, shoving at my chest. I don't budge. Her gown slips lower, caught at the curve of her hips, the loosened corset hanging as nothing but her thin shift separates us.

"Kieran!" she hisses. I don't know that I'll ever grow accustomed to hearing that old name on her tongue. Every time she says it, I'm dragged back to a life so far gone I hardly recognize it. "Please," she whispers, her sapphire eyes lifting to meet mine.

I relent, setting my hands on her shoulders and turning her as she raises her corset and bodice. I make quick work of securing her dress, tying it looser than before. She needs to breathe, after all.

"I may want to ruin you, Princess, but I'll never harm you," I say, letting my hands linger on her hips as I press my lips to her temple.

She leans into my touch, a small whimper escaping her lips. Then her words come out in stark contrast to the way her body responds to my proximity. "Stop this pretending, Kieran. Can't we just move forward as acquaintances? You don't need to carry on like this."

I pull back, turning her toward me and pressing her against the willow. "Who said I'm the one pretending? I saw how you reacted when Leland kissed you. You're the fraud—and you're doing a piss-poor job of hiding it."

"How dare you!" she snaps, and I feel my own frustration rising. She's not even trying to hide how much she hates the false marriage she's forcing herself into. It was written clear as day on her face—the disdain for him, the way she flinched when he moved closer to kiss her.

I reach up and stroke her cheek. The softness of her skin is a caress from the past.

"You forget, Princess. I know what you look like when you want to be kissed."

She leans into my touch, and I bring my lips to hers.

"Kieran," she breathes against my mouth as I press into her, and she responds like a fuse has been lit within her. Gen's lips move against mine, and she surrenders to our kiss.

She's soft perfection, just as I knew she would be, and I want her touch to consume me.

Gen gives me an exhilarating rush, and yet I've never felt more at home than when she murmurs my name and traces my chest with her gloved hands.

18

Genevieve

Kieran looks at me curiously as we sit on a bench near my window, overlooking the full moon. It's the first time in a year of monthly full-moon meetings that I don't have an agenda. No games, no questions to fill the silence, no books to read aloud together.

There's a strange awkwardness between us, and maybe it's the close proximity, or maybe it's this tentative newness between us, as though we both recognize that the love we share may go beyond friendship.

I know it has felt that way for me for a long time. Watching him grow into himself, with long limbs and burgeoning strength, his voice shifting from childlike to something deeper, kindled something more in me. This unknown need to cling to what's familiar between us is the only reason I haven't allowed myself to admit that there's more to my feelings for Kieran Greenbluff than simple friendship.

There always has been.

Like the full moon outside my window, Kieran has been a steady presence in my life. While other friendships feel diminished by my role as princess, Kieran has never allowed my status to have any bearing on our relationship. And now, as the pressure to be the perfect heir and perfect daughter only grows, I find myself desperate for Kieran's steadiness. For his endearing smiles and constant jokes.

"What are you thinking about, Princess?" he asks, his voice soft and vulnerable.

I want to hide my true thoughts—the admission that I think of Kieran as more than just a friend leaves me too exposed and raw. But if I can't voice my riotous thoughts to him, then is he as special to me as I believe he is?

"You. Us." The words come out with a blush that scalds my cheeks.

His face beams with a crooked grin. "Us?"

"Kieran," I protest, knowing that if I give him too much leverage, he'll tease and torment me until I confess everything I feel for him.

His hand slides against mine, and I jump at the touch. "Princess, this is the first time we've been alone without a litany of games to occupy our time. Tell me why that is."

I shake my head as he grasps my hand in his. The strength of his grip gives me the courage to say what's on my mind—what I finally worked up the courage to ask him tonight. "Is there more to us than our friendship?"

"Gen." His voice quakes. "Gen, you must know I feel more for you than only friendship. But..."

"But what?" My palm feels too hot against his skin, and I worry it may be damp with nerves.

"You're going to be queen someday. I don't want to hope for something I can't have."

I think of the crown, of the burden I'll one day carry, but I drive the thought from my mind. It has no place here, not with him.

"I'd rather remain your friend than lose you," he says.

"I haven't let anyone take you from me yet, and I won't ever allow that to happen. Kieran, you're too important to me."

He looks at me with an intensity that threatens to scorch me raw. "Very well then," he murmurs, closing the distance between us, his warm lips pressing against mine.

Kieran's lips are soft and warm—and so familiar that my heart aches with the memory of him against me. But my curse. I cannot let him, of all people, feel what my curse will do to him.

I try to pull back, but he deepens the kiss, pressing my back against the rough bark of the willow tree. His hand strokes my face, trailing down to my neck, where he presses gently.

He feels so good, so right, that I find myself forgetting all the reasons I should stop him from touching me, from kissing me. His touch ignites a blaze within me that I never thought I'd feel again. I reach out, stroking his arms, his chest, the hard planes of his stomach. My hands brush the coarse hairs on his forearms, and I feel as though I could be lost in the textures of him—soft yet firm, coarse and tender.

How did I ever think I could live without his touch? How, knowing now that he's alive and well, did I ever think I could marry another?

"Do you like this, Princess?" His voice is husky, lips tracing the same path his hands took down to my neck. "Still as needy for me as you once were."

His words make me hesitate, and I turn my head, pushing him back as I think of all the consequences this dalliance could have for my kingdom's future. "Stop. We cannot do this. I don't even want this from you."

Kieran leans his head against the willow. "I can feel how your body reacts to me. No forced kisses like the one you gave Leland."

Doesn't he understand? I have a duty to Leland—to our kingdoms—to make this alliance work.

"It doesn't matter," I say, my voice traitorously breathy as I try to clear my mind. I need space. I need to get away from this man. "Prince Leland and I came to a decision together that our marriage would benefit everyone."

He scowls at me, giving me the space I so desperately need but don't actually want. The look in his eyes is filled with such disdain that it stings.

"Everyone but you," he mutters.

I shake my head, knowing I need to leave. There's nothing here for me but continued heartache. "Don't you understand, Kieran? *I* chose Leland. Me. No one pushed this arrangement on me. In fact, Gabe is openly against my choosing an arranged marriage, but it's the most practical choice—and at this point, all I want is to do what's best for my country."

The growl that comes from him pains me, and he turns his back. "You, Princess, don't even understand what your country needs."

He leaves me, slipping his hulking frame beneath the willow's draping branches. This mess between Kieran and me is all wrong. Two weeks can't come soon enough—after my wedding to Prince Leland, all this temptation will be put to rest.

But part of me knows Kieran is right. I've never felt the same desperate intensity for anyone but him. Despite my best efforts, I cannot convince my heart of what my mind already knows.

For the sake of the kingdom—of my reign as queen—I must choose Leland, even if my heart wants what it can never have.

"Genny, we were so concerned about you!" Astoria exclaims when she sees me walking toward a makeshift tent set up in the far reaches of the park.

"I'm alright, I promise," I mutter, but Astoria gives me a skeptical look. I'm not hiding my own riotous emotions. She approaches quickly, blocking me from the others.

"What happened to your gown?" she whispers.

I glance down, noticing the misaligned material, the way my corset juts out at a strange angle where it shouldn't.

"I—I ran and needed to breathe deeper. I must have mussed it when I was relacing my dress."

She gives me a puzzled look. "Why didn't you stay with us?"

My mouth opens, but I can't get a word out before the two queens approach.

"You're unharmed?" Mother asks in greeting.

"Yes, I'm fine. A bit unsettled, but I'll be alright."

Queen Kalise regards me with cold condescension. "Have you seen Mr. Blackwell?"

How much of a lie should I tell the queen? I can tell by her expression that she must have seen us together. "He helped me down from the dais before I ran. I followed the crowd and got separated from everyone. I needed a moment to compose myself."

Her lips purse, and she fixes me with an icy glare. "Prince Leland is out looking for you. Your brother is dealing with the rot. As monarchs, we are always expected to show a level of decorum and restraint in the face of chaos."

Both queens' eyes trail down my disheveled dress. Queen Kalise lifts her hand and plucks a bit of bark from my hair.

"Genevieve. This isn't like you." My mother's words are a reprimand—delivered to a grown woman in front of a crowd. I want to walk away, to curse them all, but I hold it in.

"I apologize. I panicked. How is Gabriel holding back the rot?"

Mother answers before Kalise can. "He and a troop of soldiers are removing it with water. We recently discovered, thanks to Mr. Blackwell, that the rot cannot tolerate moisture."

I look at her, puzzled by her serene demeanor. "But how are we even experiencing the rot here in the first place?"

Queen Kalise replies, "There have been reports of helachite misuse throughout the continent. As you know, when the first exposures occurred, there was significant destruction until future generations were naturally blueblooded. Mr. Blackwell has a theory that others are attempting to force the gift on redblooded people. He's seen it in the mines. Prolonged and forced exposure to raw helachite results in the rot. So it appears you're experiencing unauthorized misuse of helachite throughout Naseria—now leading to deaths and, strangely enough, exposure amongst two royal families."

"Well, it must be dealt with swiftly," Mother declares, then turns to me. "Now, your engagement celebration is once again ruined. I say we retire to Fairbright for the evening."

I can't believe she isn't having a stronger reaction to the idea that people might be intentionally trying to convert from redblood to a blueblood. What would drive someone to do that?

"Mother, surely you can't consider leaving at a time like this?" I protest, but she only gestures toward my sisters.

"I need to take care of your younger siblings. Has anyone seen Darian? The boy is always wandering off these days. And Mari looks absolutely unwell."

My sister does look uncommonly pale. Her usual vivacity is gone; she leans weakly in her chair, eyes half closed. Guilt pricks me for not noticing sooner. I leave my mother's side and kneel beside her.

"Mari, are you alright? Did you come in contact with the rot?" Her lips are nearly white, her skin ashen as Astoria helps support her.

"Darian went to call the footmen to arrange a carriage. We weren't sure if Mari could walk on her own," Astoria says.

I nod, wondering whether I should wait for Prince Leland. I'm not sure what I'd even say to him, and I desperately want to be alone to sort out my feelings about both kisses. But I need to stay and help with the cleanup. One of us should, and I know Astoria and Darian will see that Mari gets the care she needs.

Mother climbs into the carriage first, hardly glancing back as the footmen help Mari in. Astoria follows, but Darian lingers.

His spectacles are askew, his strawberry-blonde hair a mess of tangled waves. "I'm staying here to help clean up. You should go back, Genny. You look like you need to rest."

I shake my head, determined to help where I can. "Let's go together."

Darian doesn't argue as he shuts the carriage door, sending our sisters and mother safely on their way. The carriage moves off, the team of horses trotting smoothly down the lane.

"Alright then," he remarks, giving me a skeptical grin. "What do you plan to do now, Genny?"

Yes, it isn't like me to stay near danger. I've always been treated like something fragile—and fragile things get tucked away when life grows difficult, put on a shelf and forgotten until it's time for a dusting.

But I'm not something breakable. I am the future of this kingdom, and if I run from its hardships, what trust will my people have in me?

"We get to work, dear brother," I say, and together we go to help our people.

19

Kieran

By the time I'm back at Fairbright Palace, I'm hopeful that my bodily exhaustion will result in a deep, restful night's sleep. I slide into the soft bed sheets, promising myself not to go to Gen's room tonight. Not after I stole that kiss from her under the willow tree, after I felt her soft body pressed against mine, the way she became pliant and willing in my arms, even after fighting against what I knew she needed most.

No, if I go to her room now, I won't be able to keep my hands off her—and I want her to be the one coming to me next. She's had a taste of what we once had, and I want her to be insatiable for it the next time we kiss.

But, of course, sleep doesn't come. It never comes easily after my time in the mines, but a day like this makes decent sleep impossible. The close work of instructing Gabriel and his soldiers on how to safely remove the rot did nothing but bring back my own dark memories of holding it back deep underground.

Then there was Gen, working side by side with the townspeople to clean up after the celebration that never happened, serving the uneaten food to those who looked like they needed it most.

Her compassion was unexpected. I'd thought she would be safely ensconced back at Fairbright before the cleanup even began. Maybe I've been too harsh on her all this time. Maybe she isn't destined to become like her mother. For Naseria's sake, I hope this wasn't just a bid for praise but a genuine desire to make a difference for the people around her.

Not even Leland stayed to help. Not after Kalise demanded they return to the palace for "private matters." Kalise wouldn't even look me in the eyes, which makes me wonder if she suspects there's more between Genevieve and me.

If she does, she's not publicly accusing either of us—but how long will that last? And do I want to see Gen ruined any longer?

My own jealous heart got the better of me this afternoon. I couldn't stand there any longer, watching Gen paraded about like a porcelain doll, only to be humiliated by that terrible kiss. Anyone could see she wasn't interested in kissing Leland, yet she'd endured it for the crown, for what she's expected to do.

Seeing Leland overcome by her touch was almost more than I could bear. If it hadn't been for the spreading rot, I might have done something very foolish, like knock a prince out for touching what shouldn't be his.

But she *is* his. She's making a mistake, day after day, choosing a life she'll soon regret. And I can't stop her. I'm the one who left her, even if it was her own words that drove me away.

I finally give up the false hope of sleep and quickly dress. The key to Gen's room sits on my night table. I shouldn't go there; I have no intention of going near her tonight, but I slip it into my pocket anyway. I can always just check on her, maybe bring a flower for her to see in the morning.

I make my way toward the garden wall separating the public grounds from the Ashcroft gardens. As I climb over the wall, the bell tolls one. Gen should be asleep by now. I pluck a bundle of bright peonies, their crisp floral scent reminding me of the way she felt in my arms, the tiny sighs she made as we kissed.

This is a mistake—coming here after I've touched her, after her lips moved against mine and she pressed her unbound breasts to me. It will take everything I have not to stroke her soft hair, not to slide into her bed beside her. But that's not why I'm here. No, I just want to bring her flowers. I need the reassurance that, after this difficult day, she's found the rest she deserves.

The hidden door creaks open, revealing an empty room. A fire crackles in the hearth, and a gas lamp burns low, making the space warm and inviting. I place the flowers on the bedside table and turn to leave. I don't particularly want to get caught sneaking into Gen's rooms. She knows I have the key; if she wants me here, she'll invite me in.

"Kieran, is that you?" Gen's voice carries from the sitting room. She steps into her bedroom wearing a lavender silk nightdress that cascades down to her bare feet. "I knew you were the one bringing me flowers. I should have thanked you sooner."

For a beat too long, I'm transfixed by her—the soft fall of her strawberry-peach tresses, the way her unbound breasts shift with her every movement, the trace of silk over her full hips. But then I notice the tension in her jaw, the weariness in her puffy eyes.

I step closer; I can't help it. "Gen, I thought you'd be asleep. Are you alright?"

She shakes her head, stepping toward me but holding herself back. "No. No, I'm not alright."

"Today wasn't easy. The rot—"

"The rot nearly took Mari from me. She worsened quickly, and I spent all evening at her bedside trying to help her find some relief from her pain. She can't sleep, can't seem to find rest. A fever burns through her, and there's no medicine that can bring her any comfort. Can you help her? From what Leland said in the carriage, it sounded as though you have more experience with the rot than anyone else."

I don't respond to what Leland shared in the carriage. There's no point in discussing that with Genevieve, even if she's shown me a different side of herself today. Instead, I ask, "Did her doctors bathe her thoroughly? The affected area should always be treated first. The fever and other symptoms should go away with time."

Her sister shows the classic symptoms of overexposure to helachite, despite only being exposed to the rot. It's strange—typically, direct contact with the rot leads to rotten skin and, if untreated, a painful death. Perhaps it's her blue blood that gives her these symptoms.

"She shows no signs of rot on her skin, so I believe she was treated right away. But I worry how she will recover. She's so terribly ill, Kieran." Gen's chin gives a small wobble. She isn't used to dealing with hardship in her comfortable life, and in moments like this, it shows. That doesn't discount the pain I now see she's endured with her gift—or the way her mother controls her every decision—but she hasn't known loss.

"I wonder if the person doing this is close to your family," I muse aloud, and Gen immediately looks at me with a cross expression, little scowl lines forming around her full lips.

"You truly hate my family, don't you?" she snaps. "You must, to say such a thing. It's obviously someone trying to harm us—someone who despises us. In fact, none of this became so serious until you arrived."

I hold up my hands, shocked that she would suggest such a thing. I returned to Naseria ready to make Genevieve Ashcroft understand what it means to feel defeated, to make her recognize that she's a spoiled brat who's never known suffering. But now, I'm not even sure that's true.

My voice comes out harsh as I say, "Gen, I would never harm you or your family with helachite or the rot. It is—I cannot begin to describe the damage it does to a person. I want the guilty party discovered, and I want them held responsible for their actions."

"The constables are working hard to find the person responsible. It will happen, I'm sure."

"It damn well better! There's a dead man who didn't deserve to die, let alone die in such a painful way. I don't want there to be another one. These attacks have been far too close to your family. You must consider whether it's not a servant or someone else who has access to you."

Gen's brows crease as she looks away from me. "You truly think it's someone near our family?" Her eyes dart back to mine, and she moves minutely closer. "No, you're right. It does seem that way."

Her face softens, and it catches me off guard. I want to pull her close and protect her. I want to explain all the reasons I'm torn between despising her and desperately wanting to make her my world again. But I don't. It's not my place.

"Be safe, Gen."

"Don't you want to ruin me, Kieran? Why do you even care?" She steps closer again, close enough that I can smell her sweet scent.

I clench my hands into fists to resist the wave of need to pull her close. She's all-consuming, and yet she's my own form of poison. So wrong for me that I know the only antidote is to stay far, far away.

"Against my own judgment, I care for you far too much, Gen."

Her lips purse tight, and she walks to the hidden doorway. "I think you should listen to your judgment. Good night, Kieran."

20

Genevieve

The glasshouse is warm on this late winter day, my seventeenth birthday, and I shuck off my wool overcoat before turning to my growing collection of rare plants. There's a peace in the stillness of this place, one I feel more and more desperate for as my world continues to become more controlled.

My twentieth birthday is only three years away, and already there's talk of what my gift may be. Last night, Mother even mentioned the need to begin considering suitors for marriage, saying that being wed before her gift manifested had been a good thing.

Gabe, being the annoying brother that he is, said I didn't need to find a suitor because I'm already in love with Kieran. At that bold proclamation, Mother suggested I should form attachments to boys of my own blood.

Blueblood.

She expects—no, demands—that I marry a blueblood.

But how is that possible when Kieran already has my heart?

The latch on the glasshouse door opens, and I turn to see Kieran step inside, a package resting in his arm.

"Happy Birthday, Gen," he says, and I rush toward him, throwing my arms around him.

"I missed you," I whisper, desperate to inhale his scent. The crisp air clings to his smooth cheeks.

"I hoped you would be here. Otherwise I didn't know if I'd be able to see you today. I'm training with your brother and the guards most of the day." Kieran's training with Gabe has continued, despite the restrictions put in place to keep us apart. Kieran, it seems, is not a threat to Gabriel.

"You know you can use the key," I murmur against his neck, the package bumping between us. Despite my eager protests, Kieran has only ever come on the full moon, and despite my growing want for more of him, he's only ever kissed me, claiming that he can't keep me. Not when I'm to be queen.

So we do this tentative dance—our love for each other evident, despite the divide between our blood.

"Open it," Kieran insists, passing the package to me. It's heavy, and I can already tell by the strange shape that it's a potted plant.

I carefully remove the brown paper wrapping, revealing the most beautiful plant I've ever seen. Green leaves are spotted with white dots and splashes of brilliant pink. Pale pink flowers arch out of a soft pink stem. "Oh, Kieran! It's beautiful!"

Nervousness traces his features, and I know it's because he's worried I won't appreciate it. "It's just for you, Gen. I've been working on it for years, and now it's yours. Begonia Gen."

"It's the most perfect gift anyone's ever given me. I love it!"

I gingerly set the pot down on the counter before I lace my hands into his hair, pulling him down into a kiss.

I take my breakfast in bed. I can't risk facing Kieran. Knowing I'll be spending the day in negotiations with Icelantica, I needed a moment alone. My heart is still racing at the thought of our kiss under the willow. Now I can't stop thinking about our conversation in my room. I suspected he was the one bringing me flowers, but now he's confirmed it.

A tingle runs down my spine at the thought of him watching me while I sleep. I should be horrified, but instead I like knowing he can't seem to resist me.

Once breakfast is complete, I change with the help of my lady's maid, then sneak away to the warmth of the glasshouse. I've been so busy lately with the upcoming wedding that I've neglected my plants.

The scarlet begonias are in full bloom, brilliant blood-red petals hanging heavy on green foliage—but it's the Begonia Gen that catches my eye today. The plant Kieran painstakingly bred over years just for me. A gift for my seventeenth birthday. Its speckled leaves and creamy pink blossoms are a sight to behold. The plant now grows across the back wall of the glasshouse, dominating the room. I've pruned and propagated it for years, and it's always been special to me.

It once represented the last piece of Kieran I could hold on to. Now, I don't know what it means to me. Part of me wishes to toss it out, if only to keep my mind from straying to Kieran.

My thoughts keep returning to that kiss. No matter what I do, how distracted I try to stay, I can't stop replaying the way his lips pressed against mine—the urge to explore him, to relearn his stronger, broader body.

But I can't let thoughts of Kieran cloud my judgment. I must prepare for my upcoming wedding to Leland, even though the kiss with him fills me with anxious energy. The way he pressed his lips to mine, as if to prove that I still want him as much as he wants me, makes my stomach churn. It pains me to admit he's right.

I know Leland is a good man. He's everything I should want in a husband, and yet, despite my best efforts, I feel so little attraction to him. I can see him as a friend, as someone I could count on—but the thought of being intimate with him makes my skin prickle, and not in a good way.

I prune some wayward stalks from the Begonia Gen and place them in a pitcher of freshwater with rooting powder before washing up at the basin and slipping out of the glasshouse. If only I could stay in the humid space with my plants all day, perhaps then I could find some clarity.

But I must make my way to the meeting with Leland and his sister, along with Mother, Father, and Gabe. Gabe will share a brief military report on Wylan, then be excused from the hours-long session meant to finalize the matrimonial terms.

I thought we'd already established a firm contract, but Queen Kalise has requested last-minute changes. I worry it must have something to do with the rot—or perhaps she's too perceptive and suspects there's more between Kieran and me than meets the eye.

I return to my rooms to freshen up and find a rare orchid bloom on my pillow. There's a note attached that reads only, *My blossom.*

Is this from Kieran as well? He has a key to my room, but surely he wouldn't be so bold as to slip into my apartment in the middle of the day—not when he knows how many maids pass through in the late morning. Not when he's already brought me blossoms in secret each night.

And yet, Leland brought all those scarlet begonias to our engagement party. Perhaps he's been researching rare flowers? It would be something he'd do, knowing how naturally he tries to please others.

I twirl the flower between my fingers, studying the handwriting on the card. It's neither Kieran's old script nor Leland's. Placing the orchid in my vase, already filled with fresh blooms, I leave for my meeting.

"Did the orchid make it to your rooms?" Leland whispers as he lays a hand on my back, guiding me toward the table where the others wait.

I feel a strange mix of regret and relief. This flower wasn't from Kieran. Of course it was a gift from my fiancé, not the man threatening my ruin. A ruin I believe he may be having second thoughts about.

"It's beautiful. Where did you find it?"

Leland smiles broadly. "Mr. Blackwell. Strangely, he's very knowledgeable about rare flowers. Once he showed it to me, I knew you'd enjoy it."

I try to hide my surprise as I agree that I did. Kieran must still be trying to ruin me, flaunting his desire for me right in front of Leland like that.

We take our seats, and tea is poured for me. I take a desperate sip, trying to compose myself before I'm called on to speak again.

"Good morning, Peach," Father says cheerfully. "I wanted to share a quick update on Mari. She's still ill, but her color is improving. It appears she was only slightly exposed to the rot and is expected to make a full recovery. She still has a fever, but she's already talking about how she wishes to leave the confines of her bed, in typical Mari fashion."

"What a relief! I'll visit her this afternoon," I answer quickly. "Is Astoria with her?"

"She stayed beside her all night but is resting in her room now," Father replies.

Mother gives him a strained look. "We're happy to hear she'll recover. Now, let's have Gabriel speak so he can return to his training."

Gabe stands, copper curls shining in the sunlight. He looks serious. "I've had reports from the Cobalt Mountains, particularly the peaks nearest the convergence of Naseria, Icelantica, and Wylan. There have been disturbances along the Naserian border—creatures attacking remote villages—and there are also reports of the rot spreading in the region."

Queen Kalise purses her lips and rises. "Prince Leland and I have heard these rumors. There is a powerful blueblood in the area, and I've often wondered if she could be the cause of the creatures. Her power exceeds most of our abilities and includes the control of animals. I suspect she's working with Wylan. There are reasons she'd want to see my kingdom fall." Her face hardens as she turns to me, and I can't help but wonder if she and I have more in common than I thought. The weight of a kingdom rests on both our shoulders, and there are people who would like to see both of us fall. Kieran's face flashes in my mind, and I draw a deep breath, trying to clear him from my thoughts.

Kalise continues, "Mr. Blackwell should be used as a consultant as well. He's seen the creatures you speak of while visiting his Wylan mines. If they are crossing the border, we are closer to war than I realized."

Gabe nods, then whispers to a footman, who quickly leaves the room. "We need to seal this alliance as soon as possible. If the rumors of what Wylan is creating are true, we will only find strength in our shared numbers. How many troops do you have near the border?"

Queen Kalise gives him a scathing look. "That is not something I'm willing to disclose at this time. Until the wedding is finalized, I prefer to keep Icelantica's military movements private."

Gabe's eyes flash. "Then we have no alliance? Not until my sister sells herself off to a man who—" The door cracks open and Kieran steps inside. He's dressed in simple dark grey and black. Professional attire for a businessman.

"How were you planning on finishing that sentence, Prince Gabriel?" Kalise hisses. "Do you not see how much my brother is losing in choosing this alliance? His kingdom, his position, his family—his freedom to have a normal marriage. And for what? For a woman who—"

"That's quite enough," Mother interrupts from her seat, her face stony as she stares at the other queen. Slowly, she turns to Kieran. "Mr. Blackwell, I apologize for interrupting your morning. I know you were busy with business matters. Could you take a few moments to share what you've seen in Wylan concerning these strange creatures?"

Kieran's face hardens, and Kalise sits. "I've only had glimpses, but it appears someone is using helachite to breed blueblood animals, forcing them into something vicious and unnatural."

Mother frowns. Gabe asks, "For what purpose?"

Kieran glances at me for a moment, but I keep my composure. I don't want him to know how sick with dread I feel about what this could mean for my kingdom. "You could ask why anyone would expose themselves to helachite to become a blueblood—perceived power, the chance to raise their station. I believe the people breeding these creatures are doing it for the same reason."

Mother's eye twitches so rapidly, Kieran must notice, but he continues, "The better question is when those in power will accept that nobody—human or animal—should be a blueblood. It's abhorrent that helachite use isn't more regulated across the continent."

Mother lets out a harsh laugh. "Fine words from a man who made his fortune through helachite. Tell me, Mr. Blackwell—would your blood really run red?"

His gaze shifts from my mother to me before he answers, "If I had my way, I would close all unregulated helachite mines until infrastructure was in place to keep them from harming anyone. It's never been about the money for me. I've developed processes to use helachite to better people's lives, not to bring about unnatural curses in the name of an arbitrary hierarchy."

The room stirs into chaos as Queen Penelope shouts in outrage at Kieran's bitter words. He looks at all of us with spite in his eyes before taking a seat. The small scar on his forehead seems to darken as he keeps his gaze fixed on me.

Prince Leland stands, quieting the crowd with an obvious use of his gift until we all settle calmly into our seats. It reminds me of the moment his lips met mine—the way I hadn't wanted his touch, yet suddenly relaxed into it, even knowing what my gift would do to him.

"Mr. Blackwell means well," Leland says. "Please understand that he wants what's best for the citizens of both Icelantica and Naseria—Wylan and Malin too."

Only slightly pacified, Mother argues, "But he's insulted bluebloods, comparing us to wild creatures who should never have been formed!"

I hear Gabe let out a stifled cough. He's experienced Mother's disappointment in his lack of a gift far too often. Despite that, he still has blue blood and could potentially pass a gift on to his future children. Sometimes I wonder if that's the only hope Mother clings to—making a good match for him in hopes of breeding the blueblood gift back into her legacy.

Kieran clears his throat. "I see no purpose in continuing the inhumane practice of prioritizing bluebloods over redbloods."

Prince Leland seamlessly moves on from Mother's complaint. "You're right, Mr. Blackwell. I think we have much to consider regarding our shared border with Wylan. With that being said, Queen Kalise and I want to ensure that our countries have certain protections in place before the marriage."

"Protections?" I echo, worried where this might be going.

"Yes, I'm sorry to insist, but I want a wife in every sense of the word. I'm a faithful man, and I'm concerned that after we've produced offspring, you'll have trouble fulfilling your marital duties."

I blush crimson, shocked that Leland would say such a thing in front of an audience. I try to keep my eyes on him, but from the corner of my vision I see Kieran—his face tight with a scowl, his bare hands gripping the arms of his chair with such force that the upholstery looks ready to unravel beneath him.

I peel my attention back to Leland. "Have I given you any reason to think I wouldn't be willing to fulfill my marital duties?" The words come out in a rush.

Queen Kalise rises, moving to her brother's side. "I want my brother to be happily wed. Please don't feel embarrassed by his words. If your gift prevents you from doing your duty, there are other options."

"Such as?" I stammer, trying not to look at my parents.

"I would like to add a clause to the contract stating that if you feel unable to perform your marital duties, we will be free to make a different arrangement between the Ashcroft line. This will ensure our alliance continues, whether it is between yourself and my brother or one of your siblings."

Mother stands with a huff. "This is unnecessary! Genevieve has no intention of remaining unwed!"

I swallow the lump forming in my throat. The humiliation of once again addressing my incapacity for intimacy in such a public manner is almost more than I can bear. What I thought could be a partnership built on friendship and a shared desire to do what was best for our kingdoms may not be that at all. I force a stiff smile and signal for Mother to sit.

"I have no doubt that I will be able to be a wife to you in the fullest sense of the word, Prince Leland. I have no problem with an addendum to our contract stating as much. However, I will have to discuss the terms of another match with my family before we can agree to that."

The words sting as I say them, and I feel betrayed by a man who isn't even my husband yet. But I have a duty—to my kingdom, my family, even Icelantica now.

Kieran rises, and it feels as though a frisson passes between us as he looks at me and says, "Pardon me. This conversation doesn't concern me. I have more pressing matters to attend to."

He turns toward the door and leaves without another word. I want to run after him, to tell him I'm making a mistake. I've never wanted anything as much as to call Kieran mine. But I don't move. I sit frozen in place and let him walk away. Then I do what I always do: bury the hurt in my heart, knowing I must put the crown before my own desires.

21

Kieran

Seeing Gen in that meeting this morning nearly undid the composure I'm trying so hard to contain. She looked beautiful in a soft blue dress, accented with lace detailing. I wanted to pull her close and do wicked things to her that would have her moaning about the impropriety of it all.

That was all I could think about until the conversation began. It was the same shit I've dealt with since arriving at Fairbright—the Ashcrofts' inability to see that continuing a blueblood line is weakening these countries. Then the insulting, vulgar way the Frostclaws openly demanded that Gen be willing to fuck Leland at his leisure. I was so close to speaking up, to blowing my cover and letting go of this false ruse.

Until Gen spoke up.

Until she once again chose to go against her own desires. I saw how she looked at Leland when they kissed, and I felt the difference in our shared kiss, in the way she was drawn to me last night in her bedroom.

I saw the dread on her face again when she pretended not to look at me as she agreed to marry a man whose touch makes her uncomfortable.

That's why I'm waiting for Queen Kalise in my study, a room I use for charting geography, completing correspondence, and making business preparations. I don't know if I'm capable of staying here much longer. I'm writing to my business manager to arrange my departure and to send a team to oversee the project without my presence.

A knock sounds at my door, and I call for them to enter. It's Queen Kalise, as I expected. She's alone, and I'm thankful for that. I don't want to try to explain to Leland, or anyone else, why I need to leave.

"This is an unexpected request," Kalise says as she takes a seat across from me, her gloved hands resting primly in her lap. She wears a brown dress cut with a high neckline and long sleeves. Although it would look drab on another woman, Kalise makes the dress look stylish. Her short silvery-blonde bob nearly touches her shoulders, longer than she typically keeps it.

"I wanted your opinion on the state of things here in Naseria."

She gives me a wry look. "Would you like my opinion on how they handle their kingdom or on whether the princess is terribly suited for Leland?"

I study her with as much disinterest as I can manage. I wouldn't put it past Kalise to see that there's something between Genevieve and me. Perhaps even Leland notices. That was the point, at least when I first arrived.

"The kingdom, of course. Your brother's betrothal is of little consequence to me. Would you like a drink?" I move to a decanter of brandy.

"Yes, that would be welcome after this morning. But I know you well enough to see you are attracted to the princess—the dance you shared, your interactions, and how you saved her from the spreading rot. The way you could hardly contain your anger at that meeting. I think you care very much for my brother's betrothed."

I keep my back turned as I pour. Steady. Casual. She doesn't need to know my pulse quickens at the thought of Leland's hands on Gen. I let out a harsh laugh as I carry the drinks back.

"Saving her from the rot is hardly a sign of attraction. You know how I feel about the abuse of helachite—I'd save anyone, even my worst enemy, from that fate. As for the rest, it's nothing. She's an interesting woman, but ultimately she's Leland's fiancée. I'll never think of her again after I leave."

I hand Kalise the brandy, her silver glove brushing my bare skin. I've never seen the queen without gloves, never seen any piece of her skin other than her face. Rumors in Icelantica suggest she bears the marks of her gift, a delicate pattern like a snowflake.

Of course that's rubbish. Still, it's strategic—hide yourself so completely that even your skin becomes legend. She cultivates the image she presents to her citizens. I wonder who the true Kalise is.

She sips the brandy and studies me more closely than I'd prefer. Kalise has a way of disarming a person with her glare, and I've avoided it while working with Icelantica over the years.

"I saw you pull the princess away that day. When she returned she was disheveled and flushed. Leland considers you a close friend. If you harm my brother, I will be forced to hurt you back."

The room grows cold, and the queen does something I've never seen her do: she slowly slides one glove off. As I suspected, there are no unusual marks on her skin—just alabaster-smooth flesh. Her hand cups the brandy glass, and immediately the brandy freezes solid.

Kalise looks at me with such frosty disdain that it stings. I nod. "You've made yourself clear. I value my friendship with Leland as well and have no intention of hurting him."

That's true. I never want to hurt Leland. I wanted to uncover the Ashcrofts' ugliness, while also placing Naseria in capable hands. I can't solve all the problems in this continent alone. But, it seems Leland and Gen may bring out the worst in both their powers.

Kalise sets the glass on the table and slides her glove back on. "I hope, for your sake, you don't give me reason to cause you harm. It would be a terrible waste of a brilliant mind."

"Of course not. Now—back to Naseria, the real reason I called for this visit. Your demonstration, however, has been enlightening." I take a sip of brandy, savoring the warmth.

"What about Naseria?" She narrows her eyes.

"What are your opinions on how the kingdom is run? Do you find anything alarming?"

She drums her gloved fingers on the arm of the chair. "It's not my place to say. Do I believe you should choose Naseria over Wylan for the railway expansion? Of course. Either way, you will struggle with how these kingdoms treat their miners—and eventually their railway workers."

This isn't new information. It's something I've weighed carefully. I've purchased as many helachite mines in Wylan and Naseria as I could, and the conditions for both are terrible.

"Will the Ashcrofts allow Leland any influence? That was your purpose in agreeing to this arrangement."

Kalise looks toward the door and lowers her voice. "The current queen won't allow any opinion but her own. She treats her grown children like toddlers, and her husband is nothing but a pet. I worry how Leland will fare in that family. My deepest concern is that when

Princess Genevieve takes power she'll be a figurehead while her mother retains control."

It's what I've suspected. Once, when we were younger, the royal family seemed happier—the queen more relaxed, more willing to hear dissenting views. That's changed since I returned. One thing is clear: Gen will ruin herself without my lifting a finger.

22

Genevieve

The cold rain beats against the carriage window as I look out at the passing townspeople hurrying through the deluge. If there were any rot left in Covington Park, it's surely gone now.

The rain has continued for two days, and it's left me in a desolate mood. Two more flowers greeted me each morning when I awoke, and I assume they're from Kieran. But between caring for Mari, making final arrangements for the wedding, and working with the constables to uncover who is spreading the rot, I've been far too tired at night to notice his late visits.

I also had to sign the marriage contract. I accepted the stipulation that I must marry Prince Leland and invite him to my bed—or relinquish the match so one of my siblings might take my place. It feels wrong to put our marriage in such stark, unequivocal terms. So binding that I feel stifled at the thought of marrying him.

I've needed time and privacy to sort through my feelings, and I've let myself reflect on what I truly want. I want what's best for my country.

I want to provide stability and peace to both our kingdoms. But most of all, I want a loving partnership. I've hoped that Leland and I could reach that point, but I fear we misunderstand each other more than I expected. Yet if I don't marry him, I'll be forcing someone else into an arranged marriage.

I'm still hurt by the way he brought up such an intimate matter so publicly, instead of coming to me privately to discuss his concerns. It makes me worry what sort of partnership we'll have.

Then there's Kieran. He's all I think about when I allow my mind to wander. There's a magnetism growing between us—a fusion of our past and the connection that never died. I know a path with Kieran is impossible. No one would allow it.

The carriage comes to a halt at The Wild Rose, and a footman opens the door for me. Another holds an umbrella over my head as I walk into the blissfully empty shop.

Clementine greets me with a tight hug. "Oh, Genny! I'm so happy you came. I was worried when I read your letter. Is everything alright?"

I step back, placing my gloved hands on her bare arms. "Yes, well, there's nothing urgent. Mari is healing well. She even took a walk in the gardens today. But I needed my friend."

"Of course. Come, sit." She directs me toward two high-backed chairs near the back of the shop. They're private enough that no one from outside will see I'm here, especially since I told the coachman to park in the alley.

Clemmy brings over a tray of pastries, and I choose one topped with candied cherries. "Now, tell me what's on your mind."

I don't hold back. I came here for a reason; I need to share my heart with someone. Usually that would be Astoria, but she's observed too much. I need a fresh perspective if I'm to make the right decision.

"I think I may be making a mistake by marrying Leland Frostclaw. He's everything I wanted in an alliance, and he's a suitable husband, but I fear we'll never have that spark couples in love carry. I thought I could live without it, but my mind has changed."

Clemmy studies me carefully between bites of pastry. "But you've said yourself that you could never fall in love again—not with your curse preventing true feelings from developing. What changed your mind? Is it nerves about the wedding?"

I bite my lip, then tell her the truth. "Kieran returned."

She gasps, choking on her pastry. Taking a sip of tea, she stares at me incredulously. "But that's impossible. He's dead."

I shake my head. "He won't tell me why he stayed away, but he's taken on a new identity. He's Morris Blackwell."

"The helachite businessman? But that's impossible! He doesn't even look like Kieran. Maybe a little around the eyes, but Genny, don't do this. He's not Kieran. He's a swindler and a liar. He must have learned about Kieran and is playing you to ruin your chances with Prince Leland."

She looks at me as though I'm gullible—a princess without worldly sense. It stings, knowing even my closest friend sees me as naïve. Yet everyone around me expects me to run the kingdom. Shouldn't they want me to be less gullible? Shouldn't they treat me like the rational adult I am?

"If only it were that simple," I mutter. "I'd never fall for such a trick. It's him, Clemmy—and to make matters worse, he kissed me at my engagement party. He saved me from the spreading rot and kissed me to prove that I still felt something for him."

Clemmy's eyebrows lift, and she purses her lips. "Well?"

"That's why I'm so confused! I felt dread when Prince Leland kissed me, but with Kieran, it was as if my soul were afire. I haven't felt that way since... since I was nineteen. These last few weeks have made me wonder if we could become something great."

She looks at me with such pity that I want to tell her to stop, but I hold my tongue. I don't want to be rude, not when she may still offer clarity. "Do you know what he wants?"

I blush. "All I know is that he claims he wants to ruin me, but he's done nothing to demonstrate that. He's still as affected by me as I am by him."

She shakes her head. "I'm in a mixed redblood and blueblood marriage. The court doesn't accept me, and while Griffin tries his best not to show how it bothers him, I know it does. I don't know how you'd ever gain your mother's or the council's approval to marry a redblood."

I sigh and drop my gaze to the table. "I know. The idea of marrying Kieran feels as impossible now as it did when I was nineteen."

"Then marry the prince. Send Mr. Blackwell away and don't let thoughts of him linger. You've said yourself you don't have the luxury of marrying for love. Why would it be any different with Mr. Blackwell? He'll still be affected by your curse, just as any other man has been. Don't you think it will hurt the love you feel for him—wondering if what he feels is false?"

Tears well in my eyes. I know my duty, and I've feared our shared kiss was only Kieran's reaction to my curse.

What if he truly does hate me?

Betraying this arrangement with Icelantica, only to have my heart broken, would be too much to endure.

"You're right. I can't cancel my wedding."

She nods, then stands and wraps me in a warm hug. I don't stop the tears that run down my cheeks onto her shoulder.

23

Kieran

The garden is still, the midnight silence something I now crave as I walk the perimeter of the Ashcroft family gardens. I want to choose a flower for Gen that might draw her from the dark mood I saw cloud her face during supper.

Plucking a soft pink rose, one of the earliest blooms of the season, I begin making my way toward her staircase. This nightly ritual is something I can't seem to stop, even knowing it will lead nowhere.

I'll be leaving in two days for my country house in northern Naseria, finally allowing myself to admit that staying through the wedding is nothing more than a personal form of torture.

Gen doesn't care whether she ruins her life with an ill-suited marriage, and my intentions have nothing to do with ruining her. She's doing an adequate job of that on her own.

No—Genevieve Ashcroft is my own poisonous bloom, and if I remain, I'll only give in to a fatal attachment to the woman who showed me her true self nine years ago.

The thorns of the rose bite into my palm as I take quick strides toward her room. Up ahead, limned in moonlight, I see Gen slip through the slightly ajar tower door. She scans the garden, her eyes meeting mine, and I shrug, caught once again in what's become my nightly habit.

"Mr. Blackwell, fancy meeting you here," she murmurs, her tone lighter than I'd expect after her dour mood at supper.

She already knows what I'm doing. There's no point denying it. I hold out the rose, feeling the catch of the thorns as she reaches for it. But she doesn't pull away; her hand is warm against mine as she rubs the stem between her fingertips.

"It's lovely," she says softly, "but you must stop this. Please."

I shake my head, knowing I'll willingly let her curse me, ruin me, destroy me. I've learned nothing in nine years from the venom this woman can extract. "You know I can't do that, Gen. I've tried."

Her fingers linger against my skin, the contact charged in a way that makes me want to pull her closer. Then, as if she senses it too, she pulls away, leaving my hands empty. The loss of her touch cuts through me like a bitter wind.

"Walk with me." Her voice is resolute, and she looks at me with a fierceness I can't help but admire.

"Of course." My voice is rough, betraying the emotion coursing through me.

"I couldn't sleep," she explains, her eyes on the rose. "I signed the marriage contract today, and I know what you must think of me—for choosing this life, for agreeing to the Frostclaws' demands. You don't need to ruin me. I've done an excellent job of it myself."

"You're doing what was always expected of you. And as we both know, Genevieve Ashcroft is nothing if not obedient."

She lets out a biting, false laugh. "Do you remember the time you came to my room after my mother removed me from shared lessons with you and Gabe? We were probably fifteen."

I smile, thinking of that first time I snuck into her room. We were friends then, but I already knew I loved her. I'd always loved her, if I'm being truthful. "I'm still surprised no one heard me banging on that old wooden door at the bottom of the stairs."

She laughs—a bright, joyful sound—and it makes something in me ache in a way I haven't felt in years. Like my heart is cracking open from the hard shell I built around it.

"We snuck out of the palace and walked all the way to Crawford. Do you remember how terrible my disguise was?" she asks, and I think back to her attempt at dressing like an ordinary redblood girl. Her clothes—even her simplest frock was far too fine, and her brilliant peachy hair gave her away long before we reached town.

"Of course. Not to mention we were both far too young to pass as old enough to order ale at that tavern. Remember how angry your mother was when reports of our adventures got back to her?"

Her shoulder brushes mine as she looks up, her smile fading. "We didn't see each other for nearly a month after that. Twenty-seven days apart. It felt like a lifetime—but in that time, I was reminded why I must be obedient. The lesson was strictly enforced."

"Gen." My voice drops to a whisper as I catch her hand in mine. "I'll say this only once more. You don't have to do what they expect of you. For fuck's sake, you're an adult—the future queen."

She pulls her hand back, and I know my words are lost to her. "I know. This was my decision, and with the Frostclaws' amendment to the marriage contract, I don't want my choice forced on my sisters. I want them to find love."

Her stubborn refusal to find another way out makes my blood heat, and I look down. "This is why I must go. I've already decided to take on the railway project under your reign, but I cannot watch you destroy yourself."

She nods, her expression resolute. "I understand why my wedding will be difficult for you to see. You were the only one who ever got me to follow my heart—but my heart has been broken for far too long to trust it anymore. In time, I hope you'll understand why I'm choosing Leland."

I say the truth, the part my insecurities have always known. "You never would have chosen me, Gen. Why is it any different this time?"

I turn away, unable to face the hurt I know will be in her eyes—because despite her words, a part of Genevieve Ashcroft still wants me.

24

Genevieve

My nineteenth birthday celebration feels like a death sentence. After years of secrecy, Mother has finally realized that Kieran and I still find time to be together, and the lashing she gave me for my lack of propriety—for the disgrace of choosing a redblood gardener's boy over any number of bluebloods—was reprehensible.

She'll never understand how deeply I love Kieran, or how cautious we've been with each other. She'll never know that, despite finding ways to show one another with our bodies how much we love, Kieran has never taken that last vestige of propriety from me. She doesn't deserve to know how I've begged him to enter me, how much I've wanted to feel him inside of me—to be joined to him.

Even after years of coming to my rooms, he's always insisted that we not cross that line, afraid I'll someday desire a blueblood husband who would see me as ruined by the gardener's boy.

Deep down, I know I can never accept Kieran as my husband. Mother, Father, the council and the kingdom would never accept a redblood as king consort. Not when the bluebloods fought for our right to rule.

But it isn't fair.

There's nobody else for me but Kieran, and if I cannot marry him, then I want to savor the time I have with him before I'm forced to choose the crown over the boy I love.

The lights are low as I walk through the palace toward the banquet hall with Astoria and Mari. Mari leans on my arm, and I'm happy to support her as she continues to regain strength after the attack from the rot. She insisted on joining this supper and the ball that will follow, despite her slow, tentative recovery. There have been no further reports of the rot, and the guilty party is still at large.

"Can I help you in any way?" I ask softly. We've done all we can to keep her illness from the public eye. I understand her wish for privacy. The court gossip is already relentless when it comes to our family, and there's no reason to add more fodder to the flame.

"I'm quite alright, thank you, Genny. I just worry how I'll go from dancing all night to being a wallflower without anyone noticing."

Astoria replies, "I'll stay close. And Darian said he'll dance with you as much as you like. Do you think Prince Leland or Gabe will be willing to help her dance with support?"

Mari looks surprised. "I couldn't ask that of Prince Leland! Besides, he'll be busy dancing with Genny. Tell me, has your affection for him deepened? He's such a kind man—I really don't see why you're hesitant about the arrangement."

Astoria gives me a knowing look. She hasn't missed the stolen glances between Kieran and me, or how I seem to be pulling away from Leland. She even gently suggested she would take my place as Leland's betrothed if it pleased me. I dismissed her. I chose this arrangement, and I will see it through, even with the new addendum to the contract. I purse my lips. "I still hope we'll grow in affection over time."

"But," Astoria adds, "Mr. Blackwell is proving something of a distraction. Don't give that man the attention he seeks, Genny. Especially not tonight!"

Mari giggles. "He is a rather distracting sight to see. Oh, and here he comes!"

As we approach the doors to the banquet hall, I see Kieran and General Pryor ambling toward us. Kieran's eyes lock on mine, and I try to calm the energy buzzing through me at the sight of him. His evening wear is immaculate—black, of course—with a steel-grey silk cravat. His ungloved hands make my skin tingle at the thought of them against me.

Both men bow, and General Pryor offers Mari his arm to escort her into the hall. "Oh, you must take Astoria's arm as well!" Mari insists. "I wouldn't want to draw unnecessary attention."

"Of course," General Pryor says, and Astoria gives me a nervous look as she takes his other arm, leaving me alone with Kieran.

"Can you see that Princess Genevieve is properly seated, Blackwell?" General Pryor calls over his shoulder.

Kieran looks down at me, his brows furrowed. "I think I'm capable of the task, if Princess Genevieve doesn't object."

I swallow as I brace for his touch. "Of course not," I reply, offering him my arm. The heat of him beside me makes my blood stir, and I have to resist leaning into his solid frame.

We enter the room to low candlelight and dark floral arrangements. The décor is a deep purple and black, giving it an air of mysterious elegance. Mother has outdone herself for this small court banquet and ball. Everything around us speaks of decadence and romance, and I squeeze Kieran's arm a little tighter. He looks at me expectantly.

"She decorated it so similarly to the night you snuck me out of the ballroom. My nineteenth birthday—do you remember? I wanted to dance with only you, but she wouldn't allow you to attend," I say quietly as he leads me to my seat.

Next to my name card is one inscribed with his. His eyes grow distant, and his brow creases. I can feel the tension in his muscles as he releases my arm and steps slightly away.

"Yes, it's all very familiar," he remarks, tracing his fingers across the letters. "And we're seated beside each other. Did you share my true identity with the queen? Is she making a mockery of us both?"

I take my seat just as Prince Leland enters, guiding his sister to hers. "Of course I didn't."

But it is strange, the similarities. The same sensual undertones linger, as if the flower choices themselves have created an alluring perfume in the air. That night she'd meant to entice me toward her preferred blueblood suitors. It hadn't worked, of course. It had only emboldened me to take Kieran to my bed.

Tonight, I'm not sure what message she's trying to send.

"Why ever not, Princess? Is it because you'd hate to see her remove me from Fairbright? Would you miss me too much? Or are you beginning to realize she's keeping things from you?" Kieran's voice is low and deep, his breath tickling my skin.

He's too close, far too close for proper behavior at a dinner party. His face, illuminated by candlelight, is hard and beautiful. I want to trace the differences in his changed features, to feel the ridge of his altered nose and the scar. I want to press my lips to those changes and learn them with my tongue.

Leland takes his seat across from me, a stiff smile on his face as he looks between us. I sit up straighter, turning toward Lord Griffin Hanford. Of course, Clementine isn't seated beside her husband; she's next to Prince Leland. She's noticed Kieran's closeness as well. Her voice rises, loud and bright, drawing Leland's attention and sparing him from Kieran's impropriety.

Clemmy is playing her part. She's the redblood baker—a crass nobody who wormed her way into the princess's life, only to rise above her station and marry a cousin of the crown. She knows very well that all the blueblood gentry in the room expect her to talk too loudly, ask inappropriate questions, and make a mockery of the court.

Just as most expect Kieran to be too close to me, to make improper comments and crude jokes. To them, he's a boorish redblood businessman, not a gentleman bred with the understanding that one never gets too close to a blueblood princess. Even now, I see the subtle glances and hear the whispered comments as I feel Kieran's large frame lean close to mine. His leg slides against my own, and I turn my attention to my empty glass. Maybe if I stare at it long enough, someone will bring me something to drink.

"Everything alright, Genevieve?" Griffin asks quietly. "That Blackwell fellow seems to be getting rather close."

"Yes, it's fine," I answer, forcing my most contained smile.

His eyebrow arches as a footman pours wine into our glasses. Staring at the glass must have worked after all. I take a deep drink, feeling the slightest burn in my throat as I swallow.

Griffin continues, "I know that expression all too well—it's the look of a woman hiding her true thoughts. Unfortunately, it's far too common in you Ashcroft girls. With the exception of Marielle, of course. But even she appears more demure this evening."

Clemmy lets out a loud giggle at something Leland says and meets her husband's eyes, raising her glass to him.

"Is that why you needed to seek a bride from outside the court, cousin?" I ask, taking another drink and stealing a glance at Kieran, who looks bored as he talks with one of the councilmen's wives.

"Clementine, as you know, is unlike any woman—redblood or blueblood. She's a force that swept me away."

I smile at my friend as she gestures animatedly, and Prince Leland snorts in a most ungentlemanly manner. "She has a way of sweeping everyone into her force. We're just the two she's chosen to keep hold of."

"Aren't we fortunate?" Griffin laughs, but his attention remains fixed on his wife. It's odd, seeing my once-serious cousin so smitten. Even after a year of marriage, he still looks at Clemmy as though she's a precious jewel.

I feel a hand graze my skirts and turn to Kieran. "Mr. Blackwell," I say in a low, warning tone as I scoot away from his touch.

He smirks. "Please, say that again. I like it when you call me by *my name.*"

I scowl, trying to ignore the hand nudging my thigh. "Is this how you plan to ruin me?" I whisper. "Still aiming for a public display, even after your confession last night? It's been weeks, and you've done nothing to make good on your threats."

He gives me a teasing pinch through my skirts, sending a jolt through me. I let out a small squeak, and the woman beside him scowls. "You ruined me in a night," he murmurs. "I plan to play out your ruin slowly and rapturously, Princess."

I give him a pointed look. If anyone was already ruined, it was me. He *chose* to leave. He refused to see me before he departed, and I was the one who mourned his death. Last night, I made it clear there was nothing he could do to change my mind. Now he's leaving, and it's for the best.

"I think nine years has been slow enough, Kieran."

He lets out a low, scathing laugh as his hand finds my hips, his thumb stroking along the thin fabric. His touch feels so good that I want to lose myself in it—even here, surrounded by people.

"I want you to beg for me," he whispers. "I want you to cry out from the torment of wanting me, Princess. We're far from that point yet. Perhaps it will happen after you take your wedding vows."

"I'll never beg for you," I retort.

He withdraws his hand, and the loss of his touch chills my senses just as our food is served.

"I look forward to the moment when you beg for ruin."

25

Genevieve

I see Kieran across the ballroom—even though he wasn't invited, even though I know Mother would be horrified to see him here, dressed as a young blueblood in all his finery. Finery, I'm sure, that he borrowed from Gabe.

I can't stop myself from going to him, knowing he's snuck into my nineteenth birthday ball just to see me. He's never done anything so bold as to push beyond his status in a public room. That boldness in him awakens a boldness in me.

"Kieran, you came." The words escape me in a hushed urgency.

He stares down at me, taking in the way my deep purple bodice fits snugly against my flesh, boosting my breasts before it flares into a full skirt, giving the illusion of generous hips.

"You look—" He pauses, swallowing. "You look perfect, Gen." Then his eyes dart around the room before he murmurs, "Maybe I shouldn't have come. I can leave. I can—"

I don't let him finish. I pull him close, drawing us both onto the ballroom floor, where a melodic song beckons.

I can feel the crowd's heavy gaze on us as we move together. A suitor I've snubbed in favor of Kieran looks ready to interrupt, but none of that matters because Kieran came to me.

Kieran has publicly taken the risk to be in my arms in front of all the court.

After our meal, Prince Leland makes his way to my side, an indiscernible expression on his soft features. "May I have the first dance with you?"

"Of course." The words stumble from me as the prince guides me toward the ballroom. The room is cast in the same dark, mysterious shadows as dinner—romantic and sensual, a setting sure to make people think scandalous thoughts and perhaps act on them, only to become the subject of salacious gossip by morning.

Gabriel walks beside Queen Kalise, and it's obvious they're having some sort of dispute. Every time I've seen them together, they've done nothing but argue. It must be a novel feeling for my brother, having a woman not fall instantly for his charms and graces.

"Do you think Gabriel is alright?" Leland asks as we walk behind them. Gabe scowls at Kalise with such disdain I'm afraid he might burst into flames.

"Our siblings seem to have a proclivity for hating one another," I remark.

Leland chuckles as the instruments begin to warm up. He hands me a glass of sparkling wine from a passing footman, and I take an eager drink. "Yes, I think you're right. At least we're the ones who agreed to this arrangement—and not them."

"I don't think anyone could make Gabe agree to marriage. He's far too busy bedding whomever he pleases and preparing for the next conflict that may arise. He'd make a terrible husband."

"And Kalise is far too afraid of herself to let a man get close. Their mutual hatred would lead to a bitter arrangement, I'm sure." He pauses, glancing around the room. His eyes fall on Kieran and a beautiful blueblood—a duke's daughter, if I recall correctly. Seeing Kieran hold her close makes my skin prickle.

"Speaking of mutual hatred," Leland says, "I can't help but notice you and Mr. Blackwell seem to be at constant odds. He's become a friend, but if you'd rather not work with him, I'm sure we can find another organization to build the railway through Naseria."

I set my empty glass on a passing tray, wishing for another drink. My mouth feels dry as the music begins, and Leland leads me across the room in steady steps.

"No, of course not. He's the only one capable of completing the project anytime soon, and I'd prefer we connect our two countries. It will make travel easier when we wish to visit Icelantica."

"Were the two of you acquainted before? There's something familiar about your interactions."

My breath catches. I should tell Leland the truth now. He deserves to know.

The music quickens, and Leland sends me into a spin. The words stick in my throat as he catches me, pulling me closer than I'd typically allow a dance partner.

"He reminds me of someone I lost," I reply quietly. "I hate that he does, but that person was close to me—and he hurt me deeply."

Leland's face hardens. "A former lover?"

"I had lovers before our betrothal, and I assume you did as well. I'd never question you on your past, and I trust that you're committed to this arrangement, as I am."

His breath escapes in a hiss. "My apologies. It's different now, after I've kissed you. I feel less of myself when it comes to you."

My heart sinks. My gift has already ruined what we might have been before we're even married.

"I've worried about that," I admit. "It affects each person differently. Some become possessive, while others hate me for what my gift did to them. It's why I stopped allowing anyone to touch me."

His cool eyes settle on me as the music fades. "I can learn to control the urges. I promise."

"I hope so. I've never tried to work past my curse with another person."

His lips press into a tight line. "You have to trust me for this to work, Genny. I can't make our marriage succeed if you're too scared to try."

Then he turns on his heel, leaving my side as he cuts across the ballroom toward his sister. My breath comes in short spurts, my heart heavy with the realization that I will never be able to let myself be close to Leland—not with my curse looming over our marriage.

Astoria approaches, two glasses of sparkling wine in hand. "Here, Genny. Are you alright?"

"Yes, of course. Why do you ask?"

"Well, I believe that's the first time I've seen Prince Leland look anything but amicable."

I nod. "My curse is taking some getting used to for him."

She arches an eyebrow just as a young blueblood noble approaches and asks her to dance. Astoria looks at me, reluctant to leave if I still need her.

"Go. Have fun," I say, knowing dancing isn't exactly her idea of enjoyment. Still, she agrees, and he whisks her away. I'm about to find Mari when Kieran steps up beside me.

"May I have this dance?" he asks.

I should say no. I'm not as composed as I'd like to be, the edges of my emotions raw from my conversation with Leland.

But I don't want to tell him no. I want to feel Kieran's hands on me. I want to get lost in the music with him, if only for this one moment. If only to remember what we once had—and what we'll never have again.

"Yes, of course," I say as he places his bare hand on my back. I can feel the heat of him through the fabric. The warmth of his touch and the strength in the way he leads us across the ballroom are things I can never resist.

The music begins, and Kieran grips the fabric of my dress, pulling my body flush with his, forcing me to tilt my head up to meet his jade eyes.

He smells spicy and clean, and there's a trace of stubble along his cheeks that I ache to touch, to feel the textures of him against my bare skin. But that's impossible, even as I grow more desperate for it with every contact between us.

The ballroom is draped in deep purple fabric, creating private spaces in the alcoves. As we move, I see couples slipping away into those secluded corners. Yet whenever my eyes stray from Kieran, I feel an irresistible pull back to him, to his green eyes. The other dancers blur into a muted stream of color as everything else seems to melt away.

"You're staring, Princess." His voice is rough, as if he's just as swept away by our closeness.

"I could say the same of you, Mr. Blackwell."

His lips curve upward as he leans closer. "Twice in one night you've used my name. I never thought I'd enjoy hearing the sound of it spill from your lips."

"But it's not truly your name, Kieran."

He flinches slightly and pulls back. "As I told you, Kieran died long ago." His lips brush my hairline, and I shiver at his touch.

"Then why have you allowed me to call you Kieran?"

He withdraws a fraction, his mouth quirking into a faint grin. "Perhaps from you, the name Kieran reminds me of all I've lost."

His hand slides to my bare shoulder, and I recoil from the skin-to-skin contact. I shouldn't let him be this close. If my curse courses through him here, I don't know how I'll stop either of us from giving in to my own desires. He's always been my weakness, and even now, I can't stop myself around him.

"Gen, I—" He stops, letting the words fade.

I look at him expectantly, but he doesn't continue, leaving us suspended in silence. "What, Kieran?"

"Reconsider the wedding. Not because of me—but for yourself. Think about what you truly want."

I shake my head. "You want me to beg for you? And yet now you're the one who seems ready to beg."

"You haunt me, Gen. I'm not myself around you, but none of that matters. What matters is that you need to do what's going to make you happy."

"Leland is a good man. He's the best husband I can procure."

He exhales in frustration, his strong hands tightening on my gown. "He's a good man, but I'm afraid your gift will ruin both of you—and not in the way I intended."

"Perhaps you'll get just what you hope for, then," I retort, trying to pull away. But he holds me close, frowning, still keeping us effortlessly in step with the music.

"You don't even allow yourself one small happiness," he murmurs. "You're choosing to put a good man through a loveless marriage—and for what? To prove a point? To show that you'll sacrifice everything for your country? Don't you see that your country needs more than an advantageous marriage?"

It wasn't easy to refuse Kieran in the dark of the garden last night, not when he asked me to give up this marriage. But now, hearing the same plea in public, I'm reminded just how high the stakes are for me to marry Prince Leland. Even though every fiber of me desperately wants to choose Kieran, the truth is that seeing my curse invade his senses—ruining everything that was once pure and true between us—would break me more than being forced to visit Leland's bed.

Last night I saw how my curse would twist him into a possessive lover. When our touch lingered too long, he looked at me with such obsession that I realized there was no future for us. The love he once felt for me would become a sickness, and I couldn't bear it, knowing what I felt was real while his was cursed.

"You don't understand!" My tone is sharp, and for the first time, a pair of dancers glance our way, but I can't stop as the words pour out. "I can never be with you. You're a redblood, and I will never force my curse on you. I couldn't live with it!"

I break away from him, pushing through the crowd—and see Leland staring at me. His face is shadowed, his expression hard enough to send a chill down my spine. His sister whispers something in his ear, and he shakes his head before turning away and striding out the door.

He knows.

"Prince Leland! Wait!" I call, rushing after him.

26

Genevieve

I walk quickly through the crowd, waves of dancers and observers parting as I make my way out of the ballroom into the hallway. A small waiting room stands with its door ajar, and I peek inside. Leland is there, leaning against the wall. His eyes are brilliant ice, his brows furrowed. Seeing him like this hurts. I shouldn't have agreed to dance with Kieran, not when I know how drawn I am to him.

Leland exhales sharply. "You're not telling me something, I know it. There's something between you and Blackwell."

I almost shake my head, ready to deny it again—but Leland doesn't deserve my lies. He doesn't deserve the hurt I'm causing him.

"You're right. He reminds me so much of a man from my past because he once was him."

Lines crease Leland's brow as he looks at me in confusion. "What do you mean he once was the man from your past?"

I sigh before letting the truth spill out. "We were friends as children, and later we fell in love. We were so young, and I knew I'd never be allowed to love him—he was a redblood gardener's son. But I did. I loved him more deeply than I've ever loved another person. Then he left me, and I never understood why. Word reached me that he'd died, and shortly after, I turned twenty and received my gift. I think the loss of him caused it to manifest the way it did."

He looks at me with little sympathy as he nods once. "And now? Do you still love him?"

I shake my head. "It's not like that. I know we need this alliance, and I want to marry you. I believe he's jealous, or maybe still hurting. He always knew I could never choose him. I just didn't think he would still care all these years later."

Leland's voice snaps. "Blackwell knew who you were all this time. He's used me to get to you."

His jaw tightens, the coldness in his eyes cutting. It stings, but I've hurt this man—I deserve his contempt.

"Why would he encourage me to make an arrangement with you?" he finally asks. "He could have come here on his own for Blackwell Industries."

"I don't know. He could have returned at any time, but coming back to Fairbright now feels deliberate—as though he's trying to ruin our chances of success." I think of how he begged me to abandon this arrangement.

"You both have lied to me. I—I don't think this will work, but the contract is already signed. Either I have to marry you, or one of your sisters. That feels wrong, to switch brides like that."

My shoulders sag. I can't force this arrangement on them. "I'm not going to let you do that. It doesn't matter how you got here. I just want to move forward with our alliance, for both our countries." I push down the nagging doubt that makes my stomach churn, thinking of being intimate with Leland. "Blackwell is leaving tomorrow morning."

He grunts, then asks incredulously, "Did no one recognize him?"

"No. His appearance is different. Only Astoria, Gabriel, and I know Blackwell's true identity. We haven't told my mother."

He looks chagrined as he leans against the wall. "Blackwell worked in the mines for years—that must be where he went after he left you. But I don't understand why. Did you force him to leave?"

My head feels light, the realization sinking in that I may have caused Kieran's suffering. I think back to the night I gave myself to him. How he proposed and promised to protect me from any backlash against our engagement, only for me to tell him it was impossible. The letter the next morning said he was leaving Fairbright. I tried to speak with him, but he refused to see me.

"Not in so many words. No. We quarreled, and he left of his own accord. I needed time to decide what to do, and he wouldn't give it to me. We were both so young."

Leland sighs, rubbing his eyes before meeting my gaze again. "You're right. We need to follow through with what we've agreed on—but Blackwell can't stay here. Not now that I know your past. Genevieve, I want this alliance to work for both our countries, and I know you do too. But I *cannot* have your former lover in the palace with us."

"Of course, I understand." My heart sinks. Losing him once nearly destroyed me—but I don't have Kieran again. Not really. I can let him go a second time. "He and I spoke about it last night. He plans to return after the wedding, but I can tell him that's not possible."

Leland gives a curt nod. "He has people who can represent Blackwell Industries during the railway construction in Naseria. The important thing is that we present a united front."

I reach for his hand, silk on silk. "I want that."

His fingers move over the top of my gloved hand, a slow, deliberate caress. "I'm glad. I've also been thinking about your gift over the past few days—and what I need as a husband."

I stiffen. How can he go from agreeing to remove my former lover from the country to talking about my gift? Why can't he just let that part of our relationship progress at a slower pace? My skin prickles at the thought of allowing his touch on my bare flesh.

"I have as well," I manage. "I agreed to the marriage contract, but intimacy will be difficult. I've tried to control my gift, but it isn't something I'm good at. It overpowers me in those moments."

He brings his hand to my waist, and I force myself to stay calm. The small room feels too tight, too stifling.

"Would you be open to trying?" he asks. "I've had to practice controlling my own gift over the years, and I think I can help you."

"Now?" The word stumbles out, my anxiety rising as my body begins to tremble.

"Just a touch," he murmurs. "Nothing more."

I don't want to. I want to retreat and deny him this one small ask. But I don't—because if I refuse him even a touch, how will he believe I'm truly committed to our marriage contract? I nod and begin tugging off my gloves. I have to do all I can to ensure he'll still have me, even if it's the one thing I despise. After all, it will be expected of me soon enough.

I take my bare hand and touch Leland's cheek. His skin is soft and smooth, likely thanks to the close shave his valet provided. His face relaxes, and he leans into my touch, a sigh escaping his lips.

I can feel my gift stir within me. The pupils in Leland's eyes dilate, the icy blue nearly swallowed by black. I take a deep breath, trying to tamp down the power flowing through my caress. Leland's hands tighten on my hips, shifting me slightly until I'm leaning against him, a hard bulge growing between us. A moment later, I feel his own gift begin to seep into me—the only explanation for the calm resolve spreading through my chest.

Everything will be alright. This is good for both of us. I let out a stifled moan as I press my body closer, desperate for the false peace that nearness brings. He lowers his head toward mine, our lips nearly touching.

"How is this?" he asks, his voice roughened. His hands move up and down my lower back, dipping lower and lower, a frenzy building in his touch that I feel compelled to appease.

I shake off the haze of calm. "It—I'm trying to suppress my gift, but I can see it overtaking you. Let me step back for a moment."

He nods and slowly releases me, allowing me to put space between us. "May I ask you a personal question?" His words come out in shallow, uneven breaths.

"Yes, of course. We need to be open with one another if this is to work."

"The feeling your gift gives me—it's a frenzy, almost a madness to have you. It's more lust than love." He pauses, raking a hand through his hair as he struggles to steady his breathing.

I frown. "That's not a question."

"I know. Let me finish. Do you feel the same sensation when you touch a man, or is it purely one-sided?"

I blush, remembering the time I allowed myself to believe that what a man felt under my touch was more than lust. I remember being swept away by the same heat, letting down my guard as I hoped to fill the hollow Kieran left behind. "When I first received my gift—or my curse, truly—I tried to convince myself I could feel what a lover felt. But now I cannot."

"Because you lose control? Has someone ever harmed you?"

I draw a deep breath. I've never spoken of what happens when I touch a man. "It's been a long time since I've allowed myself to be intimate with anyone. My gift, and the loss of control, make it dangerous. I don't think anyone meant to harm me, but it's difficult for a man to stop once he's overcome by it."

Leland curses under his breath and turns away before stooping to pick up my gloves. He hands them to me. "Genevieve, I could not live with myself if I harmed you—or did anything without your consent. I didn't understand how deeply your gift could affect a man. I could never—" His voice breaks as he slowly shakes his head and slides his own gloves back on.

I cover my mouth, trying to hide the tremor of fear at what he might say next.

"I know you want this alliance," he says softly. "I do as well. But I fear our gifts may be too incompatible. I can temper mine only so much when we touch, and I could feel your reaction to it. I was taking away your choice as much as my own." He strokes my cheek with a gloved hand. "I couldn't live with myself, knowing what I might do to you when I'm no longer in control of my own actions."

My chin quivers as I fight back tears. This is my first real choice—my first act as a future queen—and it's slipping through my fingers. How can I lead a country when I can't even maintain a successful engagement?

My voice sounds hollow as I say, "I understand. The wedding is a week away. Do try to come to a conclusion before the ceremony."

He nods once and turns toward the door. "I'll let you know my decision shortly. Your sisters..."

His voice trails off before he changes the subject. "I want you to know that, regardless of what happens, I believe you'll make a remarkable queen."

The door clicks shut, and I sink to the floor as tears spill down my cheeks, splashing onto the carpet.

27

Genevieve

"Genny, what's happened, my dear?" My father's voice is soft and gentle as I look up at him from the floor. "Prince Leland suggested you might need some help."

My face feels swollen from tears as I sit up straight. "I'm sorry you're seeing me like this. I'll be alright in a few moments."

Father kneels to my level and brushes his gloved hand along my arm. "You don't need to be alright. Cry if you need to. Tell me what's hurting you—or don't. I'll be here for you because I love you, and I won't leave when I see you like this."

He takes a seat on the floor beside me, and I rest my head on his shoulder as I try to stifle my sniffles. He removes a handkerchief from his breast pocket, and I take it, blowing into it in the most unladylike fashion.

After a long silence, I say, "Prince Leland is reconsidering our alliance because of our incompatible gifts."

My father nods. "Ah. I thought as much when he sought me out. He looked shaken."

I lean into him, feeling his warmth and remembering what it was like to climb into his lap when I was upset or lonely. He was always attentive when we were children, always there when we needed a parent's comfort or someone to show us the best hiding places in the palace.

Something changed as we grew older. Mother began to demand more of him, and now he's entirely devoted to her. I wonder what their marriage will look like when she passes the crown to me. Will he be there for me when I need guidance navigating the burdens of ruling, or will he consumed by my mother's every mood and whim?

"Father, I don't know what to do. I want this alliance to work. We need it for the kingdom—and I want a husband before my coronation."

He gives me a sad smile. "Yes, I know, darling. But marriage isn't something you can force, and some matters are beyond your control. You'll learn in time that wearing the crown doesn't mean you can solve every problem. If you try, the weight of it will crush you."

"Yes, but I cannot fail at this!" My voice comes out harsher than I intend.

"No one will see a mutual decision between you and Prince Leland not to wed as a failure."

I shake my head. "But I will."

"Genevieve, you've always been your own harshest critic. Take some time to think about what you and Prince Leland discussed. He's a reasonable fellow, and there's already that clause. Perhaps Astoria will have him?"

I let out a slow, steadying breath. "You're right. Of course you are. No wonder Mother relies on you. It's just... I'd hoped Prince Leland could be my own King Hugo. A man I could depend on to share the burden of the crown—someone who could understand the pressures I'll face as queen."

My father takes my chin in his gloved hand. "I do those things because I love your mother dearly. I want to help her as best I can—and that, my dear, is what you need in a husband. Someone devoted to you."

I turn away and rise to my feet. Kieran's crooked smile flashes in my mind—not the boy I once knew, but the man who's returned. The man trying to convince himself he wants to ruin me, yet whose every action shows he's still devoted.

"I should retire for the evening."

He stands as well, leading me toward the door. "Would you like me to escort you to your rooms?"

"Yes, Father. Just guide me through the ballroom so no one stops to speak with me. I don't think I could bear conversation right now."

He opens the door and leads me into the dimly lit ballroom. Music swells through the room, couples drifting into shadowed alcoves. It's all so sensual, and I want no part of it.

I see Kieran standing alone against a column. His eyes catch mine, and he bows from across the room, but I turn my head forward and walk resolutely on.

I cannot risk my heart any further until Leland and I reach a mutual decision.

Kieran

"What did you think of the ball, Mr. Blackwell?" Queen Penelope asks from behind her desk, sipping a cup of strong tea. I take a sip of my own, the delicate cup clinking as I set it down.

Her eye twitches, and she puts on a false smile as she looks from the cup to me. How have any of the Ashcroft children lived their adult lives under such scrutiny? I remember her indifference to their childhood and the devotion their father once showed, but even that has been replaced by an unwavering devotion to his wife.

"As far as balls go, it was fine," I say. The evening was a statement, a trap to ensnare her people into behavior beyond propriety. I wonder which of them she intended to target with such a sensuous setting.

"Did you find a young miss to enjoy the evening with?" she inquires, her lips tugged into a sneer.

I tap my fingers against my thigh and sit up to convey my annoyance. "Your Majesty, with all due respect, I am a very busy man. If you prefer to gossip about the evening's activities, I'm sure you can find more suitable company than me. As it is, I'm shortly due to inspect the mines in northern Naseria and don't have time for idle chat. My offer still stands for you to send a representative along with my envoy."

She sips again and sets the cup down delicately. "Fine. Business it is. I'm afraid I can't spare anyone to send with you. We're deep in preparations for Princess Genevieve and Prince Leland's wedding. In fact, that's why I suggested you come *after* the wedding."

The nerve of this woman—denying my only request to have someone, *anyone* from her government take interest or accountability in the mines of her own country. She doesn't need to know I have no interest in seeing this mockery of a wedding through.

"Why should I be denied seeing a good friend married? From my perspective, this was an excellent opportunity to enjoy the celebrations while gauging Naseria's prospects as my next investment. Unfortunately, your government seems unwilling to take this project seriously."

I rise when a knock sounds at the door. Queen Penelope waves me back down. "I'm quite busy at the moment. Come back in thirty minutes."

I stand anyway. "That won't be necessary. There's no reason to continue this farce, Your Majesty." I open the door—and Gen stands there in a simple white and blue day dress. Her eyes are swollen, as if she's been crying, and she gives a stilted gasp when she sees me.

"Excuse me. I didn't mean to interrupt," she says, looking down. She looks hurt, and I want to pull her close despite how often she pushes me away. The need to hold her—to be the one to comfort her—doesn't go away. Still, I don't touch her. It's not my place to tend Genevieve Ashcroft's sore feelings, even if once that was all I ever wanted.

"You weren't interrupting anything. I was just leaving," I reply, giving her space to enter.

"Mr. Blackwell, do take a seat," Queen Penelope commands. "You should as well, Genevieve."

We both take seats, close enough that I could reach out and touch her if I wanted to. The greed to feel her skin against mine is almost too much.

"Now, I know Genevieve is busy with her upcoming nuptials, but Mr. Blackwell, you are correct in saying that I haven't been eager to take greater interest in the helachite mines or the railway. I'm nearing the end of my reign and look forward to living in relative peace, turning my attention to my four other children while Princess Genevieve assumes the throne."

Genevieve shudders, disbelief flickering across her face—a sure sign this isn't a typical conversation with her mother. She has the sense to stay silent, but I don't. This woman is up to something, and from everything I know of her, I don't trust a word that leaves her mouth.

"If I dare say so, you've been criminally neglectful of the helachite mines, Your Majesty." The queen regards me as if she could incinerate me on the spot.

"That is your opinion, Mr. Blackwell. Plenty would attest that I am a thorough and compassionate ruler. But that aside—Genevieve, you asked me to hand this project to you. You can have it. Decide for yourself how you'll proceed with Mr. Blackwell. I'm no longer interested in working with a man who demands more from me than he deserves."

"But—" Gen begins, looking between me and her mother.

"But what, Genny? Speak your mind!" her mother snaps. Gen seems, for a moment, ready to fold in on herself. Then she sits up with the public confidence she always carries.

"I came to discuss Mr. Blackwell's departure," she says. "I was informed he'll be leaving this morning, and I think it would be best if he chose a representative from Blackwell Industries to oversee the project moving forward."

"And why would you want to remove me from my own project?" I ask. Genevieve won't even look at me; she continues speaking to her mother.

"Prince Leland and I have discussed it at length, and we prefer to go in a different direction. If it is truly my undertaking, I'd like to consider other options before moving forward with Mr. Blackwell's recommendations."

She turns to me, her deep-blue eyes cold in a way foreign to her. "Mr. Blackwell, that is all for now. Thank you for your time."

I rise. "That's disappointing, Princess Genevieve. I expected you'd be more willing to hear my suggestions than your mother."

She doesn't watch me leave. I need to strike something—anything—knowing the Ashcrofts are again content to harm their country rather than improve it.

There's only one Ashcroft I can strike without recourse, and I know just where to find him.

29

Kieran

"Blackwell, you're incorrigible!" Gabe shouts as I parry another strike, my training sword landing squarely against his chest. "What has gotten into you?"

Since the first day we fenced together, I've made a habit of joining Gabe as often as my schedule allows. He's also continued to use my new identity—at least in the presence of others.

"The damned Ashcroft women!" I blurt out. I shouldn't reveal that much, but Gabriel was once my closest friend and confidant. Why shouldn't he know how maddening those two are?

"Ah, you spent the morning with the crown princess and queen, I assume?"

He strikes again, but I block his sword and push him toward the edge of the room, landing another blow.

"Enough!" he calls, letting his weapon drop. "You'll have me resembling tenderized meat before long!"

He walks to the water pitcher, pouring us both glasses. I wipe the sweat from my brow and join him, handing my sword off to a waiting servant.

"I'm leaving," I say. "You should know that despite my best efforts, I'm no match for your sister."

Gabe smiles, pushing back his dark red locks. "Good. You never were a match for her anyway. You've always underestimated her stubbornness."

I shrug. "I won't be part of her ruining this country. If she's so willing to follow in Queen Penelope's path, then there's no point in me returning."

Gabe gives me a quizzical look. "This is about business—not your past?"

"Of course it is. Your sister is just as unwilling to prioritize helachite reform as your mother. She made that painfully clear this morning."

Gabe shakes his head. "That's a mistake. I thought this was about your vow to ruin her or some nonsense. Everyone sees your attempts at breaking her composure, but I knew that was impossible. She's determined to make this alliance with Prince Leland. Once you stop that embarrassing display, I think she'll be willing to work with you in a professional manner."

I growl, like a trapped animal on its last defense. I really do need to get out of here. The Ashcrofts are once again making me forget myself. "She isn't. She said so herself—even asked me to abandon the project. She's afraid to do the hard work."

"You absolute ass! Have you even tried to have a professional conversation with her? Genny's always been guarded—she was trained to be. But if you keep treating her like a lovesick teenager, I understand why she won't tolerate you any longer."

I shake my head. Gen and Leland are all wrong for each other, yet they're both charging forward with a plan that will make them miserable. Meanwhile, Gen is willing to let her mother keep making terrible decisions that harm the country. I need to get out of here, if only to clear my head and stop letting Genevieve Ashcroft haunt my every waking thought. "If she were willing to do the work, she'd try harder."

Just then, the door slams open and Prince Leland strides in with General Pryor. Leland's face is tight, his expression angrier than I've ever seen it.

"Blackwell! There you are!"

"Leland."

"Choose a sword. I want a match!" he shouts.

I walk toward the prince, already knowing the cause of his outburst. "Think that through. You know I'll best you—and quickly."

"You've lied to me in the most egregious manner! Every suggestion, every word of support for this arrangement has been nothing more than a ploy to gain access to Princess Genevieve—not to benefit me or my kingdom!"

He grabs a sword from the rack. It's not a practice blade. Of course it isn't. He lunges, and I reach for a weapon of my own. His attack is easy to block. Despite Gabe's teasing, I am a skilled swordsman—far better than Leland.

"What are you on about?" I ask, though I know perfectly well. He must have finally realized that Gen and I share a past. When I first supported him, it was from revenge, hoping to hurt Gen the way she hurt me. But now, I don't even want that. I just want her to be happy. And I know that will never happen with Leland.

I block his strike with ease. Leland isn't a fighter. He's not one to lose his temper, and I've never seen him spend his leisure time practicing with a sword. Pistols, perhaps—any young Icelantican lord knows his way around a gun.

I push him back, hoping he'll realize he's outmatched and put the weapon down. Instead, he presses forward with a ferocity I've never seen in him.

"Don't give me that shit! You're her former lover—a fraud who's been using me to get close to the princess. I won't have it!"

He swings again, his blade grazing the fabric of my shoulder as I twist to counter.

"I won't deny any of it."

"Careful, Blackwell," Gabe cautions, but I ignore him and take an offensive position. Leland isn't fast enough; I knock the sword from his hand and bring the tip of my blade to his throat. A single drop of deep blue blood beads on his skin, and the prince sucks in a sharp breath.

"I'm finished with this," he says, his voice placating. Reason returns to his tone, though it's edged with disdain. Good. I deserve his disdain for what I've done to him. It's been wrong of me to carry on this pretense. But I know, deep down, I'd do it again. "Have her or don't. I no longer want her, and she's certainly not worth dying over. But you—I trusted you. I saw you as a friend, and all this time you've been using me to what? Win her back? Hurt both of us?"

I let the sword drop to the ground, shaking my head. I've wanted revenge for so long. Now that I finally have it, it's an empty victory.

Gabe and General Pryor rush toward us, but I shake off Gabe's reach.

"You're right, Leland. I never should have encouraged your match with the princess. I should have stayed out of it. She—she hurt me, and I thought I saw an opportunity to hurt her in return. I never should have involved you. It was wrong of me."

Leland scoffs. "You've done an abysmal job of trying to hurt her. You haven't been able to take your eyes off her since that first night. I've been in denial by not confronting you sooner."

Gabe frowns, and Pryor looks ready to take up a pair of dueling pistols to finish me off properly, no swords necessary. My voice catches as I think about Gen, about how helplessly drawn I am to her. The truth is, some part of me will never stop loving her, even after everything that's happened between us. Even now, when she's still fighting what we both know exists between us.

I don't need to share all the tangled feelings my heart holds for Genevieve Ashcroft, but Leland deserves an explanation.

"Right again, Prince Leland. I was arrogant to think that what I once felt for Princess Genevieve was dead."

Now it's Gabe's turn to scoff. "You could have returned to her at any point."

I shake my head. "It's not that easy. A part of me died in the mines. I couldn't return to my former life, even if I wanted to. I am sincerely sorry, Prince Leland. I'll be leaving in a few hours for my home in the north."

30

Genevieve

I water my blooming begonias with a tenderness reserved only for my plants. After all, my plants never disappoint me. They never work to harm me or turn away from me because of my curse.

The past few days have been too much, and all I want is the comfort of my glasshouse. I've not only lost Kieran for a second time, but I fear I've also lost any chance of marrying Leland—and may have forced my sisters into an arranged marriage neither of them wanted.

I turn toward a rare orchid, wiping its leaves with a soft cloth, when I hear the click on the door.

"May I come in, Princess?"

I turn to see Leland, dark circles under his eyes and a severe expression on his face. "Of course. Are you well?" There's a small trail of blue blood on his throat, evidence of a fresh wound.

"Not exactly, but I will be." He takes in the room, brushing his fingers across the leaves of a philodendron before delicately touching the blossoms of a freshly potted Begonia Gen. "These are beautiful."

"Thank you. This is my refuge. I often come here to think and es-cape the court." I want to ask him to leave—to keep this sanctuary free from regret and pain—but I know we need to have the conversation that's coming.

Leland looks at me with a cool stare, his usually warm countenance gone. "I can see why. I hate to intrude on your peace, but I need to speak with you."

Of course, even now, Leland would recognize that this conversation could tarnish my one escape from the world. "Would you like to go somewhere else?"

"How about a walk?" He gives me a sad smile that doesn't reach his eyes, and I know our engagement is over. I've lost the alliance I worked so hard to secure and may have forced one of my sisters into a fate they never wanted. Will they live here, or will Leland now return to Icelantica to continue supporting his sister?

"A walk sounds lovely." I remove my work gloves and apron, wiping my hands before checking my dress for stains. Then I pick up my silk gloves and slide them on as Leland holds the door open for me.

The air outside is sweet and warm—not nearly as stifling as the glasshouse, but fresher, carrying the promise of new life and abun-dance.

"I wanted to let you know I've asked Mr. Blackwell not to return," I say as we walk toward the topiary.

He nods thoughtfully. "I encountered him this morning as well. I wasn't quite myself when I saw him. I'll admit I had far too much to drink last night—and far too much time to wallow in my own self-pity this morning."

"Leland, don't do that." My tone softens. I don't want to be the reason this man hurts. He's a good man who deserves happiness.

"No, it's true. I fought him this morning, and he left this little reminder that he bested me." Leland touches his throat, and a chill crawls over my skin.

"He wouldn't!"

"It was my fault, really. I lost my senses when I saw him and didn't choose a practice sword. It should be no surprise he did the same. He could have hurt me worse if he'd wanted, but he didn't. The thing is, though, the damage is done. He's betrayed me, and I've lost all trust in him."

"Because of me? I'm so sorry, Leland."

He shakes his head, slowing his pace. "No, not because of you. I hope I can be honest when I say our engagement is a political one—one I hoped would grow into deeper affection. I have great respect for you. But his betrayal is my own burden. I thought of Morris as a good friend, someone I could trust and who shared my ideals for the future. But it seems that was all a lie to get closer to you. He's hurt me, and for that I don't know if I can forgive him."

We stop on the path. Sunlight filters through the trees, and birds are singing. "Please, give us another chance—free of Blackwell's presence. I want to give our countries the best opportunities moving forward, and I still believe our marriage is the best way to secure this alliance."

I don't add that I feel guilty placing the burden of the alliance on one of my sisters. I don't know how Leland feels about switching one bride for another, or how much he must resent his own sister for pushing such an agreement.

Leland looks toward the palace in the distance. "There are two matters I've been wrestling with. One is Blackwell's betrayal of our friendship. The other is the incompatibility between us. I cannot marry you, knowing that any attempt at intimacy would leave us both unable to make clear decisions. It isn't fair to either of us."

A sinking feeling grips my chest. This is it. I've ruined my chance at marriage.

"I understand," I whisper. "Is there any way you'd reconsider?"

He shakes his head, his gaze steady but kind. "I want us to move forward with a different marriage. My sister and I talked last night, and I believe we'll have an arrangement by the end of the week."

"We should let both queens know. The wedding is so close—I don't want anyone to continue preparing for something that won't be happening."

My cheeks burn crimson as embarrassment floods me. I've failed at the one thing I thought I could control as a future queen.

He reaches for my hand, and I resist the urge to pull away and close myself off from him. "Genevieve, I'm sorry. I don't want to hurt you, which is why I'm making this decision. I hope I can still call you a friend, even if I can't call you my wife."

I relax a little, knowing he's telling the truth. He's a good, decent man, and I shouldn't have tried to force this arrangement. My mind drifts to Kieran—he's probably already gone by now, thanks to me pushing him away again.

I want to run to him, to feel his arms around me, his lips press a kiss to my hair. I want to hear him tell me again what he believes I can do as queen. How he believes in me, despite what everyone else says. I want to tell him how he makes me feel braver, more reckless, more like the person I'm meant to be.

I never thought Kieran could be my future when he's always felt like my past, but perhaps this is the chance we could have. He's never flinched from my curse, and maybe there's still a part of him that loves me for who I am.

"Friend, yes. I'd like that, Leland."

We walk side by side toward the front of the palace, silence between us as I think about my next steps.

A coach is being prepared to leave, and I turn to see if it's Kieran's. He looks at me through the window, his expression resolute as he tips his head in acknowledgment. I nod before turning away.

Leland gives me a curious look. "You don't need to send him away on my account. It's evident to everyone there's more between you two than you've allowed yourself to believe. Despite what he's done to me, I still believe he wants the best for the miners and railway workers—but he doesn't trust that you do. Go to him. Show him you aren't your mother."

I shake my head. "That's impossible."

Leland's brows crease. "You're going to be queen of this kingdom in two years' time. It will be your decision how you reign, not your mother's. An advantageous marriage won't solve the problems in this country. Only you can do that."

I pull back, a burst of laughter escaping me. "You're right! I'll ask him to stay."

Leland smiles. "Best of luck, Genny."

I take his hand and give it a squeeze before turning from one choice and walking toward another—to the man who's never left my heart.

Kieran has told me all along that all he wants is for one of the Ashcrofts to take the mining problem seriously, to believe he's working to fix this country's injustices, and even I've discounted him.

No longer. I want nothing more than to be a queen who values all her people—bluebloods and redbloods alike. This is my chance to prove to Kieran that I care.

I lift my skirts, my delicate slippers flashing as I run toward Kieran's coach. The air is warm, far too warm for running, but I smile as the breeze rushes through my bound hair. Running to Kieran Greenbluff feels like the most reckless thing I've ever done. But perhaps I've lived long enough without taking chances.

Kieran opens the door, a satisfied smile curving his lips. "Princess," he says, pulling me in and signaling the coachman to drive.

31

Kieran

"Kieran, stop the coach. Let's talk for a moment," Gen says, her tone measured, as if she's trying to be reasonable without losing her temper. From her expression, I can tell she didn't expect me to direct the carriage away from Fairbright.

"No, I don't think I will. You were the one who ran toward me, after all."

I still can't quite believe it. When I first saw her, she avoided my gaze—as usual. Denying our connection has been her plan all along.

She shakes her head in frustration, her loose curls bouncing. "I ran to tell you I want you to stay, so we can make arrangements for me to travel to the mines—not for you to kidnap me."

I chuckle, leaning back in my seat, trying to hide the way my heart barrels against my ribs. Gen ran to me. She left Leland and chose *me*. My nineteen-year-old self used to dream of this—of her choosing me over the crown, over her duty, over her mother's expectations.

As the carriage rattles through the bustling streets of Crawford, I say, "Princess, I had no intention of staying. I have business to attend to in the north. In fact, this little turn of events is perfect. I've been telling the queen we need a representative to inspect the mines, but she hasn't taken my request seriously."

Her eyes widen in surprise. "I want to join you—that's what I was coming to suggest. But I have nothing packed, and it's supposed to be dangerous! I need to speak with my mother."

I shrug. "If it's too dangerous for you, then why do you allow your citizens to work there?"

Her lips purse. For a long moment she says nothing. Finally, in a softer tone, she replies, "Kieran, please take me back. I'd be happy to go north with you, but not like this. I didn't mean to imply that I was above anyone who works in those mines. I want to help, truly—but not like this. Let me make plans and coordinate a proper tour."

I shake my head. "Come with me now. Forget the plans. Show me you actually want to improve Naseria."

"My mother will be furious. She's already going to be apoplectic when she finds out the engagement is off. She's going to think I ran away with you!"

The engagement is off?

I suspected as much when I saw her running toward me, but hearing the words from her lips sends a rush through my veins. She didn't go through with it, whether by her choice or not.

"Well," I tease, "you did run toward me, so it could accurately be considered running away."

She groans, burying her face in her hands. It's the same gesture she used to make whenever I pushed her too far. Back then, it was usually when my plans for us crossed one of the countless boundaries of propriety that ruled her every waking moment.

"Surely Prince Leland can explain this in a way that doesn't look like an absolute disaster." She exhales, lifting her head with a weary sigh. "Why did I behave so impulsively?"

The carriage rattles as we take the northerly highway toward the mines. The rolling hills beyond Crawford open before us in a verdant mosaic of farmland and open pasture.

"You've never done well with impulsive decisions, have you, Princess?"

She closes her eyes, leaning back and letting her hand fall so close to mine I can almost feel the silk. "Don't tease me, you horrid man."

I chuckle, wrapping my hand around hers. "It's true, isn't it? Remember when we were ten and decided to go swimming in the lake? It was your idea, if I recall. Astoria tried to talk you into asking permission first, but you insisted as the future queen, you could make your own decisions."

She squeezes my hand and lets out a small laugh. "I ruined my silk gown, but my lady's maid didn't tell Mother. I felt guilty for weeks for being dishonest."

I stroke her gloved hand in mine, the weight of her engagement ring pressing between us. "There's never been a more serious child—always thinking of expectations and following orders."

"I don't think I would have had any fun at all if it weren't for you and Gabe. You were my everything, Kieran."

She looks at me with a softness I've only caught glimpses of since I returned to her. But this time it lingers, her deep sapphire eyes studying me like I'm a puzzle she can't quite solve.

I slowly slip her glove from her fingers, and she doesn't stop me. Not even when I tug the heavy stone from her ring finger and slide the ring into my pocket. She stares at me with eyes that seem to enchant me into doing whatever she asks. She's always had this power over me, and I'm beginning to realize she always will. She looks down at her bare hand, stretching it in front of us before reaching for her glove and sliding it back on with a muffled huff.

Turning her head, she looks out at the countryside rolling by. "I'm already failing, and I haven't even taken the throne. I can't even have a proper wedding."

I reach for her hand, turning her toward me. "You're trying. Your people don't need a marital alliance and a brood of heirs. They need a queen who cares about them—whether they live in Crawford or on the northern coast, whether they have red blood or blue blood. Don't you see that's what actually matters?"

She closes her eyes, shaking her head. "I've always been told the most important thing I can do is ensure the blueblood line continues—to preserve our family's lineage—and that the rest can be left to my council. My worth is in making this alliance and leaving a strong legacy."

Her words disgust me, and I want to shake her, to make her see that she could be so much more than this. She's been fed this lie all her life, and it's so deeply ingrained that I don't know how to untangle the falsehoods she's turned into truths.

"Gen, you're like a blossom cursed—cursed to wilt into rot and never bloom into your true potential. If you truly think your worth is as shallow as making an advantageous marriage, then I'll turn this coach around and bring you back so you can rot with the rest of this forsaken kingdom."

She looks at me, her eyes shimmering with tears. "I'm frightened. Nothing has gone according to my plans, and I don't know if I'm strong enough to be everything this kingdom needs."

"Then forge yourself into it! Starting with taking what you actually want!"

Her expression shifts into something hungry, something I've longed to see in her.

There's the fire I know lives within her, the iron resolve buried beneath years of self-doubt.

"You're right. You've always been right about that," she says.

Gen shifts on the bench, seizing my shirt and pulling me into a searing kiss. A kiss so powerful I tumble headlong into the unrequited desire I've been holding inside for far too long.

32

Genevieve

I pull myself closer to Kieran, nearly climbing into his lap as I let my tongue dart between our parted lips. His mouth opens to me, and I can't stop the gasp that escapes as I press against the hard ridges of his body.

I let the feel of him consume me, not even thinking about my curse or the consequences it might have on him. None of it matters—because I want him. I want to be devoured by my own insatiable need for him.

He's always been right: I am a cursed blossom. Cursed never to feel the love I once had. But if I allow myself, I know the only person I can risk my gift with is Kieran. He's the only one I've ever felt safe with. The only one who understands that I can let myself simply feel what exists between us.

Kieran takes my silk gloves and slowly pulls them off, one finger at a time. When the first glove is gone, he peppers kisses across my fingers, my hand, and up my arm to the crook of my elbow before beginning on the other.

The gesture is worshipful, filled with more reverence than I expected from a man who's claimed to want to ruin me. That, of course, I've always known was never his true intent.

I still don't understand why he returned when he did. Perhaps even he doesn't understand his own decision. But it was never to ruin me. To force me to choose myself over the crown, maybe. Or maybe it began as a desire for revenge.

It hardly matters now, with his hands gripping my hips and shifting me into his lap. I clutch at his cravat, loosening it as I unfasten the top few buttons of his shirt. I want to touch him, to feel the heat of his chest and trace the changes in his firm, muscular body.

I can feel the hardness of Kieran's erection against my inner thigh as his hands roam higher, cupping my full breasts through the delicate fabric and squeezing until my nipples peak.

He lets out a deep rumble, then looks at me intently. He's handling the fervor of my curse better than I expected—better than anyone ever has. Perhaps it's because we once were in love, because when he looks at me, it's with such genuine devotion and attentiveness that I almost believe he still loves me as much as he once did.

"What do you want from me, Gen?"

"What?" The word stumbles from my lips, my hands still pressed against his chest. It's not at all what I expected him to ask. No one—not even him as an inexperienced, lovesick young man—had ever asked what *I* wanted.

He meets my gaze with searing heat. "What do you want? Do you want this? Right now?"

"Isn't it what *you* want? My curse doesn't leave much open for discussion."

He slides me gently from his lap, his expression so full of concern that I want to turn away in embarrassment. "I'm not going to descend into a beast just because you kissed me and I touched your breasts, Gen."

I suck in a breath, thinking of how disgusted Leland had been by what my gift made him feel. How must Kieran feel now, knowing that what I'm giving him isn't what he might feel on his own? Knowing how different this must be from the nights we spent together all those years ago?

"I'm sorry," I whisper. "We shouldn't do this. I know it isn't like it once was."

Kieran seizes my face, his voice low and fierce. "Look at me, Gen. I have never stopped desiring you. I've lived every day of my life wanting you—and knowing that after everything between us, I should hate myself for how you make me feel. Your gift isn't going to stop me. But *you* will. I'll go back to the gentleman you expect me to be, if that's what you want."

My heart is beating so quickly I fear it might leap from my chest. He's saying exactly what I've dreamed he would say, yet I've denied myself for so long that I never thought Kieran could possibly still desire me after all this time.

"You're the only man I've ever wanted."

Curse be damned, Kieran leans in and kisses me, and I feel a desperate need to preserve this moment—to catalog it away so I can always remember what it felt like to be kissed, to be desired without wanting to pull away. Without feeling dread blossom in my chest. To have my desire for this man eclipse anything my curse could cause.

Kieran pulls me back onto his lap, his mouth trailing down my neck, leaving hot kisses and caresses until he reaches my breasts. I let out a shudder as he squeezes the weight of one through the confines of my dress.

"I've fantasized about you for nearly a decade," he murmurs against my skin, "but never did I imagine how exquisite you'd become."

With a tenderness that borders on adoration, Kieran lifts my breast from the confines of my corset, squeezing the soft weight slowly, as if he were holding a precious object. His fingers rub my nipple, making me gasp with anticipation. Then his mouth is on my breast, sucking and licking, worshipful in his attention and ardor.

How can he keep such control over his own desires, pouring pleasure into me in a way I've never known? And he hasn't even touched me between my thighs, yet the attentive way he sucks and licks at my breast makes me wonder if he isn't in any hurry at all.

"Mustn't leave the other without attention," he mutters to himself as he fixes my breast back into place and pops the other out of its constraints. By the time he's giving this breast the same attention as the last, I find myself wiggling in his lap, desperate to feel his hard length against my core. My skirts, though lighter than a ball gown, are bunched between us, stifling my anguishing need to feel him against me. I rock against him all the same, mortifyingly desperate to feel friction in my hot center.

He doesn't stop me as he reaches down to adjust my skirts and lifts his hips in such a way that gives me the friction I'm desiring.

"Please!" I beg. My voice doesn't sound like my own, all my composure wilting away. The carriage lurches suddenly, and Kieran catches me as I nearly slip off his lap.

Kieran tuts, teasing my nipple between his fingers. "Aren't you eager, Princess? Haven't you learned over the years to be patient?"

"I've never—" I cut myself off, unwilling to admit that I've never desired a man as much as I do in this moment.

"You've never what? Never been fondled in a carriage? Never allowed yourself to enjoy pleasure? Never thought you'd have me again?"

I let out a keening laugh. "All those things, I believe."

But it's true. I've dreamed of having Kieran more times than I can count, yet even after he returned to Naseria, even after he kissed me under the willow, I still didn't think a moment like this would be possible. Not when I'd already signed away my future. Not when I've always done what was expected of me.

His wicked tongue sweeps over the swell of my breast, sending me shuddering as the ache between my thighs leaves me pressing my center into his straining length. That must be uncomfortable. While pressing his mouth to my skin, he says, "Well then, if we're making confessions, I'll confess I never thought I'd have you on my lap, my cock aching against you and your breasts in my mouth."

I reach for the fastenings on his trousers, but his hand catches mine, and he gives a quick shake of his head. Alarm courses through me. How is he showing this restraint? Why—now that I feel desired and adored—would he want me to stop?

"No, Princess. I refuse to fuck you for the first time in nine years while in a carriage. Perhaps when I was nineteen I wouldn't have been able to show that much restraint, but I'll be damned if I don't do this properly."

Something sinks inside me. Perhaps I've been mistaken about his feelings. He must truly hate me if he can resist my curse so easily. My disappointment must be evident, because he brings his thumb to my lips, a wicked grin on his face.

"Don't pout, Gen. It's a damn travesty to see you look so disappointed."

I let my bare hands glide through his thick locks, trying not to feel rejected. His composure is disorienting. How can he be so steady, so exacting, while my gift pours into him in pounding waves? I've never felt myself slipping so far from control—and yet so desperate to feel the man I'm with lose control.

Just as the carriage bumps again, Kieran lifts me and lays me flat across the bench. Instinctively, my legs clench together, and he gives me a look that threatens to set me ablaze.

"Spread your legs for me, Princess, and I'll tell you an even more illicit secret."

"Kieran," I reprimand him, but it's halfhearted as I let my legs fall open and Kieran's hard body comes between them. This feels familiar. He can't resist my gift after all. "You at least need your pants off for this part, you know."

Kieran chuckles, shaking his head. "Don't you want to know my secret, Gen?"

I nod, and he moves my legs so my knees are bent, tugging the skirts of my dress up around my waist. I feel so exposed to him as he stares down at my stockinged legs and the bareness that lies between my knees and the juncture of my thighs. I expect him to lose control at this point—for the rushed need to be inside me to come over him, leaving me feeling discarded. But he continues to hold his composure, a hungry smile growing across his face as he slowly glides his hands up my thighs, reaching my underthings and pulling them down. The lace trim of my undergarments scrapes across my thighs, and I hiss out an exhale as the callouses of his hands join the lace. His touch is firm, yet languid, like he has all the time in the world.

"My secret is that I've wanted to have my mouth between your thighs since I held you in the ballroom. Smelling you, feeling your body against mine. All I've wanted is a chance to have another taste of you."

His finger trails back up my leg to my slick heat, and he dips it into me, only to remove it and suck his finger into his mouth, a greedy eagerness in his eyes. "Yes, just as I remembered. You taste exquisite, Princess. Like one of your exotic blooms."

"Kieran, don't tease me," I whine, because surely this isn't what he wants from me. "You don't need to…"

"Shh… I want to hear you moaning my name, not ordering me about." His hands tighten on my thighs, and he drops to the floor of the carriage, adjusting me so that my legs rest on his shoulders and my head against the firm back wall. A quick flick of his tongue over me already has me bucking on the bench. He shifts his weight, pressing one hand on my hips, keeping me locked in place as he begins a steady rhythm against my aching flesh.

I'm left in disbelieving pleasure as he moves to my clit, sucking the sensitive bud into his mouth.

Never.

Never have any of my previous lovers had any interest in *my* pleasure—in what would make *me* feel good. Even when I took Kieran to my bed at nineteen, it was all unskilled fumbling and blazing, quick pleasure. It was something I desired, something I wanted, yet there was none of this languid desire, none of the patient skill he displays now.

It makes something inside me crack open, knowing I have never had someone give my own pleasure this sort of attention.

My mind also can't help drifting to where this practiced skill developed. Hot jealousy floods through me as I let that thought slip through my mind. That past doesn't matter. All that matters now is this moment with Kieran. This way he makes me feel precious while also making me feel rippling pleasure I've never experienced before.

He lets out a soft moan when I allow myself to rock against his face, and I worry I've taken things too far. I freeze, and Kieran's eyes meet mine, heavy-lidded with his own desire. "Gen, Princess, don't you dare stop."

"Are you sure? You're not uncomfortable?"

His eyebrows raise before he sucks my clit into his mouth, giving it a bite that has me reeling and rocking harder against him. Goodness, that feels *divine.*

His finger slides into my core, and he pumps and curls deep into me before adding another. I feel a tightening coil in the back of my spine. Kieran sucks my clit again, this time in rhythm to his pumping fingers, and I let out a stifled cry as I fall into ecstasy. I can't hold back his name on my tongue as he continues to pump and lick me until I feel as though I've been unraveled, nerve by nerve, until I'm made of nothing but fragmented remains.

I feel hot tears streaming down my cheeks as I reel from the pleasure Kieran has given me. I know I should stop crying—who *cries* after the most pleasurable moment of their life?—but I can't help it. My emotions are too splintered to contain the tears.

I hardly notice when he sits up and straightens my skirts, satis-faction softening into concern as he brings his hands to my cheeks, wiping the fat tears from my face. He kneels before me, and I know I should stop somehow—but the tenderness in his eyes nearly breaks me, and I let out a sob.

Kieran moves to the bench opposite me, care written across his features. "Gen, my darling, did I hurt you?"

"I'm so sorry. I don't know why I'm crying," I say, covering my face with my hands. "I shouldn't be crying. It's just—the first time I've felt such pleasure in a long time."

My cheeks burn with embarrassment and the lingering rush he's drawn from me. He looks at me with such concern that I feel splintered all over again. This is too much. I've revealed too much of myself to him. I want to hide away. Only this morning I was sending this man away, and now I'm crying in his coach. He should turn the carriage around immediately and bring me back to Fairbright, where I can stitch all these excessive feelings away where they belong.

"I'm so sorry. This is mortifying. I don't know what's gotten into me," I mumble through my fingers.

The carriage shifts with his weight as he moves to my side and wraps his arms around me. I don't try to stop him, too emotionally exhausted to think. I let my head rest against his chest as my tears dry in his firm embrace.

"Hush now, my darling. Princess, don't try to rationalize this. Just let me hold you."

My voice comes out in a gasp. "I never thought I'd have you again. Never. Kieran, your death broke me."

The truth escapes before I can pull it back, before I can bury it where it belongs. Because the truth is I never recovered from the loss of Kieran Greenbluff. I lived my life feeling like a piece of me had been snapped off, beyond repair. But now, a small part of me feels reattached, repaired in a way that hurts through the sheer unexpectedness of its mending.

He stiffens slightly as he continues to stroke my back and hair. "I'm here now. I'm not leaving you."

He presses a gentle kiss to my hair, murmuring again and again, "I'm not leaving you."

33

Kieran

The remainder of our ride to Huntley House is quiet—reflective. Gen's response to pleasure nearly brought *me* to tears, seeing how it broke something inside her. Knowing I was the first and only man to think of her desires hurts in a way that makes me want to rage, to kill any man who ever deigned to touch her. I had to bite my tongue to keep from asking for a list of her past lovers, just so I could hurt them.

This damned blueblood culture that exalts a gift over a person has forced Gen to live her entire adult life believing her worth is tied to a curse that makes her a tool for men. Has no one considered how this "gift" is destroying her?

Hell, I want to kill her own family for not seeing that she's so much more than her fucking blueblooded gift. I even hate myself for the part I've played in her suffering. If I'd stood my ground—if I hadn't run when she told me to leave—I could have protected her.

But in the end, we both carry scars from what happened after I left. What matters now is the present, and I'll be damned if I *ever* let anyone harm her through that cursed gift again.

After hours on dusty roads with only a few short stops to stretch, we finally arrive at Huntley House. The old manor, with its red-brick exterior bordered by rocky hills, was once my refuge as I built my empire around helachite. I haven't been here in months.

"Where are we?" Gen asks groggily, sitting up from where she'd been leaning on my shoulder.

"My home, actually. Welcome to Huntley House."

She peers out the window at the moonlit manor. It's nothing like Fairbright, or any of the Ashcrofts' other residences. It's not even as impressive as my home in Icelantica. But there's no place I'd rather be than back in these rocky foothills, the mountainous border still capped with snow and the smoke from the mines drifting through the night sky.

This place took my father from me, forged me into the man I am today. I should hate it, yet I keep returning—drawn back by the lives here, by the people I've worked tirelessly to give a better life to. Because I knew if I didn't, no one ever would.

"Your home? You've owned a home in Naseria all this time, and you never thought to contact me?"

I shake my head. "Perhaps I didn't want to be in contact with you, Princess."

It isn't that simple. At first, it was impossible to reach her. Then, after I heard about her gift, I was angry and jealous—I had no way of knowing what that gift was doing to her. Had I known, I wouldn't have hesitated to come for her. Instead, I poured everything I had into building this business and eventually grew numb to Genevieve Ashcroft.

But now that she's back in my life, I cannot imagine living without her. Still, that isn't rational. Even after our time in the carriage, I know she'll choose the crown over me. It's what she does—and I no longer have it in me to stop her.

She slides her hand into mine as a footman opens the door. "Why wouldn't you want to contact me if you could?"

I swallow and tell her the truth. There's no point in keeping secrets anymore. "Once I learned of your gift, my pride kept me away, Princess. It was wrong. I see that now."

She studies me, as if searching my face for something. "We've both been wrong about many things, I'm afraid."

I step out of the carriage, taking in the hills glowing in the moonlight, and offer her my hand as she follows.

"It's beautiful here. So wild."

"Quite unlike Fairbright."

"What's that smoke in the distance?"

"The mines. We've developed a process to smelt the tracks and train components so they can absorb the natural helachite from the ground—allowing trains to run safely without risking workers or passengers to overexposure."

Gen cocks her head, a grin spreading across her face. "Kieran, when did you become so brilliant?"

"I've always been brilliant, didn't you know?"

She laughs, shaking her head. "And so humble."

I rest my hand on her back, guiding her toward the housekeeper and butler—both survivors of the old mining operation and its egregious mishandling of raw helachite. I see how Genevieve takes in their scarred skin, their slow, careful movements, their disfigured hands. She doesn't waver, only approaches with that quiet confidence I'd hoped she still possessed.

Both look at me in surprise. I've never brought a woman to Huntley House, always keeping this life separate from my former lovers in Icelantica.

"Princess Geneveive, I'd like you to meet Mrs. Andrews and Mr. Bridge."

Andrews looks shocked, but Bridge maintains his composure as he bows. "It's an honor, Your Highness." Andrews catches herself and curtsies deeply before giving me a pointed, questioning look.

"Excuse me, Your Highness," she says. "We were not properly prepared for you." Her eyes narrow at me in unfettered disapproval.

Gen smiles widely and replies, "It's no trouble at all. I apologize for catching you off guard with this visit." She gives me a teasing look before leaning toward Andrews and whispering, "I wasn't prepared either I'm afraid."

I shrug. The truth is, Andrews keeps this place in perfect order—always ready for guests, even though I rarely have reason to entertain. "Give her the Lavender Room and have some clothing sent up. We had a mishap with Princess Genevieve's luggage."

"Of course, sir. How long can we anticipate your stay?"

Gen looks at me, then back to Andrews. "I apologize, but it may be quite a few days. I'm interested in better understanding the helachite mines and how Mr. Blackwell runs his operation. Then there's the railway. I'd like to learn more about the infrastructure involved."

"Of course, Your Highness. We're honored to have you for as long as you choose to stay."

I guide Gen into my home and bring her to the parlor. I know Andrews and Bridge need time to prepare the other staff for the princess's arrival. If I don't make us scarce, they may just turn on me.

"Well," she remarks, looking at me expectantly as she smooths her skirts and sits on the sofa, "this is quite the surprise."

"What part is surprising?" I ask, taking a seat across from her. A footman brings in a tray of refreshments, and I wave him out of the room.

"I think the most surprising thing is that I thought you were dead for so long. Then I came to terms with it, knowing you were in Icelantica, but to see that you have a manor just a day's carriage ride from Fairbright? I'm unsure what to think. Do you truly hate me so much that you couldn't even pen me a letter?"

"Gen," I say, moving toward her until I'm kneeling before her, "you gave me no reason to think you wanted me in your life any longer. Just this morning, you were playing the part of the haughty princess, turning me out again."

I hate that I'm already putting distance between us again, but whatever happens next—whether she accepts me or chooses the crown over me—won't be decided tonight.

She presses her hands to my chest, pushing me lightly. "That isn't fair! You've been nothing but the demanding redblood, planning my ruin!"

Despite her words, her tone is playful, and the smirk on her lips reminds me of all the times I used to tease her until she teased me back. Riling Genevieve Ashcroft out of her stuffy, composed crown princess role is something I'll never tire of.

I give her a knowing look. "You've tried to drive me away twice now, Princess. What more evidence do I need that a correspondence wouldn't have changed a thing?"

She keeps her hands fisted in my shirt, and I can't tell if she wants to pull me closer or push me away. Hell, I don't think she knows either.

"But—but..." She shakes her head, then looks away from me, the old pain I saw in the carriage returning. "When I heard you were dead, I didn't know how I'd survive it. Until then, I was so sure you'd return to me eventually. I told myself you just needed new experiences, and then you'd see that you belong to me."

I stare at her in confusion. "What part of you pushing me away made you think I'd ever return?"

"I think back on that often. We were so young, and my mother was adamant I make an advantageous marriage to continue the blueblood lineage. If I could go back, I would have fought for you. But I can't go back—I can only look to the future. What you said earlier today is true. I haven't allowed myself to make decisions I actually want. I always think of the crown. I can't help it. Even this morning, I tried to force myself to accept a marriage I already knew would be disastrous. In truth, I wish I could have felt something for him, but my heart hasn't been mine to give for a very long time."

I swallow thickly. The shell I've built around my heart threatens to crack under the weight of the woman who caused it to harden. Despite her rejection and the circumstances that nearly ruined me, I've never stopped thinking of Genevieve Ashcroft. She dug her way into my life long ago, and I could never let her go.

I ask the question that's been on my mind all day. "Who has your heart, Gen?"

She lets out a soft laugh, a smile playing on her mouth as she leans forward, so close her words brush my skin. "You do, you fool! You always have."

I grin before pressing my lips to hers. "I'm no fool. I knew from the moment you fainted I still had your heart. I just wanted to hear you admit it."

She tilts her head, then kisses me again. I want to stay in this moment forever—in this fragile illusion that she's truly mine—but I know it won't last. Even as she claims I have her heart, I can't quite trust her words, or the heart that once turned mine hard.

I pull back. "Let me show you to your rooms. Tomorrow, we'll visit the mines, then decide what comes next."

She gives me a quizzical look. "You don't want to share a room with me?"

"I would love nothing more than to share a room with you, Gen. But we shouldn't—and you know why."

"Propriety has already been damned by my running toward your carriage, away from my fiancé."

I huff a laugh, standing and pulling her up beside me. "I wasn't thinking of propriety."

"My gift, then? Did it bother you too much?"

I shake my head. "You'll be more comfortable alone."

"No, I don't think I will," she says, pressing her body against mine.

I stop her, even though the urge to hold her all night is almost too much to resist. "I've been exposed to high levels of helachite for many years. I'm not the same as I once was, and I don't sleep beside others because of it."

She gasps softly, studying me. "What do you mean?"

"Did you notice Mrs. Andrews's and Mr. Bridge's features? They worked in the mines from childhood until I closed off the dangerous mines. I brought them here and gave them employment that allows them to live comfortably. I've employed dozens of former miners—too injured or ill to work elsewhere. We're all damaged in ways you can't see. We all have restless sleep, insomnia, or both."

I want to admit that's why I kept returning to her room at night—that seeing her sleep safely gave me the only peace I've known in years. But saying that aloud would make me sound mad, even though she must understand now why I couldn't stay away.

Her brow furrows as she looks at me with a stifling amount of pity.

"Don't pity me, Princess. I won't have it."

"It isn't pity. I just feel responsible. I ruined your life—no wonder you wanted to ruin mine."

But I don't want to ruin her life, not really. Far from it. I want her to fill mine, to make all this damn work and suffering mean something. I want what I lost and thought I could never have again.

But not until I know she wants it too.

Because I may have Geneveive Ashcroft's heart, but that means little if she's not willing to let me take it.

34

Genevieve

"Gen, are you sure?" Kieran asks against my skin, his lips pressing tentative kisses along the crook of my neck. We left the ballroom together as soon as we finished dancing, my desire to be with him—and him alone—filling me with reckless abandon. I don't care if the entire court knows I've chosen to spend my birthday with Kieran Greenbluff.

"I've never been more sure of anything in my life, Kieran," I reply, my thighs falling wider as Kieran's hips meet mine.

His breath releases in a raspy exhale. "Promise me you'll be mine forever. I can't—I can't have you if I know someone else will claim you."

"I promise, Kieran. I'll always be yours."

My words are punctuated by the roll of my hips, a sharp cry as our shared promises fuse with our bodies.

I wake to a groaning cry in the night. Listening closely, I know it must be coming from down the hall in Kieran's rooms. No one else occupies this floor of Huntley House, but I'm apprehensive about leaving my bed. He clearly wanted privacy, refusing to let me share his room. Then comes a louder cry, the sound of pain—or panic—followed by a sharp crash, glass shattering into tiny fragments.

I can't lie here, listening to him suffer. He could be injured and in need of help. I slip on my robe and slippers, provided by Mrs. Andrews, and pad down the hallway toward the sound.

A muffled moan fills the air as I push open the unlocked door. The room is large and sparsely furnished, making it feel all the bigger. I see a figure on the floor, rolling and groaning.

"Kieran?" I whisper as he shakes violently. His shirt is off, and he's writhing in agony across broken porcelain.

"No, Kieran! Let me help you!" I rush to the gas lamp, lighting it quickly before moving toward him to assess his injuries. What I see makes me suck in a sharp breath: blue blood splatters his chest. It cannot be possible. Kieran isn't a blueblood. He's always been a redblood. I think back to all his skinned knees and fencing injuries from our childhood—*always*, his blood flowed crimson.

He thrashes against what appears to be a broken pitcher, embedding the shards deeper into his chest, his arms, his back. It's everywhere, indigo streaks slashed across his bare skin.

"Kieran!" I cry, shaking him gently, but he doesn't respond. He moans some incoherent words, and all I can make out is my name.

"Yes, it's me. It's Gen. I'm here, Kieran—you're safe."

Slowly, his eyes open, but he lets out an anguished cry. "I'll take care of you," I murmur. "Come now—there's a broken pitcher, and you've managed to injure yourself." I pull him up to a seated position, guiding him forward and away from the fragments. He's disoriented, and I'm not sure if he recognizes me, but I continue speaking softly as he groans in pain.

I go to the basin on his bureau, pour water into the bowl, and wet a cloth. Then I kneel beside him and begin to clean his wounds, extracting the shards of porcelain as gently as I can. He growls, but remains still, his head hanging low.

"I'm here, Kieran. It's going to be alright," I reassure him. After painstaking minutes of removing fragments and wiping away blue streams of blood, I finally exhale, realizing I've done all I can.

"Come, let me help you into bed," I insist. He moves without speaking, allowing me to tuck him beneath the covers. His low moans fill the room as I turn the light down and slip off my robe. Climbing in beside him, I feel the tension in his body—his muscles seizing and straining even in rest. I begin to rub the tightness from his arms, then his chest, until he finally relaxes into sleep.

I wrap my arms around him and whisper his own words back to him: "I'm not leaving you."

He's kept this secret from me, and I can't help but wonder why. If he's a blueblood, how could Mother refuse our match? And why wouldn't he have come back to tell me that somehow, impossibly, he's become one?

Morning light streams into the room, and I hear a quiet shuffling sound. A maid is here, cleaning up the broken glass and bloodied toweling. I cringe, wondering what she must think of this gruesome scene. I pretend to be asleep as she hums to herself, apparently unfazed by the blood—or by the princess in Kieran's bed.

Finally, I hear the click of the door. I turn to Kieran. His face is smooth and relaxed in sleep. Across his chest and arms are little blue nicks from his injuries last night. He looks like a fallen angel, and I allow myself a few moments more of this peaceful unreality, curling closer to him.

He rolls onto his side, pulling me into a tight embrace, his rhythmic breathing warming my exposed neck in a way that feels both comforting and foreign. I've never slept like this with anyone—not even Kieran—and it feels forbidden, like I don't deserve this sort of comfort. I close my eyes again, allowing myself this one small indulgence before I face the truth of why Kieran has kept such a life-altering secret from me.

When I wake again, it's to Kieran releasing his hold and stretching his taut body. "You're actually here?" he asks. "I thought it was a dream."

I roll over, meeting his green eyes, and stroke the scruff of his unshaven face. "Not a dream, actually. I woke to find you injured and helped clean you up. You didn't seem quite cognizant, and I stayed to try to soothe you. Eventually, you rested without crying out."

He sits up, examining himself, and I trace one of the slices on his chest with my finger. "You cut yourself on some broken porcelain. There was quite a lot of blood."

"Blood?" His rich, olive skin fades to ash.

"Yes—surprisingly, it was blue. Kieran, why didn't you tell me you're a blueblood? How is that even possible?"

He looks stricken and turns his back to me, placing his feet on the ground. "I'm not a blueblood. Not really, anyway. My blood was poisoned in the mines, and when I got this"—he turns toward me, tracing the faint scar on his face—"when I was sliced by a falling chunk of ore, I woke up with a fucking gift."

My heart thrashes in my chest as I move to his side, slipping my hand onto his shoulder. He doesn't jerk away, though I expect him to.

"You have a gift? How is that possible?"

He shakes his head. "I was young enough, I suppose. Most who are forced into becoming bluebloods don't receive gifts. Most just perish, and those who survive are too injured to work. Your people call it a gift, but it's an abomination. There *shouldn't* be bluebloods. The sooner we reduce exposure, the sooner they'll disappear completely. Look at Gabe and Mari—they carry the blueblood strain from their exposed ancestors, but it's so weakened now they don't have gifts. It's better that way, anyway. Look what it's done to you."

I stroke his arm—and feel nothing. None of my curse flows into him. In fact, if I think about it, he hasn't been affected by my touch at all. He's always just shown his own emotions, his own reactions to our contact. Every time we've touched, I've been too lost in my own feelings to notice. Even yesterday, when I was baffled by his restraint—it wasn't because he had more control than other men. He was restrained because he chose to give me pleasure instead of seeking his own. He chose to give rather than take, and felt no overwhelming urges from my curse.

"You nullify others' gifts, don't you?"

He gives me a sardonic smile. "You've finally realized it, Princess."

Heat rises to my cheeks. "I did. I'm embarrassed to admit I thought it was something special between us—that it was us, not your gift, that made our physical connection feel different."

His eyes darken, and he looks at me with such intensity I fear I've insulted him.

"Never again, Gen. Never. Promise me I'm the only one who will touch you from now on. I don't want to know what happened to you because of that curse. I'm afraid I'd kill every bastard who's ever laid hands on you—and your family, for allowing you to think it was acceptable. But from now on, promise me it will only be me."

I press my hand to his cheek, drawing him close until our foreheads touch. "There will be no other man but you, Kieran Greenbluff. Morris Blackwell—whatever you wish me to call you."

"Good," he growls before kissing me with a fierce hunger. Does he truly believe me? Does he realize that even my mother can't object to him now? I'm determined to make him understand nothing will stop me from finally making him mine.

He pulls back, all business once more. "We have work to do. It won't be easy for you, but if you're going to change this country, you need to see what's been done."

"Yes, of course," I say, rising to stand beside him. "I'm ready."

35

Genevieve

The stench of rot is so overpowering that my eyes burn and my nostrils sting. I want to tell Kieran this is too much, that I can't possibly inspect anything under these conditions. But then I think of how he fought through the night—the blue blood in his body still causing him agony from all those years of working in these mines—and I swallow my dismay, following him through the underground entrance.

"We can't go far here. I've closed this section, but I wanted you to see the conditions. Since mining ended, the rot has slowed its progress, but the helachite is still unstable."

I don't know how he can speak so calmly in the stifling, foul air with a heaviness that clings to the narrow tunnel. He doesn't even cover his face as he talks, reaching for a vein of exposed ore and chipping it off with his hand. It crumbles under his touch, releasing a sharp, gaseous odor.

"Helachite is naturally a sturdy mineral—difficult to extract and work with—but once it's pried out and exposed to the oils on our hands and the air around us, it begins to deteriorate. The more it's exposed, the more rot forms. It's useless to me now. The structure that gives helachite its power is so far gone it's essentially waste. It's well known that helachite isn't valuable in this state, but the former owner continued to force miners to work in these conditions. When people come in contact with the rot, they get very ill. You've seen that firsthand, from your sister and the death in the palace."

He guides me toward the exit, and I feel sick inside, thinking about the people who labored for next to nothing in these conditions. "Did you have to work down here?"

He shakes his head quickly, but his eyes linger too long on the space before he closes the door. "I was deemed too valuable early on. It was only the weaker workers who were sent into this mine. It was a death sentence—a quick way to rid the business of people no longer useful. But we all knew what was down here. I closed it as soon as I was able to take ownership."

Outside, under a heavy grey sky, I take a deep breath, filling my lungs with cleaner air before asking the question that's been on my mind for weeks. "How did you manage to rise to where you are today?"

"You know me—I have a way of making things work to my advantage. I started as a miner, like anyone else. I lost my father to this mine, and something in me snapped. I wanted to right the wrongs that had been done to us, so I fought in the only way I knew how. I moved up to supervisor, then began taking courses in the evenings to become an engineer. After that, I was promoted. Unlike my colleagues, I invested every coin I earned, choosing to remain in the bachelor barracks with the other miners. Turns out, I'm good at investing, and I made a significant profit."

He glances toward the horizon, the wind catching the loose strands of his hair. The haunted look in his eyes tells me every word costs him something to say.

"Then I was promoted over the mine, and that's when I made my move. I offered the former owner a deal he couldn't refuse and bought the place. After that, I secured a loan and purchased a mine in Icelantica. I knew there was potential to operate helachite mines in a more humane—and more profitable—way by reducing exposure and smelting the mineral into a stable form. I'd been experimenting in the evenings for years and knew my process would work. Once I got things running, I kept expanding, determined to reinvent the industry."

This man. How could he have the drive, the sheer determination, to make such sweeping changes after so much suffering? I know I wouldn't have that kind of resolve. He amazes me, and I try to slip my hand into his, but he pulls away.

"I touched the helachite in there. I need to wash before you hold my hand again. I'd never risk you with this stuff."

He leads me through the rocky outcroppings toward another mining entrance bustling with people.

"You're a remarkable man, Kieran. To have done all this in only nine years."

I want to ask how he ended up at the mines—why he left me, only to come to this horrible place—but I'm afraid of reopening old wounds. I must have already done enough to drive him here.

"Good morning, sir," a man says, tipping his cap to Kieran.

"Good morning, George," Kieran replies with a nod as we make our way toward the mine entrance. Inside, I immediately see the difference between the two sites. This one is lit with bright gas lamps. Along a tiled corridor are sinks with running water and soap; above them hang stacks of leather gloves in all sizes, and below are thick wool suits, clean and ready for the day's use.

"Are you ready to go underground, Princess?" Kieran asks, handing me a pair of gloves and wool suit.

I smile and assure him that I am. Despite my misgivings, I know Kieran will keep me safe. And what he said when we left Fairbright was true—if I'm too afraid to enter these mines, how can I ask my citizens to do so?

Once I've slid the suit over my dress, Kieran hands me a heavy metal helmet, fastening the leather strap under my chin.

"How do I look?" I ask, giving him a little twirl.

"Ready to work," he replies, thumping my helmet with his gloved hand. "Stay close to me, and don't touch the mineral if you can help it. It's still in its raw form down here, which makes it volatile. You should be fine, but I'd rather not risk you."

I give a small chuckle. "I am the heir apparent. It would be a national emergency if something were to happen to me."

He turns back and wraps a hand around my waist, looking down at me. "Just to be clear, I don't give a fuck about the crown. It's you I want to be safe."

"Oh," I say, surprised. When was the last time anyone valued me simply for myself and not for what I represent? Clemmy cares. My siblings do too. But still, I've always been the crown princess—even to those closest to me.

Kieran leads me to a strange metal cage and pushes a button that emits a loud chirp. A series of chirps answer before I hear the rattling of metal. A smaller cage moves up to meet us. He opens the door and guides me inside before pressing another set of buttons.

"This allows us to access the deeper parts of the mine. Before we installed the mechanical carts, we used a rope-and-pulley system. It was... precarious."

I don't know what to say to that, so I just shake my head, though he probably doesn't see the gesture. Part of me wants to ask what made it so precarious, but I also can't help wondering if recalling it would bring up memories he'd rather forget.

"The buttons and beeps let us communicate when to move the mechanical cart and where to send it. Each level has an operator overseeing the system."

As we descend deeper into the mines, darkness swallows the world. I can hardly see beyond the dim lamp Kieran carries. The cart lurches to a halt, and we step out into near-total blackness.

"I've never seen a place so void of light."

Kieran clears his throat and places a hand on my back, guiding me into a musty, humid tunnel. "Imagine if I didn't have this lamp. You wouldn't see your own hand in front of your face. Now imagine you're expected to make your way out from a distant tunnel without a light." He brings his free hand to a rope running along the wall. "That's why I had this installed throughout the mine. It's always on the right side, in every tunnel."

"Good thinking. Were you ever in the dark alone?"

I can barely make out his head shake. "If I were, I wouldn't be with you today. Not many made it out if they lost their light. Some were lucky, but more often we'd lose a miner and not find them for a week or two. The darkness is disorienting, and the tunnels are endless."

I want to cling to him, to erase the painful memories from his mind. He's endured so much here, and yet instead of turning his back on a place that hurt him, he's worked to make it better for those who remain.

More lights appear ahead in the tunnel, and we walk toward them.

"Blackwell!" a man calls. "Didn't expect to see you this far under-ground again. Missed us that badly?" He laughs, slapping Kieran on the back with dust-covered gloves.

"Just providing Princess Genevieve with a tour. She's here to in-spect the mines."

Around us, the miners bow and murmur their regards. I don't want their deference—not here, not after seeing the conditions they'd endured. These men and women are above giving me their respect.

"Please, don't mind me," I say. "I just want to better understand what it is you all do. You're making a difference in so many lives as helachite technology advances. You have my gratitude."

"I want to show her what raw helachite looks like," Kieran adds, resting his hand at my back again and leading me toward where the men are working.

He points to an illuminated section of rock. Even in the tunnel's dim light, it sparkles in a medley of colors, shimmering and shifting as if alive. I place a hand over my chest, gasping.

"It's gorgeous! How is it moving like that?"

The man who greeted Kieran steps forward. "That's the magic in it. It's what turned your great-great-grandmother's blood blue and start-ed this whole divide. It's what gives bluebloods their gifts—and what powers the railways Mr. Blackwell builds. It runs the new contraptions for tilling fields and weaving fabric. Magic, Princess Genevieve."

There's truth in his words. "I must agree with you," I reply. "How do you remove it?"

He hefts a pickaxe and drives it into the wall. The colors splinter and tremble, as if trying to escape the intrusion, but he continues striking until a hand-sized chunk falls free. Its brilliance fades to a silvery metallic sheen.

"Once upon a time, we needed larger pieces to send to the surface," he explains. "Thanks to the smelter, we can now use smaller fragments to refine the helachite into what we need—and stabilize it at the same time."

The man hands me the chunk of rock, and I feel Kieran stiffen, but I take it. "It's sad to see the rock lose its luster like that. It's almost as if it's sentient."

An older man snickers. "Almost? Princess, the helachite *is* sentient. That's why the rot exists. It doesn't take kindly to misuse, and it'll punish those who don't respect it. We miners have known that for a long, long time."

He squeezes Kieran's shoulder in a friendly gesture. "And now one of our own is making sure helachite gets the respect it deserves."

"From what I can see, he's doing an excellent job of it. What do you gentlemen think?" I ask, earning a chorus of laughter.

"Don't think of us as gentlemen, Your Highness. We're not some highborn bluebloods. We've been forced to take on the blue blood, and we all suffer for it."

I glance toward Kieran, hoping for guidance, but he offers none. His face is unreadable, and I think back to his cries in the night. "What are the long-term effects of mining helachite? Is there anything we can do to prevent them?"

"We all get the night terrors," one man answers, and the others shoot him looks as if he's said too much. "What? She's going to be the damn queen! She may as well know what's happening down here!"

Even in the dim light, I can see the scowl on Kieran's face. I lay my gloved hand on his arm in reassurance and say, "He's right. I want to understand how to help all my people—including the helachite miners."

The man nods and continues, "The night terrors. It's the body's re-action to the forced changes in our blood. Remember the stories about the mad bluebloods from the first generations? That's the terrors. Then there's those who spent too long touching raw helachite—lots of injuries there. But Mr. Blackwell's worked hard to see them cared for, even after all they've been through. The new generation of miners isn't seeing such rapid deterioration. We've even got a young man down here whose blood's still as red as a ruby. I think it's because of Mr. Blackwell's new rules."

I look at Kieran, curious. "What rules?"

He clears his throat. "Shorter shifts, mandatory three days off. Everyone wears safety gear and washes before going home. I've in-stalled running water and bathing rooms in all my mines. Any injuries are reported immediately and treated."

"Doesn't that increase the operating costs significantly?" I ask.

Kieran shakes his head. "It's more important to give my workers a good life. If it cuts into my profits, so be it. I'm already richer than any man should be. The least I can do is improve the conditions they work in."

I don't know what to say to that. I think of my own family—how much we pride ourselves on duty and decorum, yet never once have we sacrificed our comfort for our people. And here is Kieran, making a greater difference than my mother ever has.

She's never even bothered to learn the conditions these miners toiled in. In fact, she's chosen to remain willfully ignorant of the dangers of helachite mining, leaving me just as uninformed.

When we were younger, Kieran was many things—funny, caring, fiercely loyal. It's no surprise he's carried that loyalty into adulthood. My heart aches, thinking of how, at such a young age, he chose to fight—not with weapons or violence, but by transforming this industry from the inside out.

Kieran places his thick, gloved hand on my arm, guiding me toward the exit. "Drager, Cressup, Mitchum—thank you for all your hard work, and for taking time out of your day to show Princess Genevieve what you do. We must be off. It may be a while before I'm back. Is there anything you need that I can get you?"

"You've done more than we could ask for, sir. But if you must know, Mr. Jenkins passed last week. His widow's having a hard time. She's afraid she'll be removed from her home now that he's gone. We tried assuring her you'd never do that, but she doesn't believe us."

Kieran's hand tightens on my arm, his body tense. What kind of an operation would forcibly remove a mourning widow from her home? My stomach churns at the thought of such cruelty—and the lack of humanity these men and women have come to expect.

"Right. I'll be sure to stop by."

I bow to the men. "Thank you all for your time. You've been so helpful in showing me how the mine operates. I hope to come again."

"Do that, Your Highness," one of the men says as we begin our ascent back to the surface.

36

Kieran

Genevieve is too quiet as we leave Mrs. Jenkins's home. The widow cried at our feet, begging me not to remove her from her house now that Mr. Jenkins has succumbed to a lifetime of working in the mines without proper protection. That was the way of it before I purchased the mine—widows had one week to vacate the premises or be tossed into the streets with no shelter. Not that those former excuses for homes were even adequate to begin with.

Now I'm expanding the growing town of Aldridge, replacing weathered old shacks with respectable cottages, schools, and proper medical facilities. It's coming along, but not fast enough. I want these families to know they have safety and security here.

That's what has Gen so subdued. I can see it in her expression. She's realizing this mess falls on her family's shoulders. They've failed to take even the most basic interest in protecting their people, and she has to know she's been complicit in that.

It stings, knowing she sent me here and no one from her family cared to find out what that decision meant—for me or for my father. All I can hope is that witnessing what a helachite mine truly is, and all the work I've put into improving conditions, will light a fire under Gen to bring about real change across the industry. I can't own every damned helachite mine and fix them all myself. I need help—and I want her to see how important this work is.

We chose to walk back to Huntley House, despite the heavy clouds threatening to open in a deluge. I think both of us needed the fresh air and time to process the day. From what I can tell, Gen is receptive to what she's seen, and she seems to understand the larger implications of her rule. I want to trust her—I want my mind to feel what my traitorous heart has always felt—but after years of betrayal, after all the ways the Ashcrofts have failed this country, I don't know if my head can catch up to my heart.

Her hand brushes my arm, and I look down at her pensive expression. "I had no idea what this place was like," she says, shaking her head.

I grunt. "Yes, well—at least you've come now."

"But my mother's disinterest is horrid. What else has she neglected as queen? Is there any part of the country that's truly comfortable? Or is that only in Crawford?"

"I don't know what the rest of the country is like. I haven't traveled south of Crawford. But there are still mines operated by others—less willing to give their workers the arrangements I've offered mine. Without regulation, they're trying to outpace me and make a profit as quickly as possible. What they don't understand is that without proper smelting or safety standards, they'll never achieve lasting success. If you let them go unregulated, you'll have a national disaster on your hands."

Her face pales. "There's so much I still don't know. My mother prepared me for life at court—for ruling from a distance—but perhaps that's not what I want. Or what Naseria needs."

I run a hand through my hair. "You have to decide what kind of ruler you'll be, Gen—and you're running out of time."

She doesn't answer. Instead, she folds her arms around her waist, frowning as we walk the last stretch toward Huntley House.

If Gen is going to make a real impact, she'll have to rule differently from her mother—and from every blueblood who wore the crown before her. I don't know if she understands that yet, or if she's even willing to hear it. I don't want to push her, not before I know what she intends to do with what she's seen.

If she turns her back on these people—choosing courtly comfort over fighting for those who need her most—then I want nothing to do with her. I'll let her go again. I've been broken by her once; I can bear it again.

But the way she treated the miners, the way she came to my side in the night and cared for me—makes me think she's capable of ruling differently.

Last night felt like a fever dream, like an angel descending to soothe me through the worst of it. I've never let anyone stay with me during the night terrors, except back when I shared a barrack with the other single miners. That wasn't a choice; we were all in the fight together. But this—this was different. Despite my protests, she came to me, cared for me, and held me.

Rain begins splattering on the dusty road, sending little plumes of dirt up around our shoes. Heavy drops follow, and before I think too much of it, I grab Gen's hand and we start running as the wind picks up and the rain comes crashing down.

Gen lets out a gasping laugh, and I want to bottle that sound, treasure it like some rare vintage I reach for only in my most desperate moments. Her peal of laughter cracks through the storm, and I laugh with her. I want her closer, so much closer, that I turn and lift her into my arms. She gives a giddy shout as I scoop her against my chest, her ruined gown clinging to her skin and her hair plastered in sheets of coiling silk. She wraps her legs around my waist, surrendering to my hold as I run down the lane, Huntley House looming through the deluge.

"Kieran!" she squeals, but she doesn't fight me; instead, she leans in, her face close to mine. I stop on the stoop of Huntley House, studying the woman I already know I should have nothing to do with. But if I've learned anything over these past few weeks at Fairbright, it's that I can't stop myself when it comes to Genevieve Ashcroft. I've never been able to. And I still haven't learned how to live without her.

I press her against the cold stone as she tips her head up to me and catch her lips in a searing kiss.

I am a man desperate for more of her—more kisses, more caresses in the night that chase away the worst of the terrors, and most of all, more of her tight core wrapped around my cock. I'm harder than I've ever been in my life, straining against her thighs as I search her mouth with my tongue. I was patient in the carriage—so fucking patient—knowing I couldn't make love to Gen the way I wanted, the way she deserved, in that cramped space. But my patience has run dry.

"Promise me you'll never leave me again." Her words are a desperate plea against my wet skin, and I pull back to look at her. She still can't believe I ever chose to leave her willingly. Haven't I made that clear? She's the one who pushed me away. My entire existence up until my nineteenth year had been devoted to this woman.

"I never wanted to leave you, Gen. I would have spent my entire life at your side if you'd let me."

"I didn't understand what losing you would mean. I never want to be apart from you again." Her lips sear across my jawline and down my neck—hot, desperate touches to desperate words.

"We were never over. Not when you wrote me the letter that brought me here. Not when you thought I was dead. Not even when you tried to replace me with another."

She pulls back, confusion clouding her features. "Letter?"

I let her feet slide to the stone floor, the icy rain suddenly chilling both of us. "The letter you wrote the day before I left. The one that made it clear you'd never be alone with me again. The one where you asked me to leave the palace and come here to work."

Her face crumples as the truth hits us both. She never wrote that letter. She never rejected me.

"My mother. It was her." Disdain hardens her voice—something I've never heard from Genevieve Ashcroft. "She sent you away and let me believe you were dead. She watched me mourn the loss of your love, then the loss of your life."

She grips my forearms with her chilled, bare hands. "I've never stopped loving you. I've carried your loss in my heart every day of my life, and I'm so sorry I allowed someone to come between us. Never again."

Her rain-cooled fingers slide to my jaw, pulling me down into her kiss. She kisses me like I'm something to be reclaimed, to be possessed and never let go—and I let her claim me as hers.

37

Genevieve

The rage and hurt of my mother's betrayal is nothing compared to the need burning through me—to take Kieran as mine once again.

Nine years.

Nine years of wanting him, of never letting go of what we once had and what we lost. All for naught. All because my mother lied to me. She watched me mourn the man I loved and forced me into loveless arrangements with other men, leaving me more broken and lonely than before. She made me think there was something wrong with *me*, when all this time it was her—her selfishness, her greed, her betrayal—that caused the heartbreak I've carried for nearly a decade.

Kieran presses me back against the cold brick of Huntley House, and I wrap my legs around him, canting my hips to feel the hardness between us, the desire he still has for me evident even through my damp, rumpled skirts trapped between us.

"Kieran, I need you. I need to feel you inside me," I breathe into the hollow of his neck. His response is part moan, part grunt as he sweeps me off my feet. I wrap my legs around his waist as he pushes open the door to his home.

I don't care what the staff think. I can't comprehend anything beyond his touch—his lips on my bare skin—all of it without my curse distorting his reaction to me.

This is nothing but our own pure desire. A need I've harbored deep in my heart and spent the last few weeks denying, despite the stolen glances, the way he was drawn to me even in the night. Only he can fulfill the hunger in my body and the ache in my heart.

"Out!" Kieran barks, and a maid scuttles from the doorway. "Don't worry about them, Gen," he says softly against the shell of my ear. He knows me well enough to realize that, normally, all I'd be thinking about is propriety and everyone else's reactions.

"Kieran, for once I don't even care who sees me. All I want is you—*now*," I reply, my voice husky with want. I slide my hands through his thick, wavy hair, and he lets out another moan against my ear.

"Can you make it to the bedroom, Princess, or should I take you in my sitting room?"

He doesn't wait for an answer. Instead, he bars the door to the well-appointed room off the foyer. With deliberate, agonizing care, he lowers me onto the plush carpet near the crackling fire. My breath leaves me in a rush as he braces himself above me, sweeping one hand down the dripping fabric clinging to my body.

"No bedroom then?" I ask, my voice already frayed with need. I know there's no waiting for a bedroom. I would have fucked him in the carriage if he'd let me—long before I realized everything that's kept us apart. The well of emotion he showed me yesterday was only the barest edge of what I feel for him. Nearly a decade of broken hope and heartbreak, and I'll be damned if I have to climb the stairs for a bed.

He feels the same—his hands are already working at the cold, wet fabric of my dress.

"No time," he says, voice rough, "not with you trembling in these wet clothes."

"I'm not trembling from the cold, Kieran."

He cocks his head, a knowing smile tugging at his lips. "Yes, I know, Princess. You're trembling for me. And I cannot endure another moment with these clothes between us."

Kieran looks at me expectantly, as if waiting for permission to ravish me. It's endearing—one of the few things that hasn't changed about him, despite everything else in his life being upended. He still touches me the same way he always has: in whatever manner keeps me comfortable, always placing my needs above his own.

"May I?" he asks quietly, fingers poised at the first button.

I know exactly what he needs to hear.

"Yes. I want you, Kieran Greenbluff."

"Yes?" he breathes.

"Yes." My voice is confident, unwavering, as he holds my gaze.

"There's no coming back from this, Princess. I'll hoard you away if I must, but you'll be mine—only mine."

I draw my hand up to his cheek, stroking gently as I see the doubt hiding behind his eyes. He still isn't sure he can trust me. That realization cracks something raw and aching inside me.

"Kieran," I whisper, "you are all I've ever wanted. This is the answer to every dream I've ever dared to have."

As if the last fragments of control he'd been clinging to snap, Kieran kisses me, and I feel myself falling weightless into our shared desires. What I said is true. He *is* the answer to my dreams. All my fantasies as a young woman were of him, and even after he left, I kept hoping he would return.

Not even his death stopped me from yearning for him. I've longed for a dead man for nearly a decade, and now I finally have the proof I always dreamed of—the truth I always carried in my heart. Kieran is here. He is alive. And he still wants only me.

Kieran's hand curves around my neck, a light pressure that sends my pulse skittering. His thumb strokes the hollow of my throat before he moves to my drenched garments and begins the slow, steady task of unbuttoning my frock.

"I've dreamed of seeing you naked since that night in the ballroom. I've wanted to map every change in your body, to feel you writhe beneath my touch."

I feel a tumult of emotions as his warm hands glide down the row of buttons, slowly revealing my corset and the shift underneath. Once he's undone the dress, he lifts me with a reverence I'm not sure I deserve, then tosses the wet garment aside, where it lands with a soft slap against the carpet.

He shifts to his knees and offers me a hand, guiding me upright before turning me so he has better access to the corset strings. "Yesterday I was far too tempted to strip you of your corset, just so I could properly admire your breasts."

I give him a small smile. "Are they that changed?"

His eyebrow arches as he loosens my stays, letting the corset fall to the floor and exposing my shift. I lift my arms silently as he pulls it over my head with a kind of awed hunger that leaves me breathless.

"You're perfect, Gen. I thought you were then, but now? There is no equal to your beauty."

I ease back, letting him take in my nearly naked body. All that remains are the stockings that reach just above my knees. Kieran lifts my foot, drawing the stocking off in slow, reverent kisses along my inner leg before repeating the action on the other until I'm fully bared to him. He leans in, taking one of my full breasts in his hand and giving it a teasing squeeze. "I should have known, I should have fought for you."

I meet his eyes and reach out, touching his wet chest. "No, I should have known my mother was involved somehow. She was against our relationship—even against our friendship. But that never stopped us, did it? She must have been irate when I still chose you over all the other boys at her ball."

He grunts and shakes his head. "We can talk about her later. I have far more important things to do than discuss Penelope Ashcroft's venomous disposition."

He's right, of course. Despite everything that's happened between us, I don't want my mother's role to tarnish this moment.

I let my nails trail down the wet fabric of his shirt, finding the place where it bunches at his waist, and lift it up. He doesn't resist as I tug it over his head and let it fall beside my discarded dress. He's nothing like the boy he was all those years ago. Once a tall, skinny gardener's son, Kieran is now solid with muscle—muscles earned through back-breaking labor. And that labor is my fault. He suffered because I didn't fight for him, and the truth of that lances through me. I trace my fingers across raised scars and rigid cords of muscle until I reach the fastenings of his trousers. My breath catches before I begin to undo them. His gaze never wavers as I remove the final remaining vestiges between us. There's something so vulnerable in the way he looks at me, as though I'm seeing a part of him he's kept hidden for so, so long.

I don't think he's ever looked at me with such vulnerability, such softness—and certainly not since he's returned to my life. It comforts me and unnerves me at the same time. There's so much to read in his gaze: so much history, so much hurt, and yet beneath it all, there's hope.

That's what I choose to cling to as our bodies press together again, chest to chest for the first time in nine years.

Kieran lets out a low groan as my hands sweep down to his heavily muscled thighs, the textures of his masculine form so deliciously enticing.

"Gen, you don't know what you do to me," he murmurs, his lips brushing my ear.

I want to tease him, to point to his obvious erection. I want to quip that I know exactly what I do to him, to keep fighting this cataclysmic revelation that neither of us ever stopped desiring the other.

Maybe we've never stopped loving each other either—and that is the most frightening, the most vulnerable truth. Knowing there's always been love between us, a yearning that never truly ceased for either of us.

I don't give in to the temptation to cut into him anymore, because the truth is that I want to let go of the walls I've built around myself. Kieran is the only person I could ever set aside that hardness for—the only one I trust to see what lies beneath. So I choose to leap. I choose to accept that whatever this is between us, it's a lasting river of desire, of love, and I want nothing more than to submerge myself in it and never come up again.

"You do the same to me, Kieran." His heart beats like a butterfly's wings against my chest, all desperate energy as he begins to explore my body, his hands kneading and pressing into my flesh. I trace the changes in his own body in return—mapping every hard-earned line and ridge, all the ways he's no longer the same man I once gave my heart and body to.

"I want to know you as you are now," I whisper as I lean down and let my tongue brush his flat nipple. His skin pebbles under my touch, and I continue my exploration of his body with my lips, teeth, and tongue.

It's all so new, and yet familiar too. My tongue glides over the small scar on his hip—the one he's had since he was twelve and he sliced himself on a fence while helping his father patch my garden. I still remember the blood soaking through his shirt and how I insisted on tending the wound myself, even though I had no idea what I was doing.

Just above that childhood mark is a newer scar, and I skim my fingertips over it. "How did you get this?" I ask.

"Fell off the bed in the barracks during a particularly strong night terror. I was late choosing a bunk that night, working on smelting the ore, and had to take a top bunk."

I shudder, thinking of all the nights he's endured those terrors alone. Did coming to my room while I slept bring him comfort?

As I explore him, his hands move through my hair, down my back, circling my hips. I can tell by the way he touches me that he's memorizing the differences too. He follows the lines of my freckles, kissing a path along the new ones, and his fingers linger over the old marks he knows as well as I do.

He reaches a small scar on my soft belly. "What was this from?" he asks.

I shake my head, unsure if he truly wants to know it came from broken glass and a man drunk on my gift—how the sight of my blue-tinted blood on the sheets had been enough to break the curse's hold long enough to help clean me up before he apologized and left me with nothing but bloodied linens and a hollow sense of despair.

"How?" he asks again, tracing the raised skin slowly. "It wasn't because of your gift, was it?"

I give a tiny nod. "He didn't mean to harm me, and he helped me clean the wound. Nothing happened between us after that. It was the moment I realized I could never find love with my gift."

He looks toward the fire, his jaw ticking, before turning back to me. His hand caresses the scar with a tenderness I never believed possible from Kieran. "I should have never left you, Gen. Forgive me."

"Of course I do. Forgive *me*. I shouldn't have doubted you. I should have known it was my mother all along who broke us apart."

He dips his head to the scar, pressing his lips to the old wound. "If I hadn't left you, your gift might have become something entirely different. You wouldn't have these memories."

He presses me down onto the carpet, his cheek resting against my soft flesh. "I'm so sorry, Gen. Thinking about what you've been through—and I've always blamed you for my own suffering—but we were both hurt. We hurt each other just as much as your mother did."

I slide my fingers through his hair. "We have a chance at a new beginning now. Let's not waste it dwelling on what could have been. All I want is to make up for those lost years."

He begins pressing soft kisses to my belly, the faint scratch of his stubble leaving a trail of desire. "Never again, Gen. I'll never see you hurt again."

His hand explores up the inside of my thigh again, heat rising as he stokes an endless flame inside me. "Gen, you're perfect," he whispers before lavishing my breasts with kisses. "All of you—every curve, every change. I want to memorize and devour them."

The tip of his finger circles my entrance, firm and deliberate, before he dips inside me. A groan scorches both our lips as I shift to accommodate him. My core clenches around him as he begins to stroke in and out, and all I can think about is keeping him close—clinging to him, hungry for the promise of more of him to come.

Kieran continues kissing and sucking my breasts, my nipples tightening into rigid peaks as he slides another finger inside me, filling me and deepening his exploring touches.

I can't stop the whimper that spills from my lips as tension coils deep in my belly. A delicious heat—Kieran's body pressed against mine, the hard length of his cock at my hip, the rhythmic pulse of his fingers inside me—drives me to a quivering desperation. When he presses the flat of his palm to my clit, the tension crests like a firestorm, breaking as I'm consumed by pleasure.

It isn't like yesterday, when the rush of emotion—of realizing I could receive pleasure at all—was so overwhelming that I felt as if I'd gained a part of myself and lost myself in the same breath. No, this is an endless flame, leaving me desperate for *more, more, more.*

Slowly, I come down from the pleasure searing through me and pull Kieran close, our mouths pressing together, tongues tangling in a language beyond words.

I spread my thighs, letting him settle between them. The blunt tip of his cock presses at my entrance, and I shift my hips, welcoming him in. The slight burn of his thick length stretching me is a satisfying ache I'm desperate for.

His eyes meet mine, and as he fills me completely, I'm just as wholly certain I love this man and cannot imagine a life without him at my side again.

"I've yearned for this for so long, Gen," he says, pulling back until I'm nearly empty before he drives into me again.

"You're all I've ever wanted. I'll never let you go now." His pace settles into a rhythm that has me arching my back, lifting my hips to take him deeper. He's everywhere—surrounding me, consuming me—as our breaths mingle and our moans entwine.

Our words become promises, in harmony with the vow our joined bodies make.

"I'll never leave you, I promise," I murmur, my voice catching as pleasure expands and ripples through me again—and then we're both plummeting into our shared release.

Kieran's body slumps against mine, his weight a heavy comfort. "I love you, Kieran. I'll never stop loving you," I whisper, our sweat-streaked skin fused together. He presses a kiss to my temple, down my jawline, and finally to my lips.

"I love you too, Gen. We've lost years together, but we'll have them back—and more."

He slips away from me, moving to a pitcher where he wets a cloth before returning to wash my sensitive skin.

"Bed?" he asks.

A small gurgle from my stomach interrupts us.

"Supper in bed?" I offer.

He laughs as he scoops up my soaked clothing.

"Even better. No point in trying to put these back on." Kieran crosses to a side closet and retrieves two blankets, wrapping me in soft wool before doing the same for himself.

"Do you actually intend for us to walk through the house like this?" I ask. Making love on the parlor rug is one thing, but traipsing through the manor nude beneath a blanket is where I draw the line.

Kieran laughs again—and it's the best sound in the world, bright and teasing. "Princess, don't be shy now. The servants are very well aware of what we did in here."

I want to protest, to think of the scandal that would erupt if word spread that the crown princess wandered a manor wrapped only in a blanket. But then I look at Kieran, at the playful expression softening his features, and I can't bear to dim it.

"Alright then. Supper in bed under the blankets sounds just the thing."

He winks and takes my hand, drawing me close as we open the door and march proudly up the stairs.

As we pass the landing, Kieran calls for two plates to be brought to his rooms and for the fire to be stoked. The wide-eyed maid curtsies, doing her best to hide a smirk. And still, I can't find it in me to care.

Kieran is mine once more—and the kingdom will simply have to accept it.

38

Kieran

Gen leans against me, the blanket I gave her barely covering the swell of her breasts. She picks up a piece of bread, dips it into the soup on the tray between us, and reaches up to feed it to me with a tenderness that makes refusal impossible. Even if being fed like this feels strange, I'll give her anything she wants if it means she remains mine.

Earlier in the parlor had been a dream—something I longed for nine years ago. That her rejection of me had been false. That she would search for me, admit she'd made a mistake. But that never happened, and I had to claw my way out of hell to build my own path.

A path that led straight back to what got me in trouble in the first place.

I don't regret what happened today. I don't regret my words. I'd let the world burn to the ground before I let someone separate us again. But the old fear still nags: will Gen truly choose me when we return to Crawford? Will she stand up to her mother and declare she loves me?

She smooths a hand across the stubble on my cheek, her warm fingers an addiction I can't shake. "What's on your mind?" she asks, tilting her cheek against my shoulder.

"Just happy to be with you now, Gen."

A lie, but I won't break this delicate thing between us. Not yet. Not when it feels so fragile and temporary, even wrapped in the promise of tonight.

She tips her face up to mine, brows furrowed. "That is not the look of a happy man." Her fingertip traces the line between my brows. "I've seen you happy. This is your brooding face."

"Brooding?" I scoff. "I'm not broody."

"Oh yes you are—or at least worried. Kieran, are you a *worrier* now?" She tries to tease, but her words come out flat.

I lean my head back against the pillows. "We need to talk about what you're going to do about your mother."

She looks puzzled. "What I'm going to do about her? Because she lied to both of us? She ruined us, but I don't know what I can do other than confront her and tell her that it made little difference in the end."

The words sting. Her mother's lies made all the difference. They destroyed my life. My father's life. And for years, I blamed Gen for it.

"Her lies are the reason my father died in the mines. She's the reason I fought like hell to rise from the ashes of this place. But all these years, I blamed you. I hated you and loved you all at once because she deceived us."

Gen shifts away, lifting her blanket over her exposed skin like protective armor. "She's hurt us both, and I don't think I can ever forgive her, but my mother is the queen. Her word is law, and she faces no repercussions for her actions. You know I've lived under her decisions my whole life. It's easiest to just..." She pauses, hurt flickering in her eyes. "It's easier to ignore it when she does things like this.

We only have to live that way for two more years, Kieran. Then I'll be queen. She can't stop our marriage—especially now that you're a blueblood."

I shake my head, unable to believe what she's saying. "I don't want her to know I'm a blueblood. It's not something I share, and the last person I need knowing is your mother."

Gen looks at me—ready to argue, it seems—before her expression softens. "You hate her, and rightfully so. But she's still the queen, and she *can* stop me from marrying you. She's done it before, and I can only imagine what she's planning when we return together. She'll be apoplectic with rage over my broken engagement—and over running away with you."

I want to deny her, to make her see I will not, under any circumstances, submit to the queen's orders, demands, or lies. But I know choosing Gen means choosing her life—choosing the reality that the crown will always be at the forefront of her mind.

"The theatrics of choosing a blueblood husband are too great, aren't they?" I ask gently. In the end, this isn't about me or her; it's about appeasing a system I plan to dismantle. I've done it with the helachite industry—what's the difference, if admitting my blue blood means I can have Gen? I'll destroy the divide in this country once and for all, from the top down.

Her gaze warms. "I hate doing this to you. You're so much more than the blood in your veins. But it's not only my mother who would make our marriage difficult."

We've been here before—made love, fought, lost everything. I cannot, will not, let that happen again. The sigh that escapes me feels like defeat. But is it defeat, if it means making Gen mine?

"I'll do it, Princess. But not for anyone except you. I don't give a fuck what the rest of the kingdom thinks of me. It's *you* I want. If that means living with that viper of a queen for two years, if it means spilling my blood in front of some paunchy council member, then so be it."

She reaches for me, pulling me into her arms, her bare breasts pressed to my chest.

"I'm sorry it has to be this way," she whispers into my skin, her arms tightening around my torso. "My mother—she's hurt both of us, but she's the reason you suffered for so many years. We can get through the next two years of her reign, then you'll never have to see her again. I promise you."

I nod, my voice caught in my throat as I think about all the years of hurt I blamed on Gen. Foolish, to imagine she would ever want me cast out like that, even after she rejected my proposal. But my pride was wounded. My stubborn pride got the better of me when I believed she had penned the note that cleaved me from her.

"All that matters is we know the truth, Gen, and we make this right."

She pulls back and looks at me. "We'll right the injustices in this country together. We'll share your blue blood, but we'll make sure Mother, the council, and every member of the court who lauds blue blood over red blood understands the sacrifice that comes with that blood. We're going to end the divide in this country, and I need you by my side to do it."

"We have the rest of our lives to make these changes. First, we'll get through the final years of your mother's reign and ensure she abdicates. Then we start the changes this kingdom needs. Together. You can make these changes happen, Gen. I know you can."

She looks at me with those soft, dark blue eyes, and I don't know how I ever thought I wanted to ruin this woman. This precious, kind, resilient woman has quietly endured her own struggles and become stronger for them. I know I've suffered because of Queen Penelope's decision to tear us apart, but she has too. She carries her suffering in her blood, in the curse that nearly broke her.

"I'd like that," Gen says as she takes my hand in her small, warm one. With her free hand, she guides my face to hers. Slowly—as if we have our whole lives in this place—we make love, the promise of a future brighter than our past in every stroke of our bodies, in every shared breath mingling as one.

Afterward, we settle under the blankets together, extinguish the lights, and I wrap my arms around her.

Sleep has always been something I've despised, something I've tried my damnedest to avoid. But tonight, I know that for the first time in years, I'll fall asleep a contented man.

39

Genevieve

"Get out of that bed, Genevieve!"

A voice dripping with hatred rips me from sleep, and I jolt upright against Kieran's strong, warm body.

Kieran stirs beside me with a curse, then suddenly there's a cold absence where he'd been. He's already on his feet, looming over my younger brother. "What do you think you're doing here, Gabriel?"

"Arresting you, you bastard! Get away from my sister this instant!" Gabe snarls, while I yell at him to leave the room. He doesn't move. I've never seen him look at me with such spite.

"I'm not going anywhere without Gen," Kieran says, and I yank the blankets tighter over my bare skin.

Outside the door, bootsteps thunder up the stairs, followed by a woman's voice that makes my heart stop.

"What is the meaning of all this?" Kieran demands.

"Kieran Greenbluff, you're under arrest for kidnapping the Crown Princess Genevieve Ashcroft, for blackmail, impersonation, improper use of helachite, murder, and for treason."

"No!" I shout, stepping between them. "Get out of here, Gabriel! Have you gone mad? Kieran hasn't done any of those things!"

Gabe's brown eyes burn with fury. "I should have had him arrested the moment I knew who he truly was. Now he's going to pay for his crimes. Leave the room so I can restrain him. That's an order for your safety—and find some damn clothes, Genny!"

I press back against Kieran. My smaller frame isn't much of a shield, but I know neither of them will dare harm me. "There is no condition in which I leave him right now, Gabriel!" My voice hardens. "Get out. That's an order—from your future queen."

My brother sneers, a look I've never once seen on him. "So it's true? You ran away with him? You've gotten us into this mess? Oh, that's rich. Mother's going to love that."

"Leave her out of this and get out!" I retort, shoving him with both ungloved hands.

"Mother's here, Genny. She's downstairs." Gabe points toward the door. "I'll let you get dressed, but after that I'm arresting this prick and bringing him back to Crawford in chains."

He turns and leaves without another word.

Kieran immediately pulls me into his arms, shielding me as though *I* were the one in danger, as though he wasn't the one about to be shackled and dragged away.

I twist in his hold and cling to him, feeling the frantic beat of his heart against mine. "I won't let them harm you," I insist, a promise. I mean every word. I will do anything—*anything*—to protect him.

"Gen, look at me."

I lift my gaze. His expression is unreadable, controlled.

"If your mother is here," he says quietly, "I want you to follow orders. They can drag me back to the palace in handcuffs if they like—I'm sure she's always wanted the opportunity to arrest me. But we both know these charges are fabricated. We'll sort everything out at Fairbright. Just don't give her any reason to strike at you."

"No." My words are edged with hatred. "This is wrong. She can't do this to you. She's already destroyed your life once—I won't let her do it again. And Gabe?" My throat tightens. "I hate him for going along with her."

Kieran puts his hands on my arms, stroking them gently. "You said it yourself last night. She's the law. Her decisions go unchecked—but only for a bit longer. Don't resist her here, Gen."

I nod, knowing he's right. There's so little we can do to stop the queen, especially here, surrounded by her guards—including Gabe.

"I won't let them harm you. I'll get you out. I promise you." It's a promise I will die fulfilling. I will not allow my mother to separate us now, not when I know the truth. Not when I allowed it to happen nine years ago.

We dress in a silent flurry, the guards outside our door forcing us to hurry. When we're both ready, Kieran tugs me close and kisses me, frantic and consuming. I can taste his resolve, and I can sense his fear.

It feels like he's saying goodbye.

But this isn't goodbye. I won't allow her to break us again.

We walk into the hallway, and I smooth the cheerful yellow dress I'm wearing. It's too bright, too happy a color for what's about to happen.

Gabriel waits there, handcuffs outstretched. Kieran turns his back to his former friend, letting the irons click into place around his wrists.

"Smart of you not to resist," Gabe drawls, giving Kieran a hard tug that forces him backward. "We wouldn't want to dirty your home with your red blood."

"Gabriel!" I snap. "That's enough! We are cooperating, despite Kieran doing nothing wrong. I won't stand here and watch you act like an ass."

Gabe scowls at me as he shoves Kieran forward, but Kieran doesn't react. He just walks ahead with a neutral look on his face.

"You're delusional, Genny. I think your gift has addled your mind. We know he stole you from Leland. We know he coerced you into calling off the wedding. And we have evidence he's behind the rot."

My fury reaches a breaking point. I yank my brother to a stop, the guards halting with us, and I slap Gabriel hard with my gloved hand. The silk softens the sting, but the shock on his face is satisfying.

"I left on my own accord," I hiss. "If Leland claims otherwise, he's a liar. And if Mother said it, then you—of all people—know better than to trust her word."

Gabe's expression curdles. "Because of you, there's talk that I should marry that ice queen. You'd better hope it doesn't come to pass." He points at me, his anger unfurling like a dragon taking flight. "You did this, Genevieve. You chose to marry Leland—even with your curse—and if you fled your own decision, then I have no sympathy for what happens to this man who hurt all of us when he left you."

"He didn't leave me! It was Mother!" I shout, uncaring who hears. "She wrote a terrible letter, falsified it as my own, and forced him out of the palace. *She* is the reason I carry this curse—and *she* is the reason Kieran suffered for so long!"

Gabe turns to Kieran, suspicion clouding his features. "Is this true?"

Kieran gives a tight nod. "We only realized it yesterday. And now she's doing everything she can to keep Gen and me apart—again."

Gabriel curses under his breath, and I know he understands exactly what this means. "Be that as it may, there are still countless other transgressions. I have my orders. She cannot be defied."

Then he drags the man I love—the man who's held my heart for most of my life—down the stairs like a beast to the slaughter.

40

Genevieve

"How dare you!" I shout as my mother turns to look at me. I've been dragged into the parlor, the very room where Kieran and I made love only last night. She stands on the carpet, oblivious to what happened here, but fully aware that what she's doing now is unwarranted. She wears a smug expression of victory, as if this battle is already over. Already won.

Seeing the place where we connected so deeply *defiled* by the woman determined to tear us apart is almost more than I can bear. I want to rip that condescending smile from her face. I want to make her feel even a fraction of what she's made me endure.

Outside, Kieran is being loaded into a prisoner's wagon, steel bars and bolts securing him in place. As if he were a criminal—when the true criminal is my own mother. Arresting an innocent man simply for loving her daughter.

"Control yourself, Genevieve," my mother hisses as she approaches.

"It was you all along! You sent Kieran away! You watched my heart break—not once but twice. And you're the one who's always tried to pass my gift off as love. It's not love, Mother. It's—"

The words choke me. How can I even name what she allowed to happen to me? How she let me be a victim of my own curse. How she taught me to feel ashamed of it, to believe my worth lay only in an advantageous marriage—my own safety and comfort be damned.

"Really, Genevieve." She shakes her head and glances around the room before reaching for me. "Speaking that way is beneath you. Two days with this man and you're already sounding crass. Let's go. The coach is waiting, and you have a wedding in less than a week."

I pull away from her grasp, stunned by her refusal to acknowledge a single truth. "I'm not marrying Prince Leland. He called it off, and Kieran is innocent. I won't go anywhere with you unless you release him."

Mother's eye twitches, and her hands curl into fists. "I will not be disobeyed, Genevieve. You made a commitment to Icelantica. It was your choice. I won't allow you to cast your mistakes onto one of your siblings. I knew the moment I saw that upstart Blackwell there would be trouble. His disguise was so poor I'm shocked you believed I couldn't tell it was that gardener's boy."

"You knew it was Kieran all along?"

Queen Penelope rolls her eyes. "Of course I knew. Really, Genevieve—do you take me for an idiot?"

"Then why did you allow him to stay? Even after you sent him away? Weren't you worried something like this would happen?"

"Because I didn't believe you'd be foolish enough to fall for his advances again. Wasn't it obvious he was trying to seduce you into giving up everything you've worked for?"

She turns her back, gesturing for me to follow—but I refuse. I will not be commanded like a child. Not by this woman who's dictated every breath of my life for twenty-eight years. So I stand my ground, even as she pivots back, her eye twitching harder.

"You would choose to ruin the kingdom over this man?"

"Choosing him isn't ruining the kingdom, it's strengthening it. It's unity. It's choosing all our people—bluebloods and redbloods, aristocracy and the working class."

Queen Penelope crosses her arms, her gaze icy enough to freeze the room. "You are my daughter and my heir. You will be queen in less than two years. You made a commitment to Icelantica. You cannot choose this redblooded upstart. I have evidence of his crimes—whether you claim you left willingly or not. He will be tried. He will be found guilty. That, I promise you. Forget him."

A white-hot fury tears through me. "I will never forget him. And I'll never forgive you for taking him from me once. Try to do it again, and you'll learn very quickly what it means to threaten me, Mother."

"Oh, child. Even as a grown woman, you don't understand what it is to wear the crown."

She snaps her fingers. Two guards step forward. One presses a damp cloth to my face while the other seizes my arms. I try to scream, but the sound fractures into a muffled gasp as everything fades to black.

41

Genevieve

I wake in the carriage, my body heavy, something soft propping me up.

"Shh, dear. Rest."

It's my father. He gives my arm a gentle squeeze as he helps me sit. My head throbs as I straighten, still unsure how I ended up here—or what's happened to Kieran. Gabe and my mother sit across from me, both wearing matching dour expressions.

Then it slams into me—the cloth, the guards, my mother's confession, the threat of a trial. Nausea roils through my stomach, and suddenly my corset feels far too tight.

"You had me drugged!" My words come out thick and slow, my arm heavy as I try to raise a heavy hand toward her.

"Don't be dramatic. You resisted me. Haven't we discussed this, Genevieve? I am the crown. I will not be threatened, nor will my direct orders be ignored by one of my own children."

I turn to my father, who tries desperately not to meet my eyes.

"You'll feel better soon enough, dear," my mother says.

I grab at my father's waistcoat until he finally looks at me. "How could you let her do this to me? To Kieran?"

He shakes his head, sorrow pooling across his features. "Penelope..." His voice is quiet, pleading in a way that cleaves me in two.

"She knew the risks when she chose to disobey my command!"

King Hugo's hands tremble in mine—a small betrayal of everything he's trying not to say.

"Penelope," he says again, stronger now, "had I known Genny chose to leave with him, I would never have joined you in this hunt. The man is innocent, and you know it."

My mother's eyes turn chillingly cold as she looks at my father. "Do not question my authority in this, Hugo. I have enough evidence to convict him for the rot and for that servant's death alone."

I look between them, watching the battle flare in my parents' faces, taking in Gabe's refusal even to glance my way.

"That is not true," my father says. "You would see an innocent man executed for your own pride."

Queen Penelope only shakes her head and turns defiantly toward the open window as the carriage sinks into silence. I try again to catch Gabe's eye, but he stares fixedly out the opposite side, as if I'm nothing more than a burden he's been ordered to escort home.

"I'm so relieved you're home safe!" Astoria pulls me into her arms, but I feel nothing as I make my way into the family sitting room. I want nothing more than to retreat to my own rooms and devise a plan to free Kieran, but I've been ordered—pushed—into this room with my entire family.

"I was safe with Kieran." I let my voice carry as I continue, "Mother is the reason Kieran left Fairbright all those years ago. She's the reason I thought he was dead. She tried to separate us, and she's doing it again. But I won't allow it this time."

Astoria blanches, and I can't tell whether it's because of my defiance or because she's shocked that our mother could be capable of such cruelty.

"Don't spread lies, Genevieve," Queen Penelope hisses. "I didn't do any of that to hurt you. I was protecting you, and I'm protecting you again."

My rage builds, my hands curling into tight fists around the satin of my gloves. "I do not need your protection."

Darian gives my mother a pointed look. "If Genny is telling the truth, then why arrest him? Let her have her happiness."

My mother lets out a long-suffering sigh as Gabe speaks up. "Because she chose to make an alliance with Icelantica. It's already been decided, and Genny needs to stay committed to her agreements. She can't be seen as flighty or irresponsible when she'll be queen soon."

"Thank you, Gabriel," my mother says, pressing a hand to her forehead as if our presence is too much to bear. "We need Mr. Blackwell to look the part of the guilty party. It cannot be known that Genevieve ran away with this man willingly—not if the alliance with Icelantica is to stand."

Mari has been unusually quiet, her skin still ashen from her illness. "It's wrong to charge Mr. Blackwell for a crime he didn't commit."

They keep calling Kieran *Mr. Blackwell*, as if the truth hasn't already been spoken aloud—as if they're clinging to Mother's delusion of protecting me.

Queen Penelope fixes Mari with a sharp look, her eye twitching. "You will not speak of this outside this room, Marielle. None of you will. The damage is done, and Mr. Blackwell will stand a fair trial, like any accused man. I'm saying this as your queen, not as your mother."

She rarely speaks to us *as queen*. Hearing it now makes bile rise in my throat. She's crushed her adversaries with such perfect calculation over the years that I fear she sees me as more foe than heir. And as much as I want to fight her outright, I know that will not save Kieran.

I have to be strategic. I have to beat her at her own game. I need evidence—unshakable proof—that Kieran is innocent of every crime she's manufactured.

"Now, Genny, you will go to Prince Leland tomorrow and find a way to assure him of your commitment to this engagement. We will have a wedding by the end of the week, and the alliance with Icelantica will go forward."

I put on my sweetest, most demure expression. "Mother, I will go to him, but I will not force Prince Leland to accept me."

The queen seems placated by this as she replies, "He will accept you. If not—Gabriel, be prepared to ask for the queen's hand. It cannot fall to your sisters. Oh, Genny, you've certainly made a mess of things this time!"

That's all she's ever seen in me: someone to mold into the perfect heir, and when I fall short of her impossible standards, all she sees is failure.

I look at Gabe, and after how he's treated me today, I cannot help the mocking grin I give him. His face hardens. "I will not marry that woman. I won't be forced to give up my life to move to Icelantica with someone just as frigid as her country. Genny, you'd better not muss this up any further. All of this is your doing."

I ignore him, already thinking of how I'll get Leland to see reason. And until then, I need to find a way to see Kieran—and soon. The thought of him alone in a cold cell sends goosebumps skittering over my skin.

My mother gives a curt nod. "If it's settled, I'll be retiring. This has been a most trying day."

The queen turns to leave. Astoria slips to my side. "What do you need from me?" she whispers.

"Anything you can give. I have to get Kieran out of prison—and soon."

"Of course," she murmurs as we leave the room arm in arm. Mother is too deep in thought even to notice Astoria didn't formally announce her exit.

She's plotting her next move.

And I must stay ahead of her.

Kieran's life—and our future—depend on it.

42

Kieran

*D*rip.

Drip.

Drip.

The cool stone presses against my back as I try—and fail—to shift my body out of the path of that damned water droplet falling onto my left shoulder.

Drip.

Drip.

Drip.

Every two seconds another splash—another reminder that I'm chained to the wall, left to rot for the crime of rising above my station, of reaching for what I've always wanted.

What I'll never have.

It was reckless of me to return to Fairbright Palace. I should have known this would end in chains, the woman I can't seem to let go of abandoning me once again. Because even though she promised to get me out of this mess, even though I want to believe her, there's a part of me that knows she'll choose the crown over me.

There's never been a place where I fit in her life. We're two mismatched pieces, incompatible despite every desperate attempt to force us together. It was never going to work, and now I'm going to die for it.

Leaving behind everyone who depends on me to fall once more into the decay of a kingdom that doesn't give a damn whether they live or die—so long as they strip enough helachite from the earth to fuel its wealth.

Drip.

Drip.

Drip.

I try shifting again, the irons biting into my wrists until pain radiates up my arms. My body slips against the wet stone, and I barely catch myself. With how tightly they secured me, there's no give. If I fall, I'll hang by my own weight.

Drip.

Drip.

Drip.

I think of what must come next. Surely, even now, I'll still be allowed a fair trial. That's written into the bedrock of Naseria, even if its queen rules like a tyrant.

But if I'm not granted that right, then this entire country is a façade, and Gen will never sit on the throne. Her mother will steal that future away from her, just as she's stolen every other choice Gen has ever had.

A scrape of metal at my door. A lock clanks. Hinges groan as guards rush in. They grab me in a muddled tangle of arms, and I jerk back, unsure where they're taking me. I land a hard kick on one of them; he retaliates with a blow to my stomach. My breath escapes me in a hiss, stars clouding my vision. But I don't stop fighting, not knowing where they might take me if I give in.

"Stand down if you know what's good for you," one snarls. A blade is drawn to my throat, nicking through my skin until a well of blue blood surfaces.

"He's a fucking blueblood!" the guard shouts.

"You idiot—of course he is. He's in here for misuse of helachite. I heard he caused the rot in Crawford. Wasn't seen there until he arrived."

They wrench my chains tighter, another fist connecting with my ribs. I manage to grind out, "Where are you taking me?"

"You've had a special request. We're to bring you up—but no one said what condition you needed to be in. If you want to do this the hard way, we'll be sure to bring you roughed up."

"Who?" It must be Penelope. I've been waiting for her to call for me—to rip me apart, to tell me exactly what she thinks of me: a gardener's son, a nobody who dared believe himself worthy of her daughter, of her kingdom.

I've seen it in her eyes with every interaction we've had these past weeks. The suspicion was there, and I wondered if she could see past the changes in my face to the boy I once was. But I doubted her; she's never been the type to look closely at a person. And I did my best to keep her gaze off me.

"Wouldn't you like to know?" the man sneers with a grin, and his comrade drives the back of his sword into my spine, a hard crunch of metal against flesh.

They drag me through darkened corridors, lit only by waning oil lamps, until I'm shoved into a tight room.

Leland stands with his back to the door and turns slowly, a grave look on his face.

"I wasn't expecting you," I say, the disappointment in my tone all too clear.

He nods and gestures toward a small wooden table with two rough chairs. "Leave us," Leland orders the guards.

"Your Highness, we have our orders."

His face tightens into hard lines I've never seen on my old friend. "He is a friend of the crown of Icelantica, and we will not be threatened by you."

The guards bow their heads and close the wooden door behind us.

"Well, at least you're in one piece," Leland remarks.

"Where is Gen? Is she alright?"

Leland gives a curt nod. "She's being monitored closely. We both agreed it was best for me to see you."

I nod, knowing Leland would never harm Gen or put her in danger.

His voice sharpens. "You came here knowing you wanted her back, didn't you?"

My defenses rise, but this man—this friend—may be the only one who can save me. And I betrayed him in the most egregious way possible.

So I tell him the truth.

"I came here wanting to ruin her. I've wanted my revenge for so long, but it was ill placed. It wasn't her I wanted revenge on."

Leland glances at the chains on my wrists. "Queen Penelope, is it? Yes, well, you played your cards poorly, old friend. Do you still love her?"

"I—" The words stick in my throat. I don't want to admit this to him. I can't show weakness now, and what is my love for Gen but my greatest weakness?

"Yes, you do. It's been evident for some time. For a man who's hidden so much of his past, you do a poor job hiding your feelings for her."

I huff out a breath. "I never meant to hurt you."

"Then why encourage our engagement? If not to harm me in the process?"

I turn from his harsh gaze, those Frostclaw eyes cutting straight through me. I don't have an answer—because part of me has always known this was my chance to return to Gen. Sure, I hoped to hurt her in the process, but instead I've damaged one of my closest friendships.

"What's next?" I ask. "Will Penelope bother with a trial, or go straight to placing my head on a spike?"

"There's a trial set for two days' time. Execution scheduled for three. Then Queen Penelope expects Princess Genevieve and me to marry in five."

So that's how it will be. I'll be dead and out of the way in time for the happy nuptials. I think of Gen—how she won't be able to control her gift, or Leland's—and a vicious urge flares in me. I want to hurt him, to drag him down with me for even considering touching her again.

"You're going through with the wedding?" I seethe. "Even with her gift?"

He shakes his head sharply. "Of course not. The queen is mad to think I'd bind myself to Genevieve after knowing what her curse does to both of us. Our gifts are incompatible. I make her lose her ability to reason, and she turns me into something I'm not—something I could never tolerate in myself. It would be disastrous."

"When do you plan to tell the queen?"

"You must truly love her if your questions are all about her and not your impending trial and execution." He exhales. "I've hired a team of lawyers—billed to Blackwell Industries, naturally. They'll meet you in the morning to prepare your case and gather evidence to clear your name. Is there anything you can give me now to pass along to Genevieve? She's desperate to help your case and see you freed."

I think of the rot spreading, the servant's death. "Someone is misusing helachite in the palace. Find them and you'll have your answers. As for kidnapping Gen—you can attest to what really happened."

His jaw clenches. "My word has already been questioned. Servants claim you forced her into the carriage while I stood by. Some think we were working together. And Queen Penelope has threatened to use the accusation against me if I refuse to marry Genevieve."

"And what does Queen Kalise say to that? I can't imagine she tolerates her devoted brother being threatened by another monarch."

He looks away before sighing. "There's something Kalise isn't telling me. I think Penelope is holding some knowledge over her. I already signed the marriage contract and expected to be engaged to Princess Astoria or Princess Marielle. It wasn't ideal, but I was the one who added that clause. But instead my sister keeps insisting she must marry Prince Gabriel."

I mull that over. Penelope will do whatever it takes to get what she wants. But why is she so intent on joining the two countries when, for all intents and purposes, it appears she won't relinquish power when the time comes anyway?

It doesn't matter right now if I can't get free. Leland's right—my thoughts went first to Gen's safety. But I need to know my chances.

"Are the lawyers good?"

Leland gives me a long-suffering look. "Do you think I'd choose anyone second-rate? They're the best in Naseria. But there's little time to prepare. The queen ensured it."

A knock on the door. The guards step in.

"Time's up."

I don't fight. Not now—not when I finally know there are people on my side, people willing to fight for me even after everything I've done to them. It's a strange feeling, almost foreign after clawing my way out of the mines alone.

"Tell Gen to be careful," I say. "Tell her not to do anything that could put her safety at risk. I'll see her soon."

The guards drag me from the room as Leland promises he will. I should have told him to say more, but speaking the words aloud feels too much like goodbye.

43

Genevieve

My hands shake as I meet with the team of lawyers representing Kieran. Leland must notice, because he gives my gloved hand a small squeeze before releasing it.

One of the lawyers says, "The charges brought against him would take weeks to build a proper case for. If the queen is moving this quickly, she must have been collecting evidence for some time."

"What do you suggest we do?" I ask, trying not to give up hope. Trying with all my heart to do everything I can to save Kieran, to not betray his trust again.

I begged Gabe last night to let me see him, pleaded outside his rooms, but he wouldn't tell me where Kieran was being held. Instead, Astoria made him see reason, and Gabe allowed Leland to know Kieran's location—giving him the opportunity he'd taken from me.

Leland assured me Kieran wasn't injured, but there was so much he wasn't saying, his gift hanging in the air like cloying perfume meant to soothe me. It didn't. It only sharpened my anxiety.

One of the lawyers clears his throat. "We need to identify the person responsible for the rot and the murder. Once we have that, we can move forward with clearing his name of the other charges."

"The kidnapping too?"

The lawyer examines a paper in front of him, adjusting his spectacles. "Yes. That should be easy to refute. The court will listen to testimony from yourself and Prince Leland. It should outweigh a servant's accusation. You are, after all, the future monarch. In two years' time you could erase this trial from record entirely if you wished. But..."

Prince Leland frowns. "But what?"

"If we don't find the perpetrator tampering with helachite, we won't have a strong case for his innocence. And then there's the matter of false identity. He's guilty there—there's no denying it."

"So you'll do nothing to fight those charges?" I ask.

"Your Highness, he's been using an assumed name for years. Records go back eight years to when he first used the name Morris Blackwell."

"How is choosing a different identity a crime?" What harm is there in changing who you are? He's spent years trying to let go of his former self, so much so that he's no longer the Kieran Greenbluff he once was.

"It becomes difficult to verify that he owns everything he claims. Taking on a nom de plume raises questions—are there other crimes he may have committed under that name?"

"Stop this." The words come out sharp, steel-lined. All the men look at me. "Kieran has been running from his past because of *me*—not because he's guilty of anything—and I will do everything in my power to clear his name. This is my fault, and I won't lose him again."

Leland's touch is gentle on my arm, the silk of his gloves a soft weight against my skin. "It isn't your fault. It's the queen's. And we *will* get him out of this. I persuaded Gabriel to use his influence with the guards and soldiers to search for the true killer. Your sisters and my sister are doing all they can as well. Someone will come forward with the evidence we need."

I take in a deep breath, trying to ease the rising panic in my chest. We only have one day before the trial.

"When are you going to see him?" I ask the lawyers.

"After we finish up here. We just need to gather our notes so we have something more tangible to present to him. I'm not going to give you false confidence, Princess. We need to know who is behind the rot."

"I want to see him too. I need to assure him I'm doing all I can to get him out of there."

Leland shakes his head. "That's not a good idea. Even having you at this meeting is a liability to Kieran's safety. If your mother is intent on carrying out this false trial, we don't need to give her any other reason to feel threatened by your interest in him. Let her believe we'll have our wedding. Let her see us working together to free our friend, but don't give her cause to assume you'll go against her wishes for your future."

A lump forms in my throat as I think about Kieran alone in a cell, wondering if I would give up on him again. I can't stomach the thought of him believing I would betray him again—not after everything that's happened between us.

I push down my fears, nodding as I stand. "Prince Leland, will you escort me to my rooms before accompanying the lawyers to Kieran's cell?"

He looks at me with such tenderness, and once again I wonder why I couldn't fall for this kind, good man. Why has no one fallen for Prince Leland Frostclaw, when he has a heart so willing to give?

But the truth has always stood in front of me, just beyond my line of sight. I gave away my heart long ago, and there's nothing anyone could do to take it from Kieran. It's always been his.

"Of course," Leland says, offering me his arm. I bow to the lawyers before adding, "Please keep me informed of any updates, and I'll do all I can to find what we're looking for."

As we enter the hallway, Leland leans close enough for only me to hear. "He trusts you. He knows you won't abandon him."

"I just wish I could tell him myself," I admit. "Will you tell him I—will you tell him I love him?"

He nods quickly. "We'll get him out, and you'll have all the happiness you've always deserved with him."

I squeeze his arm in a friendly gesture, and he meets my gaze. "You deserve happiness and love too, Leland. You, more than any of us."

He looks away before stopping at my door. "Yes, well, that isn't as easy to come by as one may hope."

44

Kieran

The lawyers left me hours ago, without the false certainty that this trial will end in my favor. To put it bluntly, they don't know how they'll secure a win—not without evidence proving I'm innocent of the more heinous crimes against me.

"Another visitor," the guard says as he opens my cell. He holds out shorter cuffs and ankle restraints. "Just a precaution, but since you've been more cooperative, I don't think we'll need to result to violence this time around."

I scowl but let the man cuff me without a fight. "Is it the queen?" Only one of the royal family would warrant this treatment. Not even Leland got this.

"Her Majesty has granted you an audience."

"I'm to be brought to the palace?" I ask, hoping I might catch a glance of Gen, at least the comfort of knowing she's safe.

"Yup. They're sure making a fuss over you. I'd say just set the gallows and be done with it, but you're to be given a fair trial. No one will deny justice was served when you hang."

They march me through the dark, meandering tunnels of the prison until I'm loaded into a prisoner's wagon. The drive is jostling and harsh as we rattle through the back alleys of Crawford, avoiding any place where a prisoner's wagon might disrupt the pristine image the Ashcrofts work so hard to maintain. We reach the rear of the palace, where I'm unloaded like cargo and hauled through a set of servant's stairs. I haven't walked these old wooden steps in years, and the familiarity of them—of all the nights my father led me to supper or to evening entertainment with the other servants before guiding me back to our small cottage outside the palace—hits with a vividness that stings.

He's been gone for years, and though I've tried to bury the painful memories of our last months together, it's the good ones with their laughter and warmth that hurt most.

We exit into the Ashcroft family's private floors, and I'm led to the queen's office.

Queen Penelope doesn't bother lifting her head from the paperwork on her desk. She simply waves me forward. The chains around my ankles clink with every step. There's no seat for me. No polite gesture. Nothing like the previous weeks' meetings.

"Leave us," she says to the guards, who bow and exit. "One night in a cell and you already smell foul," she mutters, bringing a handkerchief to her face.

"I shouldn't have been subjected to a single night in your prison," I retort, refusing to let her insult hang unchallenged.

At last she meets my gaze, eyes tight above the handkerchief. "Your first mistake was coming back. I told you never to return. Whether you thought it was Genny telling you or not makes little difference. You weren't wanted here."

I don't let my emotions show, knowing she caused my grief and pain all those years ago. She deserves none of it.

"Your second mistake was meddling with Princess Genevieve. She's above you in both station and comportment. You never deserved her, and I'll be damned if I see my daughter married to a redblood servant. Oh—wait. That's right. A *blueblood*. A deceiving, malicious blueblood with intent to destroy the crown."

I say nothing. She's wrong about many things, but she's right about one: Gen is better than me in every way. If she offered me even a fraction of her heart, I'd worship the ground she walks on.

"You're known as a redblood, and that blue blood of yours will work against you in the trial. I know you and Prince Leland are scheming—even trying to involve Genny. Stop it. I have enough evidence against you that no lawyer on the continent could clear your name. In three days' time I'll be rid of you."

I meet her harsh gaze. "If you were so certain of your evidence, you wouldn't feel the need to tell me any of this."

She laughs. "I'm telling you to give up. You're beat. You'll be the one ruined—not Genevieve."

A small part of me fractures, knowing the odds are against me. Getting out of this alive is unlikely, but I won't show that to this woman. The last thing I want is for her to see my true feelings.

"If that's all, I'd prefer to return to my cell," I say, turning my back to her.

"You won't see her again! I'm making sure of it!" the queen shouts as I reach the door, thumping my arm against the barred frame.

It will be far too soon if I ever have to see Penelope Ashcroft again.

45

Genevieve

I pace my room—back and forth, back and forth—the nervous energy too much for me to contain.

Tomorrow morning is the trial, and we've found nothing that will save Kieran, despite a whole team of lawyers, loyal servants, the Frostclaws, and my siblings searching. I even sent word to Clementine to casually ask around about the source of the rot, and she's already orchestrated half of Crawford to seek information on the misuse of helachite.

Even Gabriel has changed his mind, coming to me privately to apologize. He sees that I love Kieran—sees that I can't imagine losing him again—and he feels sympathy for me. Or as much sympathy as Gabriel can muster, with his own fears of marriage to Queen Kalise hanging over him.

Queen Kalise has given her support for Lelend's withdrawal from our engagement, though I can still see her disappointment. Perhaps there are worse fates for Gabriel than marrying a queen.

"Will you please stop pacing, Genny?" Astoria asks as she brings me a calming cup of herbal tea.

I shake my head. "We're running out of time. If we don't find a solution, Kieran will be charged with every crime Mother's holding against him."

"Wearing a hole in the carpet isn't going to save him."

I nod, trying to stifle the anxious energy coursing through me. "I can't lose him again, Astoria. I don't think I can survive it."

She gives her head a small shake. "You're stronger than that. Soon you'll be the one making decisions for this country. Mother thinks she acts for the good of the kingdom, but you actually will."

I press a hand to my forehead. I can't even think about the responsibilities looming over me. "Did Mari find anything out from the maids who discovered the servant's body?"

Astoria's lips tighten into a scowl. "Mother pulled her away, said she needed her for something. When Mari came back, she complained of headaches. She still isn't well."

I nod. Recovery has been painfully slow for Mari since her exposure to the rot. We're grateful she's alive at all, but she hasn't slept soundly in weeks and has grown more withdrawn. I wish I had time to help her, but Kieran needs me more than ever.

"Will you check in on her?" I ask.

"Of course. I should go sit with her now."

A knock at the garden entry to my room sends a sharp pang of hope through my chest.

"What was that?" Astoria asks, but my heart is already pounding as I cross the room.

Gabriel steps inside, and the hope drains from me as he closes the door. "How did you get through that entrance?" I demand. No one but Kieran and I have ever used the outside door. Only we have the key.

"I came to show you just how sorry I am. Astoria, you may want to leave."

He swings the door fully open, revealing a tattered Kieran. Dark circles shadow his eyes and his skin looks ashen. A bruise darkens his exposed arm, and a ring of red welts marks where the irons bit into his flesh.

I run to him, throwing myself into his arms. He holds me tightly, and my cheeks are wet before I even realize I'm crying. A part of me feared I'd never hold him again—that our time together at Huntley House was the last time I'd feel his arms around me, a bittersweet memory of our too-short reunion.

My lips brush the scruff on his cheek, then his dry lips. "Are you alright? Have you been hurt?" I ask, even though I can see from his demeanor that he's not himself.

"I'll be okay. It's just good to hold you," he murmurs, lowering his forehead to mine.

A throat clears behind us, and I turn to see my siblings waiting.

"I'll be back before daybreak. Meet me at the outside door, and don't delay. I've paid a fortune to get you out, but we must have you back before the guards change."

Kieran releases me and crosses to my brother, pulling him into a tight hug. "Thank you. You've given us a final chance to be together."

Gabe shakes his head. "Don't talk like that yet. We'll get you out."

He escorts Astoria from the room, leaving us alone.

46

Kieran

The door clicks shut, and Gen and I are finally alone. There's a tentative stillness in her body as she looks at me from across the room, her face a mix of disbelief and desire.

"I didn't think this would be possible," she says quietly as I move closer. "I tried, Kieran—I tried so hard to find out who caused the rot, but we're running out of time. We have no leads, and the trial is tomorrow, and I don't know what else to do." Her voice breaks, and it feels like my own heart cracks with it as I pull her into my chest, her tears seeping through my thin shirt.

"You're doing so well, Princess. You've done everything you can. Tonight all I want is to be with you." I can't tell her this could be the end of us, just as we thought we were getting a fresh start. The reality of that is a cruel, bitter medicine I can't bear to swallow. Only two days ago she was mine in my own home. Now I'll most likely lose her forever.

She pulls back, a frantic look in her eyes. "I can't lose you again."

Before I can speak, she goes to her wardrobe and begins pulling out clothing, piling them on the floor. Her eyes are wide, her face pale and strained.

"What are you doing, Gen?" I ask cautiously.

"We should run. We should leave Naseria, flee the country together now. We can be at the border by morning."

I shake my head. It's fucking selfish how badly I want to say yes and run away with her, but I know I will not run again. I will never run—not after letting myself be cast aside nine years ago.

No. We have to face this, fight our own battles, and accept that tonight may be our last night together. I won't waste a moment of it making plans to flee.

I rest my hand on her back as she tears through her belongings. "Gen, Princess, don't do this. We aren't running. You have too much at stake, and I know how important the crown is to you."

She pushes back, insisting it's our only chance, insisting she won't live without me—and for a heartbeat I fear that if I die in two days' time, she might follow through on that claim.

But we both know my Gen is steel forged in the hottest fires. She's too stubborn and too determined to lead this country into something better to lose herself over my death.

I pull her into me, feeling the fight drain from her body as she cries. Slowly, she softens, her sobs tapering into muffled breaths.

"You're right," she finally says. "Even if we did flee, my mother would never let us go. She'd never let us slip into anonymity. If only because, in her eyes, it isn't my right to live without the crown. But, Kieran, I *cannot* lose you. I will fight for you until the very end. There must be a way to free you from these charges."

I nod, giving her the reassurance she needs. "The lawyers are working through the night. Leland is helping, and I think they're building a strong case that I couldn't possibly be guilty of all these crimes. We won't stop fighting."

All of these things are partly true. The case still isn't strong—not without the guilty party coming forward. Not when the queen is determined to see me convicted. Naseria's justice system becomes nothing but a façade if the monarch has a vested interest in the outcome.

She looks at me as though she doesn't fully believe a word I'm saying. Good. She needs that skepticism. She should be questioning everything, because if her mother can do this to me, then what has she done to others? No matter what happens, I need Gen to pick up the pieces and keep fighting for what she knows is right.

And selfishly, I just want to move on from this conversation long enough to savor my last hours with her.

I close the distance between us, sliding my hands around her full hips. "How do you want to spend our time together tonight, Princess?"

A shadow of a smile touches her lips, though the weight of tomorrow is still there in her eyes. "You're right. I don't want to spend it worrying."

I'm not letting her off the hook that easily. I want her to say it. "That didn't answer my question."

A blush rises in her cheeks, a delicious shade of rosy pink. "You'll make me answer you?" she asks, pressing her body against mine, her breasts brushing my chest. "I think you know what I'd like to do."

I grin down at her, my nose so close to hers I can feel the warmth of her breath. "Details, Princess. I want to hear it."

"Fine then. I want to make love to you until dawn breaks. I want to give you my body and take yours for my own, knowing it could be our last night together."

I let out a hum of approval as I draw her into a kiss. She's so soft, her scent sweet and delicate, and the idea of my filthy body defiling her makes shame flicker through me. I pull back, heat flooding my face as embarrassment washes over me.

"I'm filthy. Let me clean up first," I insist as she tries to pull me back toward her. My words finally sink in—or maybe it's my stench—because she steps back.

"Of course. I'm sorry, Kieran. I should have known you'd want a bath. You're being treated like an animal in that prison."

She leaves my side and walks into her bathroom. I follow without a word as we approach the large clawfoot tub. Of course the crown princess has indoor plumbing, a luxury that is rare in most homes. She turns the tap and begins filling the tub, pouring in scented soaps until frothy bubbles rise.

After she finishes with the bath, she turns back to me. There's a quiet resolve on her face as she asks, "Can I wash you? I just... I want to take care of you, Kieran."

I dip my head in silent agreement and begin tugging off my dirty, bloodied clothes. The warm water stings my healing wounds, and I hiss as I lower myself into the heated tub.

The water is deep enough, and the bubbles ample enough, that most of me is covered. I expect Gen to kneel beside me, but when I look over my shoulder she's shedding her own clothes before slipping into the bath as well. The water sloshes over the rim, making a mess of the marble tiles. She reaches back to turn off the tap, then faces me with a washcloth in hand.

"I wasn't expecting you to join me, Gen. The water will be dirty from me."

She huffs softly. "That doesn't matter. I need to be close to you, and I'm not going to miss an opportunity to join you in this tub."

Legs outstretched, she settles across from me, and I feel my cock twitch awake at the contact, at the way her breasts bob beneath the warm bubbles.

Slowly, she leans forward with the washcloth and begins wiping it across my skin. Her bare body glides against mine in a tantalizing rhythm as she works the bubbles over me. Fuck, how have I lived without her touch? How can I die knowing how much time we lost?

She bathes me with a tenderness and attention that makes my heart ache. It's as if she's memorizing every part of me, storing up this precious time for the moment when it's gone for good.

Her hands slide to my shoulders, turning me so my back rests against her front. She massages her fingers through my hair, scraping gently down the nape of my neck. Frothy water pours down my shoulders before she turns me again, guiding me back until my head rests against the edge of the tub.

I let my eyes fall closed, her touch soothing me, until I hear the soft slap of the washcloth hitting the floor. Gen's hands take over where the cloth left off, exploring and memorizing every part of me, from my forehead down to the tips of my toes. The slow, deliberate mapping of my body under her palms has me growing greedy for her touch on the one part of me she's avoided.

Finally, Gen's hands wrap around my aching cock, pumping firmly enough to drag a groan from my lips. She teases the tip before sliding her hands down to the base, the slick soap making her strokes threaten to unravel the last thread of composure I'm clinging to.

I lose the restraint I've been trying to hold onto and bring my hands to her hips, rocking her forward so my cock grazes her bare clit. My grip tightens on her ample ass as Gen sloshes water over the edge of the tub, rubbing herself along my length.

"I've never done this in the water," she says breathlessly.

"We don't have to, if you don't want to."

She reaches down and wraps her hand around my cock, her grip sure as she gives a quick shake of her head. "No. Show me."

I haven't even touched her slit yet, but she's already shifting into position, my cock nudges against her sweet heat. Water isn't conducive to this, especially with the tub's sides restricting our legs, but she's already so wet for me that she lowers herself onto my shaft, her core taking me in as she moves with shallow thrusts.

"Fuck me, Gen—you don't need any instruction. You're perfect, Princess."

She gives me a smirk, though her heavy-lidded eyes can't hide the lust burning there. The shallow cant of her hips grows more exploratory, more desperate, and I meet her rhythm, water sloshing over the edge with every movement.

Our fit is tight, and I'm still not fully seated in her. I don't know how much more I can take in this position as Gen steadily notches me deeper.

Finally, I can't stand it anymore, and I lift her off my throbbing cock as I stand. Gen lets out a soft cry of surprise as I grab a towel to dry us. Then I pull her into my arms, her ass in the air, and carry her from the tub into her bedroom. I let her fall onto the bed with a gentle thump before caging my body around hers.

Gen spreads her legs, welcoming my hips as I slide home, fully sheathing myself in her tight core in one stroke.

We both gasp at the shock of it, the perfection of our joined bodies, and I take in the sight of her naked form beneath me, my cock buried deep.

"Kieran!" My name breaks from her lips like a plea as I pull out, only to drive into her again and again. Her hands grip my back, fingers digging in, and from the strength of her hold I know she'll leave marks.

I welcome them. I *need* them—need to be branded by this woman who holds my heart, who I may very well lose again in only two days' time.

I can feel the exact moment Gen lets go—the pleasure pulsing around my cock, my name torn from her lips—and I let myself come with her, both of us lost in our shared need for one another. Both of us desperate for this final connection.

Because nothing is guaranteed tomorrow.

After I pull out of her, I lower my head to her soft belly and watch my seed spill down her thighs. This cannot be the end of us. I cannot lose tomorrow.

"Kieran." Gen's voice is only a shred of what it was moments ago, a whisper where a shout had been.

"Yes, my darling," I answer.

"I can't lose you. I don't know how I'll survive it. Come back to me."

I want to promise her I'll beat this, that I'll fight my way back to her no matter the cost. But she knows the stakes. She knows exactly what I'm up against, and I won't give her false hope.

Instead, I tuck her beneath the covers and draw her close. "I'll love you always, Gen. No matter what happens tomorrow."

Before the darkness fades to silvery dawn, I leave my love's side, knowing my fate is no longer with hers.

47

Kieran

The air buzzes with anticipation as the warden walks me toward the front of the courtroom. People gawk and whisper as I pass, making no effort to hide what they think of me. I keep my gaze fixed ahead, unwilling to be distracted by any of them.

Still, my eyes drift to the seats behind me. Gen promised she'd be here, supporting me through this. Leland sits there, giving me a reassuring smile—but Gen's seat is empty. She didn't come. After all her promises between kisses, her word feels like a bitter falsehood. In fact, none of the Ashcroft family is present, neither on my side nor across the aisle. A numbness settles over me, and my lawyer gives me a stern nod as we take our seats.

The judge enters and we rise. I try to focus on his words, but a ringing builds in my ears as the reality sinks in: she isn't coming. I sit mechanically, barely aware of the motion, until a steady hand presses my shoulder. I turn to see Leland.

"She'll be here," he murmurs. "I know it. Just wait."

My throat bobs and I give him a curt nod. His attempt at reassurance does nothing to ease my nerves.

The judge begins reading the accusations against me. A gnawing dread settles in my gut as I realize there will be no second chance. Penelope has likely barred Gen from attending.

At last the list of charges ends, and the judge addresses me. "How do you plead?"

The words leave me in a quiet rasp. "Not guilty, Your Honor."

He turns to the jury and, in full view of the court, says, "The queen has a special interest in this case and wishes the verdict read by day's end. I trust you understand what that means when she makes personal requests." The jury—a group of blueblood aristocrats by the look of them—offers solemn nods of understanding. One of my lawyers mutters a curse under his breath.

Our eyes meet. We both know this will be near impossible to win—not with the charges stacked this high, not without proof of my innocence, not with a judge and jury already leaning toward guilt.

The prosecutor calls his first witness, a man I don't recognize. From his manner and clothing he's clearly a servant, a fact that becomes even more evident as he recounts his version of Gen's alleged abduction.

"And did the princess resist his advances?" the prosecutor asks.

The man nods. "Yes. She went to him, possibly to say goodbye, but he snatched her up with his own two hands and dragged her into the carriage. She fought back, but Prince Leland ordered us to stand down, so we did. Before we knew it, the carriage was gone."

A ripple of gasps spreads through the crowd. The distortion of events spirals into something comically diabolical, painting me as some rogue redblood out to harm the princess. Leland is made to look like a dithering accomplice, a puppet working at my side to help me get my hands on Gen.

Finally, my lawyer steps forward for cross-examination. He questions the servant about Gen's body language toward Leland, how she behaved as she approached the carriage, and why, if this was truly a kidnapping, he didn't inform the palace immediately.

To that question, the servant replies, "I've seen enough in the palace to know when to keep my head down and my mouth shut."

The audience laughs—servants are notorious gossips—and my lawyer points out that if the man truly feared for the princess's safety, he would have alerted someone about the kidnapping.

A few jurors nod in agreement, and a thin thread of relief loosens in my chest.

Next, our team calls Leland forward. He's a prince, a powerful blueblood; surely his word must carry weight with this jury.

But as he's questioned about his relationship with Gen, frustration prickles beneath my skin—at him, at her, at the political game they played in the name of their countries, at how Gen was willing to sacrifice so much, even her own comfort and safety, for Naseria.

I hate this place. I hate what it's done to her. And a desperate part of me wonders if she's abandoned me again. Irrational, yes—Gen has never given up on me—but the fear is there all the same.

When the prosecution begins their questioning, I see the shift immediately. The jury doesn't believe a word Leland says.

"Your gift has a way of relaxing a person against their will," the prosecutor says. "Potent, even without touch. Are you capable of manipulating, say, the judge or jury in this case?"

Leland stares at him, stunned. Of course he *could*—but he never would. He's always been honest to a fault, fair and just, never willing to use his gift to compromise others. It's why he let Gen go. It's why the very idea of marrying her became abhorrent once he realized what their combined gifts did to each other.

He says as much, speaking of honor and integrity, but the doubt in the room is unmistakable. He was my strongest chance at freedom, and now his word has been compromised.

The judge calls for a short break. I turn to Leland and thank him for everything he's done. There's a hum of chatter on the prosecution's side—too much confidence, too many proud smiles.

We suspected they had a secret witness, but I'm not prepared for Princess Marielle Ashcroft to approach the stand.

Dread sinks in my chest. They won't have to work hard to prove my guilt with an Ashcroft willing to speak against me.

48

Genevieve

"Genny, please, I have to speak to you," Mari says as she trails after me through my rooms. I'm too nervous to sit still. I'm due in the courtroom in minutes, and I don't have time to listen to her unless it's directly about the trial.

"Is this about the trial?"

The guilt in her eyes makes a terrifying realization dawn on me. She could be used against Kieran. It would make sense. She's always been a thorn in our mother's side—the most unruly child of the Ashcroft brood—and always eager to ingratiate herself. And she was injured by the rot during Leland's and my engagement party.

"Tell me you're not speaking for the prosecution," I demand. The words come out sharp as daggers, and Mari flinches.

She shakes her head but says, "I don't want to, but I know things, and Mother expects me to speak up. If I don't, she's threatened to have me put on trial. I cannot stand trial, Genny. I'm not strong enough for that. You can't understand."

Then I see it—a tiny patch of rot where her bare hand touched my wardrobe.

"Mari, what are you not telling me?"

"It's me," she whispers. "I'm the cause of the rot. Or rather, Mother's made me into the cause. I didn't mean to kill that servant, I promise. I haven't meant to do any of the harm here or in Crawford. But if I admit I'm guilty, Mother will have me put on trial and killed. She's told me so herself."

My face scrunches in disbelief, and I back away from her. "You're the one spreading the rot? But how is that possible? You don't even have a gift."

Then I remember the stories of miners exposed to helachite at dangerous levels, the way Kieran described the agony of being forced into a gift, the scar on his face marking him as a turned blueblood.

"Mother forced it on you, didn't she?" I ask.

Mari's face crumples in a pained agreement.

"At first I wanted to do it. It was her suggestion, but I agreed. I didn't want to be like Gabriel—always taunted for being a useless spare. Then it hurt. It hurt so badly I wanted to stop, but Mother wouldn't allow it. She kept pushing me and pushing me until I became gifted with a touch that spreads death."

I shake my head, a cold certainty settling over me. There are no circumstances under which I allow my mother to continue ruling this family or this country.

"You have to share the truth. You have to speak up, or Kieran will die for something he isn't guilty of."

"I don't know if I can do it, Genny. I'm frightened."

"Mother's time as Queen of Naseria has run short. She must be held accountable for her actions and step down. I will protect you and do everything in my power to make Naseria the kingdom it should be. But you have to be brave, Mari. Promise me you'll tell the truth."

Her eyes flood with tears, and she nods. "I will. I promise."

I turn toward the door. There's hardly a moment to lose, and I can't risk the trial beginning without me. It would devastate Kieran if I wasn't there beside him, and I'm already late.

"Wait, Genny!" Mari calls. I turn back. "You're going to be the best queen Naseria has ever had."

A tinge of doubt courses through me, and she must see it, because she adds, "No, it's true. You actually care for your people, not see them as a means to gain power. That's something unique."

I bite my lower lip. I don't have a choice but to be the queen this country needs. Despite my insecurities about ruling justly, I know my time has come early. Queen Penelope must step down for what she's done to this country.

49

Kieran

I release a slow breath, trying to steady myself for whatever Marielle is about to say against me, knowing this will be the final blow to our case.

A tap on my shoulder pulls me out of my thoughts, and I turn to see Gen standing behind me. Her face is radiant, far too enthusiastic for what I'm about to face. Has she seen that Marielle is the one who took her seat in the witness stand?

I look at her, wishing more than anything that I could touch her, hold her, and reassure myself that everything is going to be alright.

"We did it, Kieran!" she whispers, the pure joy in her voice lifting my defeated spirits. "It's Mari. She's going to clear everything up, and you'll be free."

I give her a curt nod, not sure I can believe the woman standing for the prosecution will be my saving grace.

She murmurs something to Leland, and his face pales. It seems he's also skeptical of Mari's ability to save me.

Of course it's a fucking Ashcroft who holds my life in their hands. And of course it's one I've barely spared a thought for. Marielle Ashcroft has always seemed like a flighty, silly girl, more focused on getting her mother's attention through chaos and destruction than any of her siblings were. Now that chaotic young woman is supposed to save me.

She's sworn in, and the prosecution begins their questioning. As I suspected, they start with the disastrous spread of the rot at Gen and Leland's engagement party.

"You were personally affected by the rot that night, is that correct?" the prosecutor asks.

"Yes, I was. But not as you may think."

The prosecutor gives her a quizzical look. This isn't what they discussed, clearly. "How so, Princess Marielle? It's well known you came in contact with the rot and were ill until very recently."

"Yes, but I was actually the cause of the spreading rot." Her voice is steadier than anyone would expect from a woman declaring her own guilt. A shocked inhale sweeps through the room, but Marielle continues. "I spread the rot on the stage, and I am also the one who killed the servant. It wasn't intentional, I just—"

She falters, and the crowd rises into a crescendo of chaotic conversation.

"Order! Order in the court!" the judge shouts, slamming his gavel. Slowly, the room settles. The prosecutor huddles with his team, no doubt scrambling to recover.

But Mari goes on, her confidence returning. "I killed the servant, but I never meant to. I lost control of my gift."

The judge speaks next, as confused as the rest of us. Marielle Ashcroft is known as one of two giftless children of the king and queen. "Princess Marielle, are we to assume that you are, in fact, a gifted blueblood?"

"I am, but not naturally. My mother has been forcing helachite into my veins since I was twenty-one. Eventually it transformed me into someone with power, but it manifested as a spreading rot. The queen did this because she said I had no value as a fourth-born daughter without a gift. I'm not responsible for all the rot throughout the kingdom—there must be others like me, forced into helachite over-exposure. I've only been the cause of what happened in Crawford."

She turns and looks directly at me. "I'm sorry, Mr. Blackwell. You shouldn't have been put on trial for my wrongdoings. I hope you'll forgive me."

The room erupts again, and no amount of shouting or gaveling from the judge can rein in the noise.

Gen puts her hand on my shoulder, giving it a squeeze before turning. I stand and pull her close, holding her tightly across the bench between us.

Finally, the room calms to a low murmur. The judge is red-faced and panting from his efforts to restore order, and guards have been called in.

The prosecution and my lawyer approach the bench, locked in a heated discussion with the judge.

Gen walks forward like she owns the courtroom, her confidence a sight to behold, and at last I feel myself relax as the tension drains from my body.

My princess has saved me.

50

Genevieve

The prosecution looks at me like a dog who's taken a firm scolding when I insist that Kieran be freed. He's still trying to come up with a plan to carry out my mother's wishes.

"It doesn't matter if he's not guilty of spreading the rot or the murder. He's still guilty of kidnapping the crown princess."

I scoff. The ridiculous charges can't stand when I'm the one who was allegedly kidnapped.

"I am ready to stand as a witness for the defense."

The judge shakes his head. "That isn't necessary. I see now that this case was a cover-up for the queen's own guilt. We have much bigger issues to face than whether you left willingly with your lover or not, and from your word, Your Highness, I have no doubt the kidnapping charges were the one thing the queen could use to arrest Mr. Greenbluff. As far as I'm concerned, he's free to go."

My heart leaps, and I can't help turning back to Kieran and smiling at him. The dread he's been holding melts from his face as I mouth, "You're free!"

"Thank you, Your Honor." I start to leave, but he calls me back, a deep frown creasing his face.

"If what Princess Marielle says is true, she will have to be tried for murder and misuse of helachite. Queen Penelope will also face trial. This is unprecedented. We haven't had a monarch face trial since the War of the Blood. The council needs to be informed."

"It's already been done. My siblings and I met privately with the council this morning, laying out the misuse of Queen Penelope's power and the crimes committed against the people of Naseria. The queen is currently being convinced of her need to abdicate. As for Princess Marielle, she's committed a crime, but she's also been heavily influenced by my mother. Justice must be served, but it's my hope that her punishment reflects her status as a victim as well."

"Very well, Your Highness. I must say, if this is an example of your forward-thinking leadership, I believe Naseria will be in good hands."

He bows, and I give him a small curtsy before turning toward Kieran. It takes all my self-control not to run to him. I don't run. I walk, head held high, back straight, like the queen I am.

But when I reach him, I drop every pretense of royalty, throwing my arms around him as he wraps me close. "You're free!" I cry, his embrace everything I've hoped for.

Kieran's hands shake as he cups my face, his eyes brimming with tears. "You amazing, brilliant woman. You did it."

Then his lips press to mine in a bone-melting kiss that is anything but proper. I don't care. I open myself to him, his tongue meeting mine in an eager greeting. He's free and safe and mine—forever mine.

We pull back only when I realize people are clapping and cheering for us. "He's free!" I shout, and the room bursts into applause. A hand grazes my back, and I turn to see Leland smirking.

"I should still be angry with you, Morris—Kieran, I mean—but I can't seem to stay mad at you. I wish you both the best." Then he slips away through the crowd.

"There's someone you need to speak to," I tell Kieran, taking his hand and leading him toward Mari, who sits deep in conversation with several men I don't recognize.

"Excuse us, please," I say. The men bow and step aside, leaving the three of us alone.

"You know how to clear a room, Princess," Kieran quips. I could cry at the sound of him teasing me again, knowing how desperate we both were last night.

"Mari, how are you doing?" I ask.

She closes her eyes, her hands trembling slightly in her lap. When she finally opens them, she replies, "I feel good that my word got Mr. Blackwell—Kieran—free. But those men were from the court. They're saying my testimony will be used against me in a trial. Genny, I never wanted to harm anyone! Everything has been so uncontrollable since my gift manifested. I shouldn't be trusted with anyone."

I squeeze her shoulder, feeling the tension there. "Don't be frightened. I'll protect you. I have a plan."

She looks at me with earnest green eyes. "I trust you, Genny."

"Thank you, Princess Marielle, for everything you've done for me today. Your bravery saved my life."

Mari takes Kieran's hands in her gloved ones. "I could never let my mother harm another person the way she's harmed me. And I know you both deserve a chance to be together."

"Should we get out of here?" I ask, and Mari gives a quick, wary nod.

"Shouldn't I be arrested by now?" she says.

"It will be more complicated than that to arrest a member of the royal family, whether that's just or not. You're safe, Mari. If anyone should be concerned, it's Mother."

Kieran takes my hand as I lace my other with Mari's, and together we head toward a side exit. We slip out unnoticed.

I've never felt so relieved to leave a place as I do leaving the courtroom.

51

Genevieve

After an exhausted Mari is tucked into her room, I guide Kieran through my room and outside into the evening air. It's cool, with a delicate breeze that feels all the more worth savoring, knowing Kieran is free and we have a life ahead of us to share.

We walk through the gardens, arm in arm, saying so little, and yet the contentment I feel is something I want to enjoy for the rest of my days. There's a lightness between us, and though there's much to be decided, I don't want to step away from his side. We need time alone to let our new reality sink in.

"Do you believe your mother will abdicate the throne? Shouldn't you be there for the conversations?"

I cringe, knowing I've been avoiding what's coming next, then shake my head. "If a monarch is being forced to abdicate, it shouldn't come from the crown princess. It should be up to the people of Naseria. It's best that I remain out of the conversation until the decision is made."

Kieran raises an eyebrow. "Well, then. Can I bring you to your glasshouse? It's been days, I presume, since you've entered it."

"I can't think of anything better than to go to my favorite place with my favorite person."

We walk hand in hand, skin brushing skin, across the gardens, making our way toward the glasshouse. Kieran cracks open the door, and I'm brought back to that moment weeks ago when he knew exactly where to find me. It's always been my private oasis, and while his presence here once felt like an intrusion, I now welcome him into my sanctum.

"How well do you remember your plants, Kieran Greenbluff?"

He gives a light chuckle, his fingers gliding across a leaf. "More than you'd believe." With enthusiasm, he starts listing the names of the different plants, from common tropicals to rare breeds. When he reaches the Begonia Gen, his face tightens into a frown.

"What's on your mind?" I ask.

"My father's the one who helped me cultivate this plant for you. His imprint is on so many things here, and yet he was tossed aside in the end. There was no reason to send him away with me. None. I always wondered why that letter insisted we both leave. Now I know."

I know what he means too. The real reason his father left with him. "She knew he wouldn't survive, didn't she? My mother must have known enough about the conditions to understand it was a death sentence for an older man. But if he stayed here, you would have come back—and she couldn't have that."

Kieran lets out a harsh sigh, turning toward me. "I blamed you. I blamed you for so long, filled myself with such hatred, and it was all for nothing. All that wasted energy hating you, and now I don't think I even have it in me to pass that hatred on to your mother. She doesn't even deserve it."

I bring my hands to his strong body, kneading the tight cords of muscle in his arms and shoulders, feeling the tension release beneath my touch. "It's not going to be easy to move on. None of what happened to you or your father was fair, but it's over now." "It will always hurt," he says, a sorrow lingering in his eyes that's been there since his return. I can't take that pain away, nor should I.

"It always will," I whisper, working my fingers into the tightness along his neck. "But now we get to rebuild our lives into something beautiful. I want to take care of you, Kieran. Just like I always wanted when we were children."

He gives me a sad smile. "You already have. You saved me today, Gen. Saved me from your mother's final plan for me."

"But now I plan to make you mine." I take his hands in mine, look into his green eyes, and say the words I've wanted to say for days. "I love you, Kieran Greenbluff. Will you be my husband? My king consort?"

Kieran looks at me in surprise, lifting one hand to my cheek. "You want me as your husband?"

"Yes, of course. I should have asked you nine years ago. Please forgive me."

He leans down, bringing his lips to mine in a sweet, savoring kiss, like we have all the time in the world. "I would be honored to be your husband, Genevieve Ashcroft."

I grin against his lips, and he lets out a soft, joyful sound. "I hoped you would say yes. As it happens, I still have a date in two days' time and a dress to wear."

His strong body anchors against me, filling me with the sense of him—his spicy scent and clean-shaven skin. "We've lost enough time. I'd have it no other way."

"Then it's a date," I murmur, leaning deeper into him, the tips of my breasts peaking from the nearness of his heated skin. He's the only man who can nullify my curse, who's always made me feel loved, appreciated, and cared for. I loved him as deeply as a young woman knew how, mourned him like I'd lost a piece of my own heart, and now I can spend the rest of my days loving him with all the fervor and gratitude I have to offer.

"It's a date," he agrees, pulling me closer. I wrap my arm around him, bumping a plant on the shelf and sending it teetering, but Kieran's quick reflexes catch it before it can crash to the stone floor.

"Will I be Kieran Ashcroft then? Morris Ashcroft?"

I look at him thoughtfully, knowing what taking the Ashcroft name must mean to him. "You'd go by Ashcroft? After everything my family has put you through? You don't have to do that. I'll call you whatever you'd like."

He peppers kisses along my skin, and the heat of him is so consuming, so overwhelming, it feels as if my skin will catch fire. "Princess, if I'm yours, I want your name branded on my soul. The title I care nothing for. But your name—I want it to be mine. My own means so little to me now, anyway, after all the changes."

He leans down, sucking gently at my throat, my neck, and lower to my chest. My breath catches, deepening into a gasp as I say, "I could never adjust to calling you Morris. King Kieran Ashcroft it is, then."

He rumbles against my skin. "Yes, despite my best efforts, you've done a terrible job of calling me Morris—or Mr. Blackwell."

I let out a laugh, knowing how utterly I've failed at hiding his true identity. "You've always been Kieran. I couldn't change that if I wanted."

There isn't the same desperation between us as before. Kieran huffs a soft laugh against my hair before gingerly undoing my coiffure, loose tangles of waves falling across my shoulders and down my back.

"Princess, I've always wanted to have you in your glasshouse. Now that I'm to be your king, will you give me that piece of you?"

His hands settle at my hips, waiting for me to grant permission to take me in my most guarded place. "Yes. I've dreamed of making love to you here since before I should have been thinking such things."

The moan against my skin makes me burn with desire as his hands travel to the rows of buttons down my spine. "You're like a gift, Gen. A gift only for me to enjoy."

"I'm forever your gift now, Kieran," I whisper as I reach for his cravat, untying the binding at his throat just as he finishes the long row of buttons on my gown. He takes his time undressing my many layers, and in between I do the same, until we're bared to each other, nothing but the steam to shield us from the world outside.

But in here, in my safe haven, it feels as though the world no longer matters—like the two of us could sustain ourselves on slow, deliberate lovemaking and let everything else slip from memory.

Kieran lifts me onto the shelf, and I part my thighs for him. He fills the space between us with his firm, rigid body before he begins to slowly, reverently press kisses across my skin, tilting me back until I'm flat on my spine and splayed open before him.

"I thought I lost you again, Kieran. I couldn't—" He hushes me with his mouth, a moan replacing the words left unspoken. There's no space here for the uncertainty we nearly faced today. For how close I was to losing him once again, and I understand why he doesn't want me to remind him of that fear.

It will take a long time for us to forgive ourselves for the ways we've hurt each other, for how we almost let it happen again. But for now, we can allow ourselves the elation of knowing we've made it—that despite all the years apart, all the childhood doubts that we belonged together, we are once again wrapped in each other's embrace.

This time I swear I will never let him go.

"You're mine, Gen. You'll be mine forever. I won't let anyone take you from me," he murmurs against my thigh, his tongue tracing a trail upward. I feel myself rocking closer, urging him to put his lips on my center, but he ignores my growing urgency.

"Yes, love, I'm yours, and you're mine," I say. He rewards me with a swipe of his tongue across my center.

"Always," I breathe, and he answers with another lick that sends me spiraling into euphoric pleasure. "You're mine," I echo, the words tumbling out again and again until I'm breathless, teetering on the edge of my release.

Just as I'm about to fall, Kieran pulls away. "You're mine," he growls, voice thick with possessiveness, as he lines his hard cock against my center and slams home in one fierce thrust. His thick length stretches me, the sweet ache of taking him while I'm already so close threatening to unravel me completely.

Our movements together are fluid, full of promise, and leave me certain I'll never be without Kieran's love again.

"I'm yours, forever, Kieran. Always." I gasp as the orgasm crashes through me. My walls clench around his cock, dragging a guttural sound from his throat. He loses control completely, hips slamming deep one last time, pulsing hot inside me as he follows me over the edge.

Afterward, our heated skin feels melded together, and I meet Kieran's steady gaze.

"You never needed to ruin me, you know. I've always been yours, Kieran," I say.

"Princess," he murmurs, his hands at my back as he gently lifts me from the shelf, keeping me steady on my feet. "I've been ruined for anyone but you since I was eight."

He wraps his body around mine, and I can still feel the possessive claiming in his movements. I'm where I belong—finally home, in the arms of the man I've spent a lifetime loving.

52

Kieran

I don't wake with the nightmares that have plagued my sleep for years. Rolling to my side, I wrap my arm around Gen, pulling her close and feeling the way her lax body settles so neatly against mine. She's still sleeping soundly, and I want to savor the feel of her in my arms, safe and nestled close.

"I'll never let anything separate us again, Princess," I whisper, twirling her rose-gold hair through my fingers, the cascading softness of it like spun silk. She lets out a tiny sigh and shifts, her hand landing on my chest, resting over my thrumming heart.

I feel whole and happy in a way I never imagined possible. This happiness is hard-earned, and there will always be forces that threaten it. But it's my deepest hope that we can preserve this peace here in these rooms, a sacred space where I will worship Gen.

A knock sounds on the outer door. Probably a servant coming to light the fire. Gen stirs but doesn't open her eyes, so I loom in the bed, a dragon hoarding his treasure, as—not a servant but Gabriel—barges in.

Once again interrupting our peaceful morning. "Dammit, man, will I never be free of seeing you in bed with my sister?" Gabriel says with mock reproof.

"Get used to it. We're to be married in one day."

Gen blinks awake and sits up, her nightdress cascading in silky folds around her. "Gabe? Why do you keep showing up uninvited?" she asks, sleep still clinging to her voice.

"Good question. Why do *I* keep having to be the one to break major news to you? Mother abdicated the crown early this morning. Father thought to wake you, but I suspected this was what he'd walk in on, so I convinced them to give you another two hours and let me come wake you. She's abdicating and leaving for Sullard Castle—the horribly drafty one in the south? Father is joining her, but I believe the council would like to see their new queen and confer on what's to be done about Mari."

"Yes, of course. Tell them we'll be down in thirty minutes," Gen replies. Gabe bows and turns to leave. At the door he glances back. "You both deserve this, you know—after everything you've been put through. And don't make a fuss about what I suggest in there today."

He shuts the door, and Gen sinks down against my chest. "Oh, so it begins. We're going to need an extended honeymoon once we sort everything out—just to have a few more moments of quiet."

I trace the graceful length of her spine. "You've only seen one of my homes. I have two more to show you, plus a proper tour of the railway—and, of course, our own train car."

She tilts her head up to meet my eyes. "Sounds like a lovely way for you to work on our honeymoon. No, I think we should escape to the coast. Just the two of us and no distractions."

"Perfect," I murmur, pressing my lips to hers.

Another knock interrupts us, but Gen calls for them to enter. Two servants step in, carrying clothing for both of us. They bow low. "Your Majesty. Mr. Blackwell—er, Greenbluff. We're here to prepare you for the council meeting."

The man ushers me into an adjoining suite I never knew existed and begins preening me for the meeting.

With surprising efficiency, we're both ready and leaving the suite before anyone else can come looking for us. Gen wears a tightly corseted gown of fine lace over a satin underlay. The fabric is a deep forest green—the color of Naseria. A delicate diadem sits atop her head, hardly a crown but enough to give her a regal air.

"Are you sure you want this life?" she asks, giving my hand a squeeze through the silk of her glove. I wish I could pluck the fabric from her fingers, let her soft hands intertwine with mine, but I understand why she chooses to wear gloves in public.

"I want nothing more than a life with you, Gen. Don't question it again." She gives me a satisfied smile, my certainty clearly lighting her from within.

As we enter the chamber, the entire council rises and bows with shouts of "Long live the queen!" echoing through the room.

Gen signals smoothly for them to sit and takes her place at the head of the long table. But I notice the slight shake in her hand, the gooseflesh along her exposed neck. She speaks with confidence, but I can see her pushing down her nerves. That bit of fear won't stop Gen. If anything, she'll use it as fuel to make herself steadier, more confident as a ruler.

Her siblings are all present, along with Queen Kalise and Prince Leland. The cheers and smiles on their faces tell me everything I need to know about their loyalty to her. Even Gabe looks proud.

Missing from the room—though unsurprising—are Queen Penelope and King Hugo. By now they'll be making exile-bound departure. And if I never see them again, all the better. Queen Penelope deserves worse. She deserves the fate she dealt my father. But I know even a monarch who commits egregious wrongs rarely faces the consequences.

"Your Majesty, may we congratulate you on the smooth transfer of power?" an older man says to Gen. She gives him a wry smile.

"I do not yet wear the crown, Lord Fenweir. When I do, I'll accept congratulations. For now, tell me what has been decided concerning Queen Penelope and King Hugo."

The man clears his throat in a truly ghastly manner. Even I, who was never a well-bred blueblood, know better than to make those sounds in public. Perhaps he has some sort of ailment?

"The queen and king are to leave immediately, as per our agreement this morning. She has been sentenced to exile for endangering the country and for misuse of helachite. She seems willing to go peacefully—more resolute than any of us would have expected under the circumstances."

Gen nods, a seriousness settling over her that makes her seem all the more stately. She's already stepping into the role, and pride swells in my heart that I get to witness this incredible woman rise into her reign. Not only witness it—but be by her side, day in and day out.

"There's still the matter of Princess Marielle to discuss," Lord Fenweir adds. "There is interest in seeing her tried, but I wished to leave the decision to you, Queen Genevieve."

Gen answers without hesitation, her tone allowing no room for dispute. "If Queen Penelope is allowed exile over a trial, then the same will be granted to Princess Marielle. However, I want her to decide where she would like to go. I will not force her to remain with the woman who caused her so much pain."

A few councilors exchange glances, clearly disagreeing, but none voice their dissent.

"If there's no objection," Gen continues, "then I'd like to address the issue of my marriage. As you know, Prince Leland and I have amicably decided not to pursue an alliance between our countries through marriage."

She smiles at Leland, and he returns the gesture. Relief washes through me that they're able to move forward as allies and friends. If not for their cooperation, I might not have survived my trial at all.

One of the councilors stands, addressing both royals. "We would like the two of you to reconsider. Think of the power our two nations could command with a strong alliance. Only marriage can forge a bond that close."

Gen looks at me with a reassuring smile as she removes her glove before the council and slides her bare hand into mine. They all know what her touch can cause—the expressions on their faces make that clear—but we keep our composure.

"I will wed Mr. Kieran Greenbluff, also known as Mr. Morris Blackwell, tomorrow. He and I share an enduring fondness that will not be separated now. Are there any questions or objections?"

Surprisingly, Gabe stands, and my first instinct is to pummel the idiot for every doubt he's ever cast on us.

He looks resolute as he says, "The marriage contract between Icelantica and Naseria has already been signed—with the addendum that if the alliance between Prince Leland and Queen Genevieve is dissolved, another must take their place. As such, I make a public request for Queen Kalise of Icelantica's hand in marriage."

Gen squeezes my hand hard, and I look at Kalise. Her expression is unreadable as she meets Gabriel's gaze.

"I accept your offer of marriage," she replies in a clear, confident tone.

Not surprising—not after Leland hadn't been willing to propose outright to another Ashcroft sister. The room erupts into murmurs and side conversations. Gabe looks at Kalise with such bitterness that I doubt theirs will ever be anything but a political union.

Then the door cracks open, and Queen Penelope rushes in, her hair disheveled and her clothing askew as she darts toward Gen.

53

Genevieve

My mother's rage is terrifying—her hands outstretched as if to claw at me, her hair disheveled in a way I've never seen. But before she can lay a hand on me, Kieran steps between us, using his own body as a shield.

"How dare you! Move at once!" she shouts, and my father is right behind her, tugging her back. There's pain in his gentle eyes, betrayal too. This must be tearing him apart, seeing his beloved wife turn on her own child.

I never wanted to see my mother leave the crown like this, never imagined she would be forced into shameful exile for her own greed.

"I'm sorry, Genny. I'm so sorry for all of this," my father says as he holds her back. She's cursing and fuming as guards step between us. Kieran pulls me into his chest, holding me protectively. I choke back the tears threatening to burst as I watch my own mother fall apart before my eyes.

My father releases her into the guards' hold, letting them take her out into the hallway.

I let go of Kieran and fall into my father's arms. Kieran instructs the council to give us privacy, and they obey his firm, commanding voice without objection.

"I don't know what's become of your mother, but she is quite unwell," my father admits. "She seems to have lost the restraint she was holding on to earlier this morning."

My throat tightens, and I allow the tears I've been holding to spill free.

My mother has caused a schism in our family, and her own pride is the reason for it. My siblings close in around us, forming a tight circle of support. And in that moment, I know the only one truly separated from us is my mother. "You don't have to go, Father. You're not guilty. Stay with us. Stay with your family."

He looks at me with such sad eyes it makes fresh tears burn behind mine. "No, Genny. She has my heart, and I cannot leave her in the state she's in. She needs me now, more than ever."

Although it hurts that he's choosing her, I understand. His love for my mother is one of the few good things she still has.

"Mari, darling girl, what is to be done with you?" my father asks, cupping her cheeks.

She steps back, and I see the doubt in her eyes—fear of harming someone she loves with her curse. I wish I could keep her close, help her navigate this, but I know this path is hers to walk. And though all this is my mother's doing, Mari never confided in any of us. Never told us what she and Mother were secretly attempting.

"I'm going into exile too. I'll join you, Father, and help you with Mother," she replies. There's sadness in her voice, but for once, Mari is being the dutiful daughter I've always been forced to be, that Astoria has always chosen to be.

"Good. Being with family is the right choice," he murmurs, glancing toward the door. "We shouldn't linger."

Our family folds into one last close embrace before we say goodbye to Mari and Father. After they leave, I look at Gabe and Queen Kalise. They're staring at each other with such intensity I half expect one to ignite and the other to freeze solid.

"Are you both sure this is what you want?" I ask tentatively.

Queen Kalise gives me a frosty look before turning back to Gabe. "A marriage in name only, Prince Gabriel. You will reside in Whitehurst, and there will be no dalliances with women in front of me. I will not be made a fool in my own kingdom."

"A fool? You?" Gabe scoffs. "You've only ever been made to look heartless. No one will think anything of the new king taking a mistress or two with you as my wife."

I purse my lips. "So you are both agreeing to this marriage?"

They nod tersely, their gazes locked in some strange, volatile understanding. "Very well," I say. "Queen Kalise, we should discuss the alliance—if there's anything you'd like changed or amended from the original arrangement with Prince Leland."

I think of the request they once made of me—to be his wife in the full sense. That will not be an option for these two, not if the rumors about Kalise's power are true.

"Yes, of course," she replies, eyes still fixed on Gabe.

"Don't worry," Gabe cuts in. "I'd never consider trying to take your virtue, Queen Kalise. I'd rather not have my favorite appendage frozen stiff—not that you could make it stiff."

My eyes dart to Gabriel, and he gives me an arrogant smirk.

"Likewise, Prince Gabriel. I'd hate to catch whatever diseases you've collected while fucking your way across your own country." Her tone is pure frost, but her eyes gleam with a warmth I've never seen from her. She's enjoying this—the hatred, the shared insults.

Perhaps Gabe has finally met his match.

"Excuse me," I say, slipping away and making my way back to Kieran, who's deep in conversation with Leland.

Kieran opens his arms to me, and I slide in beside him, relishing our public affection. It's something I've been denied for so long that it still hits me with abandon every time we're in each other's arms. I don't think I'll ever grow tired of how perfectly I fit against him.

Kieran's lips graze my hair, and I wish we could retreat to our rooms. Leland gives me a knowing look as he asks, "Are those two going to kill each other? Do we think it's smart to arrange this match between them? I could, I don't know, offer my hand to one of your sisters."

I shake my head. "They'll either kill each other or fall madly in love. Personally, I think they're a perfect match."

Leland glances over at them, already deep in some sort of squabble. "Yes, I think you're right. I haven't seen Kalise interact so viciously with anyone in a very, very long time."

He clears his throat and continues, "Before we part, I want you both to know I hold no animosity toward either of you. Gen, you're a brilliant woman, but we were never meant to be. Morris—or Kieran, what do you prefer now? Ah, it doesn't matter. You were out of line when you worked to make this match, but I can't say I blame you. I can see now you were never meant to be apart."

I smile at the man who was almost my husband. "What will you do now?"

"Return to Icelantica and help Kalise prepare for her wedding. No doubt she'll rely on me to make many of the decisions in the coming months. Then I think I'd like to serve on the continent. Perhaps I can go to Wylan and temper the tension between our three countries."

"Very diplomatic of you," I reply with a smile.

"We should call the council back in and finish the necessary business," I say to Kieran, and he squeezes my shoulder as he heads toward the room where he unceremoniously deposited the council earlier.

After the arrangements for the transfer of power are settled, Kieran and I slip from the room together, making our way toward my suite. His arm is wrapped around me, and despite all the changes ahead, I feel a contentment I've denied myself all my life. I know it's because I have this man at my side—this strong, brave man who fights for what is right and, despite all the adversity he's faced, still has room in his heart to love me deeply.

This life won't be without its trials, I know. But a life with Kieran is a life worth living.

Epilogue

Two Months Later

My hands can't stop shaking as Kieran and I walk down the aisle of the throne room. We're both dressed in sumptuous silks and robes of mink, only lacking the crowns that will soon be placed on our brows.

"You're going to make a wonderful queen, Gen. And I get the honor of being by your side through it all," Kieran whispers as we pass crowds of bluebloods and redbloods alike.

"I feel so much more nervous than I did on our wedding day," I admit, and he smiles down at me.

"Of course, there was no doubt on our wedding day. This makes me terrified," he murmurs, and I'm grateful I'm not the only one who feels that way. Being responsible for an entire nation—for protecting and supporting everyone, from nobles to the poorest miners—will fall to my shoulders the moment that crown is placed on my head.

It's something I've always feared, the pressure of supporting so many people. But I know I can do it. I've been trained for it, and now it's up to me to decide how I will better the lives of my countrymen.

"It makes me feel better knowing you'll always be at my side," I say as we step onto the dais.

The clergyman bows before us, and the ceremony begins: the anointing our foreheads with oil, incense to clear the air of the previous reign, and finally the crowns atop our heads as we swear our oath to uphold the kingdom above all.

I take that oath very seriously, after seeing how terribly my mother squandered it in the end—how deeply she betrayed it to satisfy her own greed.

"I declare before you Queen Genevieve Ashcroft and King Consort Kieran Ashcroft of Naseria!"

***

We enter the ballroom in a flurry of illuminated lights, the announcement of our presence overrun by the cheers of the court—blueblood and redblood alike. Astoria greets me with a warm smile.

"I'm so proud of you, Genny."

I smile back, knowing how difficult these changes have been for her, especially with how occupied my time has become. "Thank you, Astoria. I only wish Mari could have been here with us."

She shrugs. "She seems happy enough. I think the change has been good for her. She says Mother is doing better too. Perhaps removing them both from court will allow them to find their own happiness."

"I hope so. I want Mari to be able to return to society someday. It would be cruel for her to spend her entire life in exile."

Gabe approaches, interrupting our conversation. "Are you speaking of my own forced exile to Icelantica? I'd much prefer the sunshine Mari is getting."

I scoff. "Oh, brother, do you forget you made that decision your-self? Is Queen Kalise still insistent on not receiving you until this winter?"

"Yes. We're exchanging correspondence on the subject. It's riveting," he says with all the boredom he can muster.

"And you still hate her?" I ask.

"Despise her. She's horrible. At least once the railway is finished, I'll be able to travel quickly back to Crawford and indulge in some actual culture. Did you know they consider standing next to a hole in the ice, hoping a fish goes by, *entertainment*? At least they're known for their generous pours of spirits on cold nights."

"I think you'll do just fine there, Gabe," I reply, laughing as I make my way toward Kieran. He's gorgeous in his silk evening suit, fitted to accentuate his broad shoulders and strong physique. It still catches me off guard to realize he's actually mine—that the man I thought I'd lost forever is now my husband.

As if sensing my eyes on him, he turns, shamelessly letting his gaze roam over me. It's indecent, really, to behave like that in front of the court, but I don't object. Perhaps it's for the best, letting go of Naseria's obsession with decency and propriety in public.

And that's exactly what I do as he pulls me into his arms, a herald announcing our first song as Queen and King Consort of Naseria.

I reach for his face, bringing his lips to mine in a long, languorous kiss that is probably scandalizing half the room. But I don't care, because the man I once thought lost to me is mine forever.

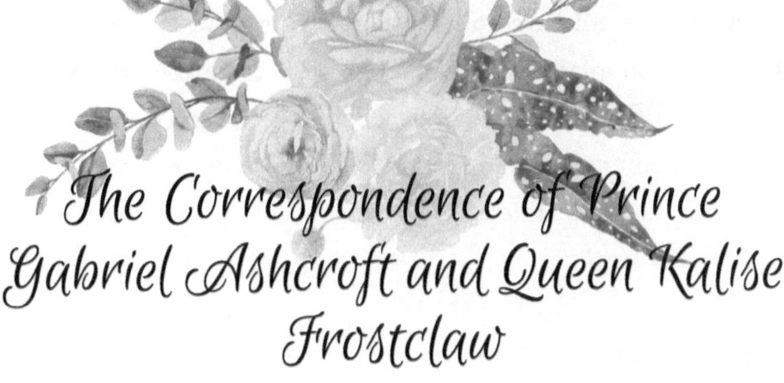

The Correspondence of Prince Gabriel Ashcroft and Queen Kalise Frostclaw

P rince Gabriel,

Your insinuation about freezing off your proud length has gone on long enough. As I've said more than once, you'll never have cause for concern where your favorite appendage is concerned.

In fact, your *humble* length will never find itself close enough to me to be threatened. Furthermore, I'd like to remind you of Appendix I in our marriage contract: at no time will you be permitted inside my private suite.

Fondly,

Queen Kalise

Dear Wife,

I see you have taken quite the interest in my proud length. (I'm rather proud of it, I must admit.) I concur that you will never have the pleasure of enjoying it.

Furthermore, I have no intention of visiting your private suite. Please keep in mind I would prefer my suite to be as far from yours as possible, if only to ensure Appendix II, my right to a mistress of my choosing, isn't interrupted by your scowling disapproval.

With much endearment,

Prince Gabriel

Prince Gabriel,

For propriety's sake, I'd prefer you refrain from calling me *wife* until we have exchanged vows. I'll see that you are housed in the farthest, most isolated wing of the castle. It's a bit drafty, but it seems you'll have plenty of company to warm your bed.

With respect,

Queen Kalise

Dearest Fiancée,

Perhaps you can direct me toward a bedfellow or two who will keep me warm through those famously cold Icelantican winters. A few hardy, full-bodied women will do well. Not all Icelantican women are as lean as you, I presume?

On another note, I'd like to plan for an annual hunt. I hear the fox population is abundant, and I'd love nothing more than to provide Queen Genevieve with a coat of snow-white furs as a token of my gratitude for this arrangement. Without her and Prince Leland stepping away from their own obligations, I would never have found myself with this perfect match.

Always yours,

Gabe

Gabe,

Is that what I'm to call the man I must marry? It's so informal.

I'll say this once, and once only: touch one of Icelantica's foxes and you will not live long.

I've had word from my council of a tradition I had overlooked for a king and queen of Icelantica, and I wished to prepare your noble length for it. On our wedding night we're to have an audience to ensure we are truly husband and wife. There's no other choice but to forfeit the alliance. The law requires it.

Sincerely,

Kalise

Kalise,

Fuck it all, then. I'm to be turned into an icicle on my first night as your husband. If I must die in service to my country, it may as well be at the tip of my cock rather than my sword.

Yours to the death,

Gabe

Bonus Scene!

THE WEDDING OF GENEVIEVE ASHCROFT AND KIERAN GREENBLUFF

If you're like me and love a good wedding scene, be sure to download the bonus scene, **The Wedding of Genevieve Ashcroft and Kieran Greenbluff** from BookFunnel!https://dl.bookfunnel.com/l2ppq4 d8lz

It covers the day leading up to the wedding, the ceremony (including the monstrosity of a dress Penelope chooses, because of course...) and the wedding night.

If you're looking for other books by Audrey Lynn, check out The Lost Realm Series.

Acknowledgements

Richie and the kids, thank you for being my biggest cheerleaders, for giving me the time necessary to write this book and supporting me as I chase this wild author career. Your support and love means the world to me!

Samantha and Ambria, you polished this girl up to perfection, and I'm so thankful for that! Seriously, I couldn't do it without you! Valentina, for the amazing, gorgeous cover art! I'm so obsessed with Gen and Kieran in the glasshouse! Elena over at Untold Stories, your help in marketing OUABC was unparalleled!

Meredith, Maddie, Myrina, Haley, Ashleigh, and all the girls in our little discord group, thanks for sprinting with me, helping me name this book, and being there for me as I took a lot longer on this book than I could have expected!

Dana, Meredith, Jennifer, and Allie, for giving me such valuable feedback on the early draft of this book. You helped it become so much better!

For you, dear reader. Your support makes this dream of mine possible.

www.ingramcontent.com/pod-product-compliance
Lightning Source LLC
Chambersburg PA
CBHW031116160726
47991CB00004B/1411